Love Like Gumbo

Nancy Rawles

Love Like Gumbo

Fjord Discoveries No. 2

Fjord Press
Seattle

An excerpt from Chapter One was published in *Raven Chronicles*, Vol. 6, No. 1, Fall 1996, in different form.

Published and distributed by:
Fjord Press, PO Box 16349, Seattle, WA 98116
tel (206) 935-7376 / fax (206) 938-1991
email: fjord@halcyon.com   http://www.fjordpress.com/fjord

Editor: Steven T. Murray
Cover design: Jane Fleming
Cover illustration: Barbara Earl Thomas
Design & typography: Fjord Press
Author photo: Nancy Perez
Printed on alkaline paper by Versa Press, East Peoria, Illinois

Library of Congress Cataloging in Publication Data:

Rawles, Nancy, 1958–
       Love like gumbo / Nancy Rawles.
             p.   cm — (Fjord discoveries ; no. 2)
       ISBN 0-940242-75-3
       I. Title. II. Series.
PS3568.A844L68   1997
813′.54 — dc21   97-31392
                                                          CIP

First edition
Second printing, February 1998

For my family

Yon sel dwet pa manjé kalalou.
You can't eat gumbo with only one finger.

Haitian proverb

LOVE LIKE GUMBO

Part One

Christmas, 1978

A ll stories begin with Death. This fact cannot be helped. Consequently, it is best to anticipate deaths and, if possible, to plan for them with the utmost care and consideration. It is difficult to die suddenly, worse yet to stagger across the stage clutching a bag of catsup to breasts before twirling to the ground in a jittery mass, legs akimbo, lips quivering. At its best, death is not fraught with anything, least of all complications. How a person dies determines how she lives.

With T-Papa dead and the family in turmoil, Grace saw her chance to get on with it. In that time of the lengthening of days, in that darkest time of the year, a light did dawn upon her: If she did not move now when everything on earth was casting about for constancy, she would wake up to find the ground resettled beneath her exactly the way it was before. She must bury her inheritance once and for all—the ball of shame, the chain of devotion, the leg iron of duty that kept her alive but motionless. Oh, how she would miss them! Already she was mourning the loss of predictability. Being a Broussard, Grace understood that the only way to beat death was to mourn in advance. She stepped up her efforts.

She came carrying flowers, a watering can, and clippers to trim the disobedient grass. A sweater was needed in case of a breeze, and sunglasses helped against weather and tears. Nothing helped against guilt, which tailed her like a devoted pet. Before the day was over, Grace would fall to her knees with the prayers of remembrance heavy upon her lips. She would rage a little and weep a little and leave with family loyalty embossed upon her heart.

The hand, the body, the hair, the foot, the eyes, the voice, the walk, the wink—these are what the Broussards missed, the physical presence, all things corporeal. The mud of this earth gives way to ashes and soot. Bones are buried, never the heart.

1

The Cemetery

Monday, December 25, 1978

Mourning was what the Broussards did best. On any given day, family members of every age and ability could be found engaged in this soulful activity. They mourned the passings of trains, the bulldozing of buildings, the demise of neighborhoods. They mourned when they were apart, when they were together, and when they were in transit. Love was tied in their hearts to mourning. Even a recalcitrant Broussard like Grace knew that love and death went hand in glove.

It was because Camille was in the hospital having her uterus removed that Grace and Yvette had come by themselves to make Christmas at their father's grave. For Camille, the most painful part of being in the hospital over Christmas was not the lack of gumbo feasting or the force-fed merriment or the pain of the surgery itself. It was the knowledge that she could not take flowers to her husband's grave. In the three years since T-Papa had died, she hadn't missed a single week of flowers. He was a man who noticed everything, and Camille feared that such a large loneliness as this one, a missing wife at Christmastime,

to grieving. He needed things like flowers. On
after an eve of no sleeping, she waited impa-
te to arrive. At forty-three, Yvette was her oldest
a.   n time. She would come at exactly 7:59, carrying a
bag of p. ents and a box of pralines. She would be followed by
her twenty-year-old sister Grace, the youngest of the seven
Broussard children, who came brooding and plotting her escape.
With little more than a glance in their direction, Camille dispatched her daughters with these words: "Go and see Papa
for me."

Yvette drove.

"They think Zippy's baby is retarded. Probably 'cause he
married so close." Yvette was reviewing the family gossip for
her sister's edification. Zippy was the Broussards' first cousin,
whose real name was Isidore. He had eloped with a second
cousin on his mother's side who happened to be a third cousin
on his father's side. They had married in a Catholic church in
Tijuana, which made the whole thing legal in the eyes of Rome.
Together, they had produced a dimwit. But so had several of the
kings and queens of Europe, and this fact was lovingly recalled
every time Zippy's baby came up in conversation.

"I hear his wife wants an annulment. Bet you anything Aunt
Julie ends up raising that baby. They won't even bring it over for
Mama's blessing, they're so ashamed of what they did. They
never should have gone against family and run off like that."

It seemed to Grace that Zippy and his wife hadn't gone
against family at all, but rather had gotten carried away with it.
She didn't bother to point this fact out to Yvette, who was taking advantage of the confined quarters to accomplish what she
couldn't get away with at home, where Grace could always
retreat to her room. Yvette liked Grace. And her goodwill was

reciprocated. But there it stopped. They had nothing in common but a last name, nine letters that served to bind them to each other for all time.

That last name. That was Grace's problem. She was a Broussard. That was her trouble in a word. She belonged to a mixed-up group of Louisiana Creoles, which was more confusing than being a Chinese Mexican-American. In post–Black Power America, it meant not knowing who you were. When the boys came home with "naturals" and cake cutters in their back pockets, Camille had accused them of "ruining" their hair. They could not bring into the house the language of the streets nor the children who spoke it, their friends and neighbors who were not, after all, Broussards. They lived *in* Watts but they were not *of* Watts. They were of Pointe Coupee Parish, where there was lots of rain and plenty of crawfish.

Grace meditated on this last thought. She could not understand why men would rise before dawn to catch such ghastly little creatures and why women would spend all day stuffing their crusty little bodies with dressing. She herself had participated in this most elaborate of rituals and, contrary to everyone else present, she felt that the meal in no way made up for the labor. She was glad there were scant crawfish in Los Angeles.

Yvette chattered on relentlessly, encouraged by her sister's lack of words. Their Uncle Claude, Camille's brother, had been honored recently by the St. Vincent de Paul Society for twenty years of outstanding service to the poor. Uncle Claude was no wealthy man himself, but he had given of his time, and that was no little thing. Patrice's daughter was getting married. Her intended wasn't a Creole, but he looked like one.

"Did you know that Brother is moving up in his company?" Yvette continued. "He's practically one of the owners, after starting out as a lowly cement mixer. My, but Lisette's son has big feet! Imagine having to buy men's shoes for a nine-year-old!"

As they drove down Slauson, Grace found herself almost looking forward to the day's work. Christmas was the best season in the cemetery. There was never any snow in this part of the world, so that particular garnish had to be sprayed onto things. But save for this one inconvenience, all the Christmas trimmings could be found in abundance. Poinsettias with their regal heads, tiny trees on wooden legs, pine wreaths that withered amidst all that manufactured joy. It took only a mild wind to scatter ornaments and tinsel and set aluminum pinwheels to spinning. Plastic music boxes replayed carols till they ran out of batteries. Mechanical birds chirped without ceasing. Lights flashed into the not-so-silent nights. The children's graves were covered with toys.

T-Papa had died near Christmas. "T-Papa" wasn't his given name but what everyone called him instead of "Henri." The stone read "Henri Joseph Broussard, Jr., March 5, 1911 – December 21, 1975." Camille Broussard had paid extra for the stonecutter to carve the words, "My presence shall go with thee and I will give thee rest," and she had meant that as surely as Yahweh had meant it in Exodus. The "T" in her husband's name stood for "*petit*," and coupled with "Papa" it meant "little father." Camille thought of this name as the perfect description of the frail and lonesome soul hiding inside the hefty pioneer she had married. (She alone had not been surprised by his death.) In actuality it was merely a telling translation of "Junior."

The name suited him. He had been the most patronizing child anyone had ever come across, inclined to tell both children and adults what they ought to do. They listened. And during the

Great Depression, when the young father and master workman determined that the only thing to do was to leave the stifling white heat of Louisiana for the dry brown heat of Los Angeles, everyone had followed him. He was the one who had taken in the endless parade of cousins, who had turned the house on Compton Avenue into a meeting hall against Camille's wishes, who had trained the young men to work wood, who had risen every morning at five and cooked a hot breakfast of grits and blood sausage after warming the coffee he kept in a jar on the second shelf of the refrigerator. He was a large man with a wide, booming voice, given as often to imparting ignorance as wisdom, but always commanding and frequently entertaining.

His people were lacking, now that he was gone. They could no more do without him than catfish can do without hot sauce, than gumbo can do without garlic, than red beans can do without rice. They missed him the way they missed crawfish bisque. Nothing about Los Angeles could make up for the lack of crawfish—not ocean, palm trees, Disneyland, not tacos, burritos, or teriyaki—and no one but no one could replace T-Papa. Family would continue to follow him. Some of them had already purchased plots in his vicinity.

If she closed her eyes, Yvette could evoke the cemetery exactly as it now appeared before her, but Grace squinted as though she were seeing it for the first time. Before she could walk, she used to sit picking blades of grass while her mother tended to the dead. Once on her feet, Grace had run laughing down the hills, tumbling and rolling over stone and ground, waiting at the bottom for the world to stop spinning. She had collected pine cones, fed cookie crumbs to the carp, taken candles to the statues, and danced in the sprinklers. She had knelt quietly and watched her mother's face in prayer. Over and over, she had heard the words, "Eternal Rest grant unto them, O

Lord, and let perpetual light shine upon them." She learned
them before she learned how to read and could recite them more
readily than nursery rhymes.

That had all been a long time ago, when Grace was still a
child, details she didn't like to recall at the distant age of twenty.
From about thirteen on, she had declined to go on the weekly
excursions to Holy Rosary. When her older children were
young, Camille would call out, "Who wants to go to the cemetery?" the way other mothers bellowed, "Who wants to go to
the store?" Various little Broussards would pile into the car and
spill out onto the holy park like marbles on a sidewalk. While
their mother made the rounds, the young Yvette at her side, the
others chased each other over coffin and corpse. But as they
matured, the Broussard boys realized that tending graves and
visiting the dead was women's work. Men's only duties were to
stay healthy till they died, bring home enough money to feed the
living, and have enough left over to flower the dead. So, while
the boys were learning how to stucco walls and plaster ceilings,
Yvette accompanied her mother with a prayer book in her hand,
and little Grace traipsed behind them practicing her "Turn oh
rests" and "Pet you all lice."

Once she was old enough to recognize absurdity in its family
form, Grace stopped going to the cemetery. It's not that she
wanted to go shopping instead. She enjoyed that activity even
less. But there was something morbid about the cemetery. She
reasoned she would spend enough time there once everything
was said and done; no need to appear overeager. Perhaps, by
paying your weekly respects, you could guarantee that generations yet unborn would make the same frequent pilgrimages to
lay flowers at your feet, but Grace was not interested in such a
fate. She thought it obnoxious the way the living constantly pes-
tered the dead, petitioning them for good health and long life.

"Rest in peace" took on a new meaning when you belonged to a group as verbose as the Broussards.

Grace would have none of it. At twenty, she was much too old for the cemetery and for the superstitions of Catholics. She couldn't remember the last time she'd been grave-hopping. It wouldn't have been at her father's funeral, because on that day they'd all just stood around the casket dumbfounded with no thought of the "good company" T-Papa had now joined. All the other dead fell away in the face of that one grand departure.

It had been a terrible occasion. Grace had only blurry memories of the Christmas landscape of three years before. Her mother, veiled and trembling. Her brothers, tall and somber, carrying their father's body with gloved hands, straining under the weight of his legacy. Yvette, hidden behind black hat and white handkerchief. The countless relatives with heads oscillating like electric fans, their eyes glossy like cellophane. The mechanical birds chirping. The tin-pan carols playing throughout the final words.

Her brother Joseph tried to strangle one of the birds but succeeded only in destroying a perfectly lovely yuletide display in his futile attempt to disconnect. Everyone followed Camille's lead and ignored him. All except Grace, who went over and took his hand and gently led him back to the service. She had worn a purple dress and black pumps bought special for the occasion. Every time she thought of her father's death, she saw herself in that purple dress, looking lost and suddenly old.

When he died, she had been dancing to the strains of *Fiddler on the Roof* in the living room of an old Communist home. A headache seized her at exactly the moment they say he fell to the dining room floor. She had not been there, and it was the only thing she was glad about. She had not been there.

Yvette had been home that night. Although it was a Friday

night, Yvette had been home studying education theory when she heard her father fall. She called for Camille and the paramedics. She summoned her brothers and their wives, drove her frightened mother to the hospital, waited with her for the priest, opened the door for the undertaker, put on the coffee as relatives rushed to the house from everywhere in that sprawling city.

Grace had come home sweaty and reeking of smoke. A friend had dropped her at the driveway, which was thick with her brothers' cars. She could see the Christmas tree blinking in the window. Someone had forgotten to close the curtains. Marc was the one who met her on the lawn, his gold eyes flashing gray. Right away, she knew someone had died and that the someone was her father. Marc held her arm as she felt her way up the stairs, choking on her own breath. Relatives had already claimed the porch. Grace searched the hollow rooms for her mother and Yvette. A wail went up from the kitchen as the three Broussard women became one keening mass. In the space of an evening, the world had changed thoroughly and forever.

Grace hadn't come to visit her father since the week he died, and she was the only one of his seven children to neglect him so. She didn't know why she had come with Yvette today, unless it was for one last look before she turned from him forever. Being at Holy Rosary reminded her of how comforted she'd felt in those days of her father's death, surrounded by her family. She didn't want to dwell on this feeling, now that her own departure was imminent. Grace knew that if she turned around now on the road to independence, she'd be reduced to a pillar of salty tears. She had to leave her family while the leaving was still good.

The way she saw it, the Broussards would probably be a nice family to belong to if you hadn't been born into them. Catholicism was probably a perfectly good religion for those who hadn't been forced to sign on at birth. Likewise, the United

States of America was doubtless a fine place to settle if you had
come of your own free will. Lack of free will was the thing that
most irked Grace about her life as a human being—both the
actual lack of free will and the persistent advertising to the contrary. As far as she could tell, freedom meant you could choose
your own toothpaste or decide how to comb your own hair.
Important things like God, country, and genes were mapped out
before you saw your first light. Well, that would all change soon
enough. Nothing was static. God, country, even genes could be
altered in this day and age. Grace was an adult now. She could
make her own decisions. She had squandered her childhood listening to other people; now she would listen to no one but herself. Dreams of deliverance flooded her heart.

They arrived just as the iron gates were opening, and no
sooner had they passed through them than Grace knew she had
made a horrible mistake. Yvette had talked her into going—
Yvette, who was afraid to visit the dead alone. Grace had
wanted to point out that she would hardly be alone since Christmas was such a popular time at the cemetery, but she stopped
herself. Something had drawn her there, something beyond herself. The cemetery looked strangely festive to her.

Staring out the car window, Grace took in the long expanse
of green, the sleepy trees, the garish decorations, the cars, the
people. This time was not so different from any other time. The
hills still rolled down into the roadways which emptied into the
pond, which sprouted water lilies for carp to swim around and
folks to stare at with wonder. Statues grew to adore the trees
that gave them comfort. Trees worshiped the fertility of this
once-desert stretch of land. The hills were watered and tended to
softness, as though they belonged to a golf course or the nearby
racetrack. They were lucky, these hills, the envy of their brethren which lined the freeways hiding truckloads of decomposing

garbage. Life was decomposing here, and in its shadow, life was being born. This was the place where calamity ended, where tragedy came to rest. Occasionally, a sprinkler would pop up right where a mourner was sitting and grieving. And sometimes that mourner would laugh. From the fake grotto atop the sacred mound, the soul of Los Angeles lay bare beneath its dusty sky. The city was never so quiet as it was from these hills, and no traffic ever bothered them. Grace's mind settled on the idea that this might be her last upright visit to Holy Rosary or to any cemetery, for that matter. The thought made her sad.

Yvette sensed her misery and began to hum a lala song, the kind they played at the lala dances that Grace never wanted to attend. This humming annoyed the younger sister. Yvette could see this, so she stopped. She noticed a stillness come into the car as they traversed the familiar roadways, and Grace had arched her back the way she did when she needed to leave a place. Yvette decided to tell a family story. The story she told was of the day twenty-two years before when Camille had decided that the cemetery was as good a place as any to give her eldest daughter a driving lesson.

Camille was unique among her contemporaries in that she could drive, and she took great pride in this fact. To get around, she didn't need her husband. When she went shopping, she saw other Creole women at the market with their husbands or sons. Camille could go twice as fast pushing the basket by herself. She didn't need a man to get in her way. She needed a man for friendship, respect, love, support, and children. She could push a basket by herself. She was determined to pass the keys to Yvette, whether Yvette wanted them or not.

So, after the two had prayed and sat awhile in silent companionship at the graves of relatives near and far, they returned to the car and Yvette claimed the wheel. The car was facing downhill, perched on a slope like a tilting boulder, scanning the city with its hungry eyes. Backing up would have been the thing to do. But Yvette, in the anxious serenity that becomes a girl who has just witnessed her mother talking to spirits, thrust in the key, turned on the ignition, and shifted into drive, setting into motion a favorite family tale. Over the mounds they careened, bouncing up and down, dragging grass and flowers after them. Yvette finally located the brake and planted the car, a queer monument in that lovely garden. By this time Camille was crying the hysterical laughter of a doomed person. Through her tears, she shouted, "Thank God these people are already dead!" And that sent both of them into fits of mirth right on top of those who slept.

Grace usually liked to hear this story because it pointed to Yvette's imperfection before Grace was born—she had made no such mistakes since—but today it was less than amusing. Grace looked to see where they were going. They were sailing past the Resurrection, the Assumption, Our Lady of Perpetual Help, Our Lady of Sorrows, and Holy Innocents. Yvette was driving to the ends of the earth, moving her head to the beat of her story, words winding up her throat with only a hint of concern that her remaining parent was confined to a hospital bed. Grace was sitting in a panic of her own. Somewhere among these hills and valleys was T-Papa, and she wasn't sure she wanted to meet him. Had the choice been anything other than that hospital room, she would likely not have made the trip. They finally came to the Redemption.

Yvette parked the car and jumped out. She opened the trunk and began unloading their provisions—pillows, blanket, watering can, and clippers. Grace grabbed the flowers from the car, and they began climbing up the hill to T-Papa's grave.

"This is where Mrs. Mouton is buried," Yvette said,

pointing down. "Last time me and Mama was here, we ran into Vincent and Simone putting up this sad little tree. Isn't it pitiful? They've been trying so long to have a baby. At last count, they had three over in Holy Innocents. Why don't they just adopt?"

Grace wasn't listening. She knew any step might fall where her father rested, and she didn't want to surprise him. The thought made her bristle.

Yvette continued. "Old Dupont finally died! He must have been 2,000 years old if he was a day. I wanted to see him off, but his service was the morning of Mama's surgery. It's a shame the way they can just keep people hanging on indefinitely these days, hooked up to everything but a gasoline pump. Poor old Dupont. He's right over there. Hasn't even sunk in good yet."

Grace couldn't keep up with her sister, a "regular" who knew everybody in the place. Yvette did her tour-guide routine as they made their way up the lonely hill. From Yvette's commentary Grace could glean that Death came in three categories—the Unexpected Tragic Kind, the Expected Tragic Kind, and the Avoidable Kind You Brought Upon Yourself. Relatives died of the first two; neighbors died of the third. Yvette knew who had smoked himself to death, who had crashed the motorcycle he was riding without a helmet, and who had been stabbed to death by the husband she never should have married. These were the neighbors. Only one relative had died such an unseemly death, their cousin who had been shot in the back as he exited a club on Western Avenue. His death clearly belonged to the first category. Any third-category intimations (what was he doing over there at that time of night?) were saved for the unrelated neighbor deaths.

Although Grace had heard all of these stories before, they sounded fresh and not altogether real as related by Yvette, who might have been inventing them right on the spot. Grace felt

herself falling farther and farther behind her sister, who was
heading with a sure stride to the crest of the hill. She teetered
as Yvette spread the blanket over what surely must have been
T-Papa.

By the time Grace arrived, Yvette was already on her knees.
Camille had been very specific about which flowers to purchase:
yellow chrysanthemums. Together with the poinsettias they had
brought on the anniversary of his death, these would make for a
handsome arrangement, one that T-Papa would surely appreciate. Yvette got busy arranging them. From the pocket of her
sweater, she took one of T-Papa's old handkerchiefs and care-
fully blew her nose. With a widowed sock, she began to wipe the
stone.

There were no standing stones here. Every one was lying
down, some close together, others aloof, all the same size but
half-sized for babies, and small, plain, sad ones for veterans.
Some of the stones had Spanish names surrounded by flowery
Spanish words. Often, Our Lady of Guadalupe appeared, etched
next to the words. Even though she was only one color here—
set against black or driven into gray—she still suggested all the
colors of her glory. The stars and rays and lightning of her robes
were not lost to this flatness. She seemed happy, that Lady. She
always appeared to be floating, her bare feet dangling under her
gown. If you followed her far enough, you'd end up in the Chinese section, which was small but impressive. Lengthy epitaphs
written in Chinese boasted about the deceased. The border was
marked by a family of Chinese Mexicans, the Wang Mendozas,
some of whom had married Filipinos. A few of the stones bore
portraits of the deceased, most of whom wore mustaches. There
was one whole section given to the nuns, buried in their habits,
rosaries in hand.

There had been no stone on T-Papa's grave when Grace had

last visited, only a mound of grass raised like the stomach of a
sleeping man. That was before T-Papa had settled in death,
when he still stood out amongst his companions. To Grace's
considerable surprise, he was now sunken down to everyone's
level. She looked at the stone. It was startling to see his name
written there. And the dates! As though his whole life had come
down to these few words. It was maddening. Worse still was the
addition of her mother's name, "Camille Marie, June 13,
1917." All it was missing was a closing date.

"How can you come here every week?" Grace shrieked.

Yvette looked truly perplexed by this question. She was a
near-widow herself, having lost the boy she loved in a construction accident thirteen years and eight months before. He was
buried in Louisiana, so she could not tend his grave. Grace had
never known her sister to date, though Yvette liked to dance and
could flirt as well as anybody. It seemed all her love was spent at
home or here at Holy Rosary. If there was any left over it was
given to the children of Watts whom she taught at St. Martin de
Porres Elementary School, where all the Broussard children had
once been ensconced. Grace was sorry for her question.

Thinking it called for an answer, Yvette tried. "Sometimes I
wish I was dead. Then I realize it's just as precarious a state as
being alive. You're still dependent on people for everything!
You need somebody to bring flowers to your grave and wipe
your stone and pray for your soul so it doesn't end up in limbo.
Somebody has to trim the grass or it'll grow wild and cover the
stones. I think the source of all evil in the world is dead people
with nobody to care for them, roaming around restless, stirring
up trouble."

This speech pierced Grace to the base of her spine. She
wanted to throw her arms around her sister, to take her hand
and beg her never to die. The knowledge that Yvette, who was

twenty-three years her senior, had wished for her own death touched Grace more deeply than any admission of love could do. It made her coming betrayal all the more indecent.

Grace was planning to leave the Broussards. She would resign in anticipation of being fired. She had a Ten Point Plan, which would have been well under way had it not been for Camille's sudden hysterectomy. (Without fail, someone always managed to grab center stage when it should have been Grace's turn.) As it was, she was struggling to launch Point One.

For nearly twenty years, Grace had labored long and hard in her quest for perfect Broussardness. She felt she was due to retire. At best her performance had been less than satisfactory. Judged next to Yvette's, it was downright pathetic. She was no good at ironing, dusting, or making beds. She couldn't even understand why beds needed to be made, although the necessity had been explained to her many times. She was of no use at home and her school record was dismal, an array of high and low Cs punctuated by an occasional B. Even the Broussard boys could be counted on for A minuses. Only Grace had brought home Bs in Religion, a shameful grade, unheard of! You could earn an A in Religion by sitting up straight in your pew at student body Masses. This too Grace had failed to do. She was given to slouching, looking around, and asking to go to the bathroom. In third grade, she had wet her pants in the confessional. In fourth grade, she'd nearly choked to death on Holy Communion. In fifth grade, she'd gotten into a fight with another girl, just outside the sacristy.

To her knowledge, no other Broussard in California or Louisiana in this era or any age past had ever struck a human being who did not belong to them. "Dogs do that," is how Camille had put it. It was inconceivable that a Broussard would condescend to roll in the dirt with anybody. Broussards walked upright into the world; they would not be bowed by anyone. What made matters worse was the fact that the other "dog" was also Creole. The Broussards knew her parents, as all Creoles know each other. For six months Grace had been treated as a pariah, made to walk to school by herself. From that time forward, it was clear to her that she was not an authentic member of her tribe. Hence, she did not revel in their doings.

Grace couldn't afford to get sentimental about Yvette, who was the most sentimental person she knew. Neither could she afford needless worries about who would bring flowers to her grave. So she chose to focus on the last part of Yvette's speech, the part about "all the evil in the world," rather than the far more revealing beginning. Grace supposed all the world's evil was caused by the living. She said so. Yvette, looking hurt, said nothing. She merely shrugged her shoulders, picked up the clippers, and began to trim the grass, which didn't really need trimming. They would need some water to wash the stone, which had gotten slightly muddy due to one day of rain. Would Grace like to go get it?

Grace grabbed the watering can and started down the hill. She felt embarrassed for herself. She prayed she wouldn't run into anyone she knew. The cemetery was full of merrymakers— Mexican girls in lace dresses and patent leather shoes, Black girls in velvet dresses and suede shoes, Chinese girls in red coats and cloth shoes, all with families of gesticulating males and discriminating females. Grace's worst fear was that one of these girls would turn out to be a cousin, a neighbor, or a fellow parishioner whose parents would inquire about her father's grave, her mother's surgery, and her own lack of wedding plans. She walked straight ahead, eyes to the ground, hoping in earnest that no one would ever put tinsel on her grave. By the time she reached the dripping faucet, she was exhausted. She filled the watering can and turned to make the slow climb back. But her feet were settled in the earth and all her strength had left her.

If she kept giving in to her family's demands, Grace would never succeed in making a life for herself. The rules and rites of Creole society were too much for her. She refused to comb her hair more than once a day. She didn't know how to sew. She was not fond of gossip and did not give or receive it well. She did not understand the concept of a secret. Grace was twenty, but she still didn't know how to set the table for a family reunion—who to seat next to whom, where to put the left-handers and the babies. Nor did she understand how to make herself presentable for company, how to apply just enough shadow to make her eyes look bigger and just enough blush to make her skin look brighter, or how to love a Creole boy.

Grace had a lover. Her name was Elena. She was not a Creole boy. Grace couldn't decide which was worse, the fact of her not being a boy or the fact of her not being a Creole. She was Mexican, which Grace considered to be close enough. Both groups were walk-on-your-knees-to-the-basilica people with shrines in their back yards. Elena's family had kicked her out when they discovered she was *marimacha*, a discovery made with Grace in attendance. Now she lived in a large four-bedroom house on Normandie Avenue with three other fallen-away Catholics—a Lebanese-American who had converted to the Baha'i faith, a Korean Quaker, and a Caucasian atheist from Michigan who was very active in the John Brown Anti-Klan Society. Elena was planning to move out in February when the lease came up, and she had asked Grace to move in with her.

At first, Grace had hesitated. Even though they'd been going together for more than four years (they'd met in their junior year at Our Lady of Fatima Girls High School), Grace doubted their love could withstand such intimacy. After all, neither one of them could cook. But life at home had become most stifling with the rising expectations of age. Where were the boys, the pristine young Creole men who came calling after other girls Grace's age? She wasn't unattractive. Why didn't she go to parties? Why didn't she fix her hair?

Camille chose to ignore her daughter's dalliance with "that little Mexican girl," and Grace's unbridled affection for Elena was never mentioned by any member of her family. Grace didn't mention it either. She told no one, though they all must have known. They imagined she was having an extended pubescent flirtation, especially given the fact that she'd achieved puberty at the age of ten. When she moved out of her mother's house and in with Elena, they would all be forced to know. Grace had no intention of being a Broussard all her life. Between her and freedom lay the Ten Point Plan. Though the implications of the Plan stretched into every area of her life—she'd already had to quit her part-time job at the Louisiana Fish Market to work full-time in a department store—she meant to see it through.

The first thing she would do was refuse to attend Mass. That was Point One. Her siblings would try to convince her to fulfill her duties, but she wouldn't hear of it. "Go without me and pray for my soul," she would mock them. They wouldn't know what to make of her.

While her family was still reeling from the shock of this sin, Grace would hit them with Point Two. She would "ruin" her hair by picking it out into a large umbrella. The effect would be as great as if she were to rend her garments and put on sackcloth. They would know then that she wasn't playing.

Grace would take advantage of the chaos caused by her "ruin" and invite Elena to a family dinner—Point Three. Elena had been to the house on Compton Avenue many times, and once, when Camille and Yvette were at the cemetery, Grace had taken her to the service porch and kissed her everywhere. But she had never invited Elena to a family dinner. That would never do. After all, Elena was not family, no matter how much Grace tried to imagine her thus.

Well, that would change with Point Four—the red dress. Elena could wear the red dress Grace was planning to buy her. This would make the Broussard brothers swoon and their wives appear dowdy by comparison. Yes, that red dress would give them all pause. And with Grace outfitted in the men's sports jacket she had bought at the St. Vincent de Paul thrift shop, they would topple right out of their chairs.

Any doubt left about her intentions to vacate the premises would vanish when she introduced Point Five. She would stay out all night. Depending on how awkward the family dinner had been, Points Three, Four, and Five might be executed on the same day. Maybe she and Elena would go dancing. (They hadn't been dancing since T-Papa died.) After working up a holy sweat, they would end up in Elena's bed, cavorting quietly so as not to attract unwanted attention. Elena and Grace had ended this way many times, but Grace had never stayed the night. She would always rush off like Cinderella. Grace and Elena were lovers who had never fallen asleep in each other's arms, never woken that way the next morning. The change would be delicious and unforgivable.

After that, there would be nothing to do but announce the move—Point Six. The family would doubtless heave a sigh of relief, for the tension created by the first five points would have brought them to the edge. They could conclude but one thing: Grace would have to go. And she would. Before they suggested it.

She would pack her things (Point Seven)—everything but the statues given her by interfering relatives, the holy cards she'd collected for years in Catholic schools and never been able to bring herself to throw away, her First Communion dress, and her rosary beads blessed by the Pope.

Then would come moving day—Point Eight. This would be accomplished with the help of Elena's brother Felipe and his rusty Ford pickup. When Elena was kicked out it meant that *she* couldn't go home to her family; it didn't mean they couldn't visit *her*. Both of her parents and each of her four siblings visited her separately and regularly, phoning ahead to make sure she didn't already have "company," reassuring her that she would have been invited home *ahorita* if it were up to the individual speaking. While the Hurtados might help Grace move, the Broussards would not be permitted to lift a box in her behalf. If they participated in her liberation in any way, the victory would not be a true one.

No, the separation had to be convincing and complete. Grace would use Point Nine to signal the permanence of her departure. She would refuse her mother's gumbo. That would be the end. Nothing to do but leave. She had been preparing for a good three months in her head and even longer in her heart, but she worried that she would falter on the judgment day.

All such worries were laid to rest when she contemplated Point Ten. She would change her name. She would exchange it for an ordinary Black name like Washington, Jefferson, or Jackson. If she was really feeling bold, she would drop the slaveowners' legacy altogether and put an "X" where the Broussard had been. (She doubted she would be feeling *that* bold any time soon.)

If pressed for time, Grace felt she could enact all Ten Points on the same day so long as she was flexible about the order. She could destroy her hair instead of going to Mass, bring a red-dressed Elena to the traditional Sunday gathering of extended family, pack her bags while her brothers swooned over her lover, refuse her mother's gumbo in a loud voice and add, "By the way, I'm moving," load her things into Felipe's truck, and drive off in a state of unadorned bliss that would culminate with an all-night dance of celebration on Elena's bed. In the morning she would wake up with a new name. This scenario exhilarated her.

Having recovered her strength, Grace started back up to where Yvette was kneeling and beseeching the saints. She carried the can of water like a knight hoisting a lance. Her mind was making monstrous plans. She would become a Unitarian. She would never kneel again. No candles or incense allowed within ten feet of her house. No more trips to the cemetery. No more pilgrimages to Louisiana. She would give her statues to the Goodwill. She would not baptize her children. She would not send them to Catholic school. She would raise them as pagan babies. And when they were grown, she would kick them out—or better yet, she would never have them in the first place. She would die alone. There would be no angels, no seraphim and cherubim, no heavenly hosts, no sniveling priests, no penitent loved ones at her bedside. She would be cremated. She would go to hell.

Grace was walking along this way, feverish with bad intentions, when she heard someone calling to her.

"Where you going, 'tite fille?"

She spun around. T-Papa. She searched the ground to see where the voice was coming from. Behind her, the ground was stirring. The shadow she was casting did not belong to her. It was her father's shadow, following on her heels. She knew it had to be him because he was the last person she wanted to see. The voice was as real as her own. And the shadow was wearing a hat.

"Where you going, little girl?"

"Stop following me."

"If you'd slow down a bit, I wouldn't have to follow you. Old man can't walk like he used to."

"What are you doing here?"

"I live here. You came to visit me, didn't you?"

"I came to visit your grave."

"So, why ain't you visiting it?"

"Why aren't you in it?"

"Person gets tired of lying down all day."

"What about heaven?"

"St. Peter didn't want me. Sent me back to look after you."

"I don't want you looking after me."

"You need somebody looking out for you. Before you go off and do something crazy."

"Oh, go to hell, old man."

"I never thought I'd live to hear my own daughter curse me. Thank God, I didn't."

"There's a lot of things you didn't hear your own daughter doing, even when you were living. And I was doing them right under your nose."

"I didn't know you so good. You was so far behind the rest of them."

"I was your mistake."

"Hush, little girl! You don't know nothing about no mistake. We Catholic. We don't make mistakes. Not that way. You a child of God."

"What god? What god am I a child of?"

"If you don't know, then I can't tell you. Acting like you don't know God! What's wrong with you, girl? Who you think you talking to?"

"There's nothing wrong with me. Nothing you can fix."

"Don't be so sure. I know about your little plans. They not gonna work."

"Why not?"

"Cause you can't leave the family."

"Oh, I can't? Watch me!"

"I'm gonna watch you try."

"Don't stand in my way, Daddy. I'm not your little girl."

"You ain't got to talk to me that way. You act like you don't want to see me."

"I don't!"

"Then what you come looking for me for? Where's your mother?"

"She sent me."

"Why she didn't come?"

"She's sick. Didn't she call and tell you?"

"Didn't get no message. What's wrong with her?"

"She had two grapefruit in her uterus."

"Did they take them out?"

"Yeah, they took the whole thing out."

"She okay, then?"

"Yeah, she's okay. Just sore, that's all."

"How y'all getting on?"

"We're doing just fine, Daddy."

"Without me?"

"Apparently."

Grace turned and headed up the hill. She could hear her father behind her, struggling to catch his breath. She wanted to wait for him, but she was afraid he would overtake her.

"Hold your horses! Why you don't want to walk with me? Old man can't keep up like he used to."

"You're only sixty-four. That's not so old."

"I was sixty-four three years ago. Haven't been that young in a while. It's hard to stand up when you been down so long."

"Then go take a nap!"

"Anger wakes me up. I visit with your mother once a week. She's still mad at me for leaving her. What you mad at me for?"

"For not letting me live."

"What you talking, girl? I gave you your life, didn't I?"

"I thought God gave it to me."

"What you know from God? I'm the one put the bread on the table. God didn't put the shrimp in your gumbo."

"How did you know I wanted shrimp in my gumbo? How did you know I even wanted gumbo?"

"You a Broussard. You gots to want gumbo."

"I'm tired of being a Broussard. I'm tired of gumbo."

"You don't know what you talking, now! Most folks would give their right arm for a taste of your mother's gumbo."

"Well, I wouldn't give my little toe! I'm tired of gumbo, jambalaya, red beans and rice, crawfish bisque, and hoghead cheese. I'm tired of marching to 'When the Saints Go Marchin' In' and praying rosaries and talking to dead people. I want to be regular. I want to eat chitlins."

"What's wrong with you? What you know about chitlins?"

"Why does there have to be something wrong with me to want to eat chitlins? I'm going to eat chitlins and pickled herring and seaweed. I'm never going to eat gumbo again as long as I live, not even at my wedding, which I'm not going to have. And I'm not going to marry a Creole boy."

"What's wrong with Creole boys?"

"They want you to act like a Creole girl, that's what."

"What's wrong with being a Creole girl?"

"Nothing. You just spend your whole life making gumbo. I don't know why I wouldn't want to do that."

"I never heard of no Creole don't like gumbo."

"Maybe I'm not a real Creole. Maybe I'm just a regular

Black person with a slight melanin deficiency. Maybe I'm really French, from the South of France near Africa."

"You a Broussard, that's all. Can't be nothing else but that. Even if you marry Irish. Even if you marry Eskimo. You still be a Broussard. And your children still be crying for gumbo."

"I'm not having any children."

"You talking out your head! You gots to have children."

"Why?"

"You a woman, ain't you? Womens gots to have the children. Mens can't have them. Who gonna have them if you don't have them? How you can say no to your own children?"

"Same way you said no. I'm just going to say it before they're born, not after. Spare them the heartache."

"You can't spare yourself children. You'll be lonely."

"Maybe."

"Nobody come to your grave."

"I don't want nobody coming to my grave. I don't even want a grave!"

"Then what you want?"

"I want you to stop haunting me."

"I didn't come to haunt you, 'tite fille."

"You been haunting me all my life. Trying to make me just like you. Well, I'm not like you. I'm not like you or Mama or Yvette or anybody else in the family. I'm like me. I want to leave and have my own life. I want you to let me go."

"All right, 'tite fille, if that's what you want. I'll leave you be. I'll go to where I'm going. But first you got to do something for me, so I can rest. I ain't been able to rest so good. There's something I left undone. I was in the middle of living when I died."

"They said you were about to taste your dinner."

"Had the spoon in my hand! That's right. I can almost taste

it. Been hungry ever since. Old man can't go to his rest long as he's hungry."

"What am I supposed to do about it?"

"Bring me one last taste of your mother's gumbo."

"You're crazy!"

"Just one last taste, that's all. Make sure you get a good piece of crab in there."

"I'm not thinking about any crab."

"And don't forget the garlic bread. I'll be waiting."

Grace snarled. Coming to the cemetery with gumbo... He must be out of his mind! A cloud hovered nearby. She supposed she would be struck by lightning for thinking the way she did. She didn't really care. They could just dig a hole and toss her in it. She was not coming to nobody's cemetery with nobody's gumbo. She turned to face her shadow, but he was already gone.

Grace marched back toward Yvette, sweating and muttering oaths. She would not bring him gumbo, she would not bring him anything. If any of the other cemetery visitors thought it strange to see a young woman talking to herself on Christmas morning, they didn't let on. Or maybe they knew she was talking to her dead, as they themselves had come to do. A few heads turned as she stormed past them, but life does strange things to the living.

By the time Grace arrived with the water, Yvette was finishing her third rosary. "What took you so long? I'm all prayed out."

"I ran into someone I knew."

"Who was it?"

"Some old man."

"From church or from the neighborhood?"

"Some old relative."

"A relative? Don't you know who it was?"

"Jesus! I haven't seen him in years."

"Don't swear."

"I didn't swear. And what if I did?"

"Like I tell my students, 'You'll have to go to confession and look God in the eye and tell Him you broke His second commandment.'"

"You're nuts. They shouldn't let you near children."

"What an awful thing to say! Grace Broussard, you're becoming crueler by the day. I hope you weren't mean to that old man. Don't you remember his name? Did he come to Daddy's funeral?"

"I don't know. I think so."

"I bet I know who it was. Was it Mr. Juge? I bet it was. He's not that old, but he looks it because he's suffered so. Poor thing. He practically lives here. Visits his two dead wives. He can't get over that last one. She was young enough to be his daughter. Cervical cancer. Thirty-seven years old. Sad. A tragedy, really. He went against his entire family to marry that girl, and now he's all alone. Nobody to love him but two dead wives. I don't know why he doesn't just jump on in there with them."

"I want to leave."

"We can't leave yet. You haven't prayed with me."

"I don't want to pray."

"Grace Broussard! I ought to spank you. Stop thinking about yourself for a minute and show some respect for your poor dead father. On Christmas Day, no less! And your mother lying in a hospital bed! The last thing she asked for was to bring you here."

Yvette was on her knees, waiting. Grace regarded her with mild contempt. Was it Camille who had conjured T-Papa to scold her? Perhaps Camille and Yvette had discussed it before picking up their direct line to heaven. Did they suspect her of infidelity? Did T-Papa voluntarily resurrect himself to tell her,

"You can't leave the family," or was he prevailed upon to deliver this message? A conspiracy suggested itself, a ploy to bring her back in line. Well, it wasn't going to work. In tight-lipped resentment, Grace refused to kneel.

Yvette waited. And shook her head mournfully. Tears came to the eyes of the older sister. What had she done wrong? How was it that this babe in her arms had grown up to be such an unabashed heathen? Would Grace just like to answer that one question?

Grace remained standing. She refused to speak to Yvette. They could spend all of Christmas Day in this penitent duel, for all she cared.

Yvette had the patience of a saint; she would not surrender any time soon. She rather enjoyed the morally superior position that kneeling sometimes implied. Besides, she was a schoolteacher and quite skilled at being uncomfortable for extended periods of time without letting on. Minutes ticked by.

Grace wondered what Yvette would look like strangled with her own rosary beads. Exasperated and guilty, the little sister dropped to her knees. Her own violent thoughts had defeated her. Next time, she'd be careful not to sink to Yvette's shameful level of bald manipulation. It was futile to argue with zealots.

"Eternal rest grant unto him, O Lord," Yvette began the benediction.

"And let Perpetual Light shine upon him," Grace replied, unable to stop herself.

"May his soul and all the souls of the Faithful Departed, through the Mercy of God, rest in Peace." Their voices collided on the day's last "Amen."

"Amen, Amen, Amen!" Grace bounded to her feet. In one deft movement, she was striding down the hill, hands shoved

into her pockets, feet traveling fast and furious. The family
ghosts surrounded her on all sides. She'd been conned into sub-
mission by Yvette's lyrical voice, Camille's prone body,
T-Papa's ridiculous request. She'd knelt to them and invoked
their God. The shame she felt was a Broussard kind of shame.

Yvette, who kept a step behind, tried to recover the moment
by musing about her burial preferences. "I want to face the
ocean, so I can step out and feel the salty breeze against my face.
I wish we had those big old tombs like they have back home, the
ones with the porches. I could sit out and smell the night jasmine
and rock myself to sleep. I want to sleep facing the sunset."

Grace turned a deaf ear to Yvette's grandiose plans. She herself didn't even want to be put in the little urn—just have her
ashes scattered over Playa del Rey. That way, she could still
make waves at the annual family beach trip, a tradition that
could be expected to last well into the next few millennia. Her
individual death would be of little consequence, since there
could be no end to the Broussards' everlasting births and deaths
and burials. She felt a stinging compulsion to flee right then in
the middle of Yvette's monologue, to run away and leave her
sister standing there amongst the powerful Broussard dead, who
were linked to each other by the chrysanthemums, bright yellow
against the reds and greens of Christmas.

"Did you know the Chinese bring food to their dead? Isn't
that a good idea? I'd like to sit out in the evening sun with a big
pitcher of iced tea and a piece of pecan pie."

Grace exploded. "Is that all this family thinks about?
Food?" In a streak she was gone, flying down the hill to the car,
away from her Creole sister and her crazy family, with endless
pots of her mother's gumbo chasing in hot pursuit.

When Yvette reached the car, Grace was still panting, but

not from exertion. She had clearly been crying. Yvette said nothing, but her eyebrows puckered as though she were regarding a downed bird.

"Do you feel like stopping by the beach, little sister?"

"The beach? It's not summer!"

"It's better than summer. Nobody'll be there."

"Nobody in their right mind. It's cold."

"We both have our sweaters. I thought it might be nice to watch the waves for a minute. We don't have to stay long. We can just make a little detour to Playa del Rey. We're awfully close."

"Why do you always have to 'make a little detour'? Maybe we could just swing by the Grand Canyon on our way to the supermarket. That's why I never want to go anyplace with you! Every time you step into a car, it's not necessary to roam all over creation. Give me the keys. I'll drive."

"Is a short excursion to the ocean too much for a godmother to ask of her godchild on the day that Christ was born? Is it too much for her to want to dip her toes in the icy water on the fourth day of the third anniversary of their own dear father's death?"

Grace hated to be reminded that Yvette was her godmother. She hated to be reminded of T-Papa's death, how they'd already been without him for three years and four Christmases, how the last real conversation they'd had was the night of his final beach trip. Yes, a short excursion to the ocean was too much for Yvette to ask.

"To smell the salt air, to hear the rush of the waves, to appreciate the mysterious workings of the Holy Trinity? Isn't it wonderful that we only have to drive ten minutes out of our way to give thanks to the Lord for his marvelous creation? Daddy so loved the ocean."

He did? Grace tried not to think about her father's last beach trip. She tried not to remember his halfhearted attempt to rescue her after her halfhearted attempt to drown. "You went out too far," was what he'd said. He had turned his back on her that day. She had watched him walk away, knowing she could no longer reach him with words or with actions, no matter how dramatic. In fact, she was the one who was out of his reach, out of the reach of the entire family. Grace was "too far out" for her family. That was the message she'd gotten that summer night in 1975 when her own body's tides had threatened to sweep her away on a sea of desire. That very night, she'd vowed to do whatever she could to avoid the fate prescribed by her father. She didn't want to become Yvette or, worse yet, one of her brother's delicate wives. Grace would have to rescue herself.

"Why don't you and Mama ever go to the ocean? You're over here every week."

"Oh, you know how Mama hates to lollygag. And she doesn't believe in mixing mortification with pleasure. Not to mention the sand. It's been such a long time since I've seen the ocean. My world gets smaller and smaller."

Against her will, Grace contemplated Yvette's world. A neat circle it was. From home to school to church to store and back home again. Once a week to the cemetery with her mother. Once a month to the beauty shop. Once a year to the beach to meet the cousins who wouldn't come to Watts. It was all too much to think about.

"I'll drive," she said, holding her hand out for the keys.

As Grace pushed the key into the ignition, a sense of doom devoured her. She would end here, buried alive with the rest of them. It could not be. *Absolument pas.* Not her. She would do whatever she had to, but she would not end here. She jerked the wheel. As the Valiant lumbered toward the wrought-iron gates,

Grace began to sweat. What if she got trapped here? She had to leave while she still had a chance. She had to get away before they closed the gates, before dusk descended and claimed her for its own. Grace tightened her grip and pumped the gas, rolling over all the graves in her mind, the graves of these people who, thank God, were already dead.

2

The Beach Trip

Friday, August 29, 1975

Hair was the Broussards' terra firma, their crowning glory, their fait accompli. Since hair was the very essence of self, the most selfish of them did everything in their power to preserve it. They shaped their hair, they did not shave it. They trimmed the ends, they did not slice them. They clipped the curls, they did not cut them. It was generally understood that to squander your hair was to squander your talents. For girl children, hair was dowry. Only the craziest of girls who wished to renounce her nativity and jeopardize her future would whack off her Creole hair. Grace Broussard was such a girl.

The Broussards lived forty-five minutes from the California coast, but they packed as if they were going to Louisiana. They visited both places with equal frequency. Springtime found them in the countryside near Baton Rouge. Summers brought them to the beach. The yearly trip "home" lasted thirteen days and took them down Interstate 10 past the Arizona desert, the mesas of New Mexico, the ranches of Texas, but not as far as the sin of New Orleans. The annual beach trip lasted thirteen

hours and began with a tour of Manchester Boulevard past the
liquor stores of Watts, the auto repair shops of Inglewood, the
doctors' offices of Westchester, and beyond the cheap airport
motels. They swung by the cemetery on the way.

Besides being located in proximity to one another, the cemetery and the beach had important things in common. Vast open
spaces, lots of sky, slow erosion. Both were holy, lending meaning to lives small and large, bringing beings ever closer to their
origins. The cemetery was a jarring, sunny reminder of mortality. The beach was a jarring, sunny reminder of eternity. Visiting
both in the same day could definitely lead to overexposure.

There may have been beaches in Louisiana, but no Broussard had ever seen one. Before they moved to Los Angeles, New
Orleans was as adventuresome as they got. One Mardi Gras was
enough for a lifetime, as far as they were concerned. No matter
how they tried, they couldn't understand the endless parade of
tourists who came pouring in year after year just to get drunk
in a strange place. The appeal of Bourbon Street escaped them
entirely, but the California beach… Now, there was something
to talk about!

The Buick, packed to the roof with humans and food, was
commandeered by T-Papa. As T-Papa was a cabinetmaker who
worked in a shed behind his house and as his wife Camille did all
the shopping and all the visiting of dead relatives—the live ones
came to their house—he only had need to drive long distances
twice a year. He knew the road to Louisiana like he knew the
grooves in his workbench, but the route to the beach confounded him. He did not read maps nor pay attention to street
signs but followed his considerable nose, which proved infallible
when sniffing out gumbo but less than proficient at picking up
the ocean scent. (Gumbo and the ocean were made up of the

same basic ingredients — salt water with a lot of seafood thrown in — but gumbo had the advantage of smoked sausage.)

The children helped when they were little by panting, "Daddy, I smell the beach!" one right after another from the back seat. But as they grew, they merely sulked and sighed, occasionally speaking up to save the family's life. "Daddy, this is a one-way street!" they would panic when T-Papa made a wrong turn after stopping to check the fan belt at some back-alley Inglewood auto repair shop. "Since when?" would come the crusty reply. "What they go and change the durn street for?" And off he would go, right foot on the accelerator, left foot on the brake.

T-Papa was a hazard; he caused accidents, but he seldom directly participated in them. For this, his family was grateful. Prayers of thanksgiving could be heard throughout the car, not to St. Christopher, the Patron Saint of Drivers, but to Rouby, the nephew who had sprayed the Buick bright green out of worry for his *parrain*. They always arrived safely, a fact for which they credited this same ingenious nephew as well as St. Christopher, God the Father, St. Anthony (the Patron Saint of Lost Causes), and the holy water a distant cousin had carried back from Rome, which Camille liked to sprinkle on the hood before leaving. (By keeping one drop of the sacred fluid, blessed by the Pope himself, in the bottom of the jar, she could refill it from the tap and ensure that the blessing remained intact.)

The journey to the beach was not a predictable one like the trip to Louisiana. Louisiana was "home" and utterly familiar, while the beach was something altogether foreign. Malibu, Hermosa, Marina del Rey were exotic and incomprehensible to the bayou-soaked Broussards. Not simple like Cane River, Lake Pontchartrain, Achafalaya, and the Mississippi. The ocean was vast and wild and mysterious, a world without end. They never quite knew how to act in such strange surroundings, and a once-a-year visit did not bring the Broussards any closer to penetrating the secrets of beach etiquette, which could be gleaned by watching a Gidget movie but never imitated by ordinary people like themselves. The California beaches belonged to White people, who were anything but ordinary.

Where the Broussards came from, anything owned by White people could never be fully enjoyed by Colored people. This seemed especially true of the beach, which for Whites meant acquiring that ever-elusive color the Broussards were trying their best to unload. They did not enjoy lying in the sun with their bellies exposed and their eyes covered. They came to the beach because it was a nice place to eat. Playa del Rey had pits where they could cook, so the Broussards went there. That was the best beach for Blacks and Browns and Yellows like themselves. They did not play volleyball, surf, or sail boats as was the custom at the White beaches. They cooked and ate and went "down to the water" in between meals, where they worried they would drown from wading on a full stomach.

The Broussards regarded the beach as the Rockefellers might regard a juke joint. They were drawn to it precisely because it was out of their realm. The silver ocean with its waves of sand, seaweed, and charcoal was the epitome of freedom and danger. Only by approaching it together, after careful consideration of its power and Catholic awe of its might, could they hope to know something of its mercy.

They began planning in June. They selected a day and invited everyone they knew. As everyone they knew was related to them, either by blood, marriage, or desire, this made for a family reunion of sorts. It wasn't a formal reunion because there was no gumbo, no speeches, and no charts linking them to senators, slaves, and sugar plantations. It was distinguished from the regular Sunday gatherings by the fact that relatives occasionally skipped a Sunday, but they never missed the beach. Here was a chance to see the year's new walkers dip their toes in the sea, to be buried alive by an ever-bulging pack of nubile boys or pushed in the water by some cousin you hated. It was the only time to spot Camille in shorts. When she turned her back, you might sneak a look at her chunky legs.

Camille set the menu, which was the same every year. Hot dogs, potato chips, and hot sausage for lunch. Hamburgers, potato salad, and hoghead cheese for dinner. Coffee, pecan pie, and pralines for desert. Watermelon and baked beans whenever you wanted them. Coca Cola, beer, and Hawaiian Punch. Marshmallows for the fire and grapes for the car. Animal Crackers for the little ones and Planter's Mixed Nuts for the men. One year, some cousins who lived in Burbank and passed for White three hundred and sixty-four days of the year brought a wooden ice-cream maker, and the entire extended family, old and young, spent the evening cranking. The result was a sweet, milky substance that tasted slightly grainy and would not stand in a cone. "Too much fuss," decreed Camille, and it was not seen or heard of again.

Going to the beach involved plenty of "fuss," but it was ritual fuss and not to be tampered with. Packing began three days before the appointed hour. Ice chests full of cold drinks, coolers full of meat, baskets full of buns. Charcoal and lighter fluid, tablecloths, blankets, coat hangers for the marshmallows, a tin pot for the coffee, peaches for snacking on, chairs for napping on, cards for bid whist. Beach balls, footballs, baseballs, buckets. Jars for collecting rocks and shells. Mayonnaise, mustard, pickle relish jars. Bottles of catsup and hot sauce. Paper plates and napkins. Forks, prongs, wooden spoons. Knives, cups, aluminum foil. Oven mitts, pot holders, towels, and wash-cloths. Soap. Ginger ale, in case somebody got sick. Sunglasses, sun hats, sandals. Scrabble and checkers. A map of the coast. Flashlights with batteries. Polaroid cameras and transistor radios. Binoculars for the sunset. Don't forget the matches. Salt and pepper, sugar and cream.

In addition to these items, each traveler carried a beach bag with a change of clothes. Suntan lotion was popular with the young Black Power set. The elderly toted their rosary beads. Women waited until after the beach trip to get their hair done; scarves were a common sight in the Broussard camp. Bathing caps were not needed because no one went in far enough to get her hair wet. Hair repair appointments were scheduled a month in advance.

Preparation was exceeded only by the time it took to recover. At least a week to get the sand out of everything. Sand was the one drawback to the beach. Once, a Broussard grand-child had jumped around barefoot in the sand and landed on a piece of glass. Her parents rushed her to Kaiser Emergency while the rest of the clan waited for word of her punctured toe. It was fine. But from that day forward, by Camille's command, shoes were kept on until they reached the water, where the sand was hard and where pieces of glass could be seen and avoided.

Camille organized the annual beach trip as she organized all doings of the Broussard clan. Every familial urge had to be sanc-tioned by her. If a couple wished to marry, they came to Camille for her blessing. If she judged them too immature, too lustful, or too closely related, the wedding never came to pass. If they wished to baptize their baby, they checked first to see if Camille was free. She was more necessary than the priest and, therefore, her schedule was consulted before his. A Broussard could not receive a diploma without Camille in attendance. (Those years when two graduations conflicted, Camille attended neither ceremony but held her own at the house on Compton Avenue, summoning each of the graduates to recount his or her achievements before all the assembled guests.) If a married couple was struggling, it was Camille who intervened. She did not grant divorces. Even T-Papa deferred to his wife in matters of blood.

Blood was at the heart of the beach trip. Mixed blood— African, French, Native American... who knew what else. They came to partake of it, to bask in it, to celebrate its purity. The Broussards might be part of a mongrel race, but they were mongrels of the highest pedigree and a damn sight prettier than most purebreds. It was their blood that made them superior. They were hot-blooded, warm-blooded, and cold-blooded at the same time. Continents converged in them, civilizations trembled. They had taken the encyclopedia's three racial subdivisions and improved upon them all. To the full, patient African lips they added the imposing French nose, the exalted Indian cheeks, eyes of every color and shape, and hair of every hue and kink. So robust and hearty was the syrup choking their veins, it was not difficult to imagine the recipient of a Broussard transfusion hopping off the table and jogging home. Like gumbo, the culinary chaos that had become a delicacy, the Broussards had taken a genetic casserole and made of themselves a feast. For seasoning, they added Catholicism, which overtook their characters like too many cloves of garlic.

These were no Vatican II Catholics, unsure of themselves and reluctant to genuflect. They were fasting, candle-lighting Catholics, shrine Catholics, novena-making stations-of-the-cross Catholics, Catholics who gathered at the Coliseum on Mary's Day to recite the rosary with thousands of their sweaty comrades, cohorts of the missionaries, confidantes of the priests, colleagues of the saints, and well-placed on Mother Teresa's mailing list. Religion figured into everything they did because everything they did was steeped in ritual, and love of ritual is what their religion had given them. Belief was not as important to this constellation as an outsider might imagine. The Broussards were cultural Catholics—what one did was important, what one ate was paramount, what one thought, believed, and felt was best kept to oneself.

It was in this state of religious non-fervor that the sixteen-year-old Grace reluctantly joined her family for yet another cultural outing, the Beach Trip of 1975. Grace was sick of the family, an affliction she shared with many other sixteen-year-olds, but one which she regarded as uniquely hers. She cramped her soul into the back seat of the Buick, buckled her powerful legs, and wished she lived in the time of Jesus, when children left home early.

By the time they arrived at the beach, Grace was so thoroughly oppressed she could barely move. The conversation in the car astonished her—her father's incessant barking, her mother's relentless hounding, her emotionally comatose brothers who spent the entire ride berating each other, her sister's valiant attempts to gossip through it all. The drama in the car was a rote one; Grace knew all the parts by heart. It soared and dipped in exactly the same way year after year, ride after ride. Brothers got married and drove their own cars with their own families in them, but the conversations remained the same; only the actors changed. Conflict was a comforting thing to a carload of Broussards. They loved to hear themselves roar. The fact that Grace did not share in this pleasure proved her deepest suspicion: she had been born into the wrong family.

The car coasted to a stop. Grace turned her head to the door and studied its handle. She could feel bodies pushing her to release them, mouths putting her down for moving too slowly. The sky in its swirling fragments danced by the window and stopped. Worn, stale, groggy, she struggled to right herself, the grooves of the seat back pressed into her face.

Grace had cramps. She'd had them for several days now leading up to the beach trip. She hadn't spotted any blood till the morning of the great event, but she knew without a doubt that her period would arrive in time. Sure enough, Camille found her doubled over in pain moments before the packing of the car was scheduled to begin. Staying home was not an option. Aspirin, tea, a hot bath, whatever it took to turn the mind from its preoccupation with pain. The sun streaming through the car window had been soothing to her stomach. Nausea had lulled her to sleep. When the car stopped, she snapped awake. It hurt to move her legs. But the fresh ocean air, which circled the car like a wary lover, made her feel strangely romantic.

Doors popped open and the Broussards scrambled out, Yvette in the lead, Grace falling behind. Several cousins had already arrived and were setting up camp. Grace surveyed the bunch of them, ranking the different branches of her extended family according to their relative whiteness.

There were the Burbank cousins, who sported thin brown hair and thick blond skin. Grace marveled at their fairness, which they mistook for prettiness. In fact, they were homely, both in spirit and in feature. There was not one remarkable attribute about any of them, and this lack of "color" represented an achievement on their part. They were trying so hard to fit in with the colorless people of the world, they had bleached themselves limpid. Only a perverse sense of curiosity and a desperate longing for relevancy propelled them to wax their El Dorado and drive to Playa del Rey once a year. There, they could mingle with the less fortunate, all the while assured that they would not be spotted by any of their neighbors, who were busy sunning themselves in Malibu.

Then there were the orange cousins from Baldwin Hills. They looked exactly like those people the nuns made you draw in Religion class—just that shade of tangerine with wide sad faces. They were a self-conscious bunch, always biting their lips in an attempt to make them smaller. If not for their lips, they might have made it to Burbank too. They were good friends with the Leimert Park crowd, whose brown skin, green eyes, and wavy hair made them the envy of shallow people everywhere. Rouby, T-Papa's much-adored godson, was one of this group. When he saw the Buick take the parking lot, he ran to greet its slightly traumatized passengers.

Rouby rushed to take Yvette's basket. Joseph, Camille's last unmarried son, helped his mother carry the meat. Raymond, the oldest of the Broussard boys, appeared at his father's side, wrested the ice chest from T-Papa's hands, and passed the bag of charcoal to his own son Gregory. At thirteen, Gregory was the oldest of the grandchildren and only three years younger than his Auntie Grace.

Nobody rushed to help Grace with the watermelon, probably because they could tell she was "in a mood." They didn't wait for her to catch up. This hurt her more than anything. Half of loving anybody was waiting for them, and nobody waited for Grace. She could walk by herself and feel just fine about it, but she couldn't wait for herself. Each year on Grace's birthday, Yvette would tell the story of how she had waited for her baby sister to come. Grace wondered why she didn't wait for her now. Her family looked even more ominous from behind.

Grace scanned the beach. She remembered every trip they had ever taken there. As though in a dream, she saw her family

the way they appeared to an outsider. A sixteen-year-old girl
with cramps, Grace was indeed an outsider now. She remembered standing amongst her brothers as a little girl, confronted
by the hairiness of their legs, ready to run before they caught
hold of her tiny arms and swung her into the hot sand. She
remembered testing the water with her toe, unafraid in her
sister's capable hands. How good the wetness had felt against
her legs! How she had run laughing from the waves! She remembered these things and began to cry. Grace was delirious. The
blood, the pain, the heat had rendered her foolish. Her family
knew this and did not try to comfort her. They left her alone.

Grace regarded her hand, the stronger one, the left one,
which was clinging to her little bag as though it contained the
meaning of her existence. The skin on her hand was what she
could see all the time. This was what was natural to her. When
her eyes looked out upon the world, things that were the color
of her hand seemed ordinary—sometimes beautiful in their
ordinariness, sometimes mean, but always natural, basic. She
followed these thoughts from the safety of her own hand—its
shape, its range, its color—back to those childhood beach trips
and all the shapes, colors, and shadows of the days before she
knew she was different.

Grace was the darkest of all the Broussard children. She had
not realized this when she was small; she had not understood its
importance. Yvette, who had been born in Louisiana in 1935
(one year before the family moved to California), had red hair
and freckles. She looked Irish. Raymond was not quite two
years younger and black Irish. Louis, exactly two and a half
years after Raymond, was every bit the Frenchman like his
father. These were Camille's Depression babies. Anthony, born
in 1941, was her War baby. His skin was leathery and he was
prematurely gray. The other War baby, a girl named Michelle,

had died four days after her birth in 1944. She was buried in
Holy Rosary. No one knew what color she was. Marc was
golden, the Victory baby, hair coarse, eyes sleepy, born two days
after the bombing of Nagasaki. Joseph, born in 1949, was the
closest to Grace in age and the closest in color as well. He was
tan. He didn't need the beach. His hair was jet black, but his eyes
were light brown. Gidget might have gone for him if she had
only let herself.

It was into this mélange that Grace was born, the most colored of all her parents' colored children, the spirit of her Haitian
foremother, a fried oyster's black pearl. She was the youngest,
born in 1958 during the Civil Rights Movement. She looked like
Joseph's sister, but her skin was a few shades darker. Her eyes
were not light but a deep, dark brown. Her hair was just as black
but not as straight. She was chunky like her mother.

In the fog of her memory, the seven Broussard brothers and
sisters appeared on the horizon like sausages on a plate. People
who didn't know T-Papa and Camille and their cluster of saucy
children didn't automatically put them together, because they
did not look alike. Lena Horne, Johnny Mathis, Billie Holiday,
Nat King Cole, Harry Belafonte, Duke Ellington, and Sarah
Vaughan had more in common physically than the seven
Broussard children. The family resemblance they had for each
other was no greater than the family resemblance most Black
people have for one another; they could have each come from a
different continent.

You only had to look at the Broussard parents to discover
the reason for this disparity. T-Papa and Camille were as suited
to each other physically as a whale is to an otter. He was tall; she
was short. She was hairy; he was smooth. In no two of their
children had their genes collided in a similar way. However,
each of the Broussard children had at least two features that

placed them squarely in their parents' home—eyes, ears, nose, chin, teeth, cheeks, a dimple, a honk in the voice, a lilt in the stride, a way of moving the body that was altogether known. The most immediate difference was the contrast in their skin colors.

Camille was as dark as a daughter of India; T-Papa was as light as a sacred cow. This made them a most exceptional pair in Creole circles. Like the people of India, the Creoles were fierce matchmakers, calculating everything from class to complexion. Husbands and wives often had a "family resemblance" before they got married. In the case of the Creoles, it didn't take a genealogist to figure out why. Any two human beings could find a relative in common if they went back far enough. Creoles didn't have to go back very far.

In the Negro society of the elder Broussards, a light male with a dark female was a combination as unusual as its reverse was common. Dark male and light female was tantalizing. It hinted at a liaison that was strictly forbidden under White law. A dark-skinned man could raise his status by acquiring a white-looking wife but, if he dared to flirt with the real thing, he would only succeed in raising a noose around his neck. But why would a light male want to be with a dark female? This was a senseless combination. Would a man bred for success lower himself by marrying backwards, by marrying his past? This liaison was doubly spurned because it hearkened to a practice that was roundly encouraged under White law—the wholesale rape of African women. No Negro wished to be reminded of this, least of all Creoles, who were the telltale evidence of so many rapes.

For Grace, being a mixed-race person in a Black-White country was a miserably disconcerting thing. The only sanity that she could see lay in firmly pronouncing her Blackness for all the world to hear. She would leave the Creoles where they

belonged—in an annotated history of France and its colonies.
This was Los Angeles. A person like her could easily be taken for
Mexican. Grace made up her mind to claim Black, not Creole.

Still, she wondered if the rest of the world would see her as
Black. How would she get on in Lagos or Kinshasa? Would she
be Black in Durban? A generous Bedouin family might invite her
home for dinner, certain she was a long-lost relative in need of
better clothing. She could carry on famously in Katmandu, fit in
swimmingly in San Salvador, be a big hit in Cochabamba. Mission magazines confirmed her suspicions. Grace looked at the
pictures and cried. She didn't know how Bolivians managed to
survive their history, but she found her task to be an arduous
one. Unlike her brothers and sister, who took comfort in their
Louisiana homeland when questions of identity arose, Grace
was not so easily consoled. America was her only country, and
she didn't know how to claim it.

Grace spread her blanket to calm her thoughts. Greeting everyone with the same wan smile, she made sure no one hugged
her too tightly. Once her enormous family was safely occupied
eating, resting, playing—generally leaving her alone—she retired to her aspirin and can of ginger ale. Nobody cared about
her, a fact which was evidenced by year after year of inattention.
Even her mother, who knew her condition, would not so much
as carry a hotdog to where her daughter lay drooping. Camille,
whose chief emotion was embarrassment, was always embarrassed by Grace's lack of sociability. As far as her cousins were
concerned, she was sickly and best left alone.

It was no coincidence that, more often than not during the
annual beach trip, Grace was on her period. A girl on her period
could not be expected to run and play with the other youth. She
would not likely be in the mood to cook or chase behind the
younger children. She would not be caught dead in salt water,

which would cause her napkin to bloat. Or worse, the rush of
the water might be enough to whisk it from between her legs and
wash it out to sea. A menstruating girl would be unmolested by
brothers carrying buckets of water or looking for victims to
bury alive. She would not be found in a bikini and she would
make sure her bra was both sturdy and loose. Her beach bag
was a cache of extra panties and shorts.

Alone on her sky-blue blanket, Grace entertained herself by
imagining what it would be like to be ordinary. She had been
careful to bring a hat today. At ten years old, when she first
realized how different she looked from her brothers and sisters,
the realization had brought her blood down. She secretly believed that her dark, dense blood was the cause of her darker
skin. Today she was careful to hide them both.

She regarded her parents as they fired up the grill. Grace was
glad they did not look alike. She looked at her mother, shimmer-
ing like copper in the noonday sun. Next to her was T-Papa, all
silver and zinc under his hat, which he could not do without, lest
he smolder and burn. They reflected one another. Grace could
appreciate their courage. They had defied their families to love
and marry. She could appreciate their love, even if it did not
always include her.

Unbeknownst to her conscious self, Grace had now joined
the wandering hordes of lost Americans trying their best to ac-
quire self-esteem from the contents of a paperback. She had
brought one of her vast collection to the beach that day, a perky
little book about learning to love yourself, even if it required
divorcing your parents. She was on page 68. Here, readers were
encouraged to appreciate the "wheat" in their parents and to
throw the "chaff" away. Accordingly, readers were instructed to
make a list of their parents' positive points before moving on to
all-out condemnation. Grace's first list was painfully short.

Perhaps her parents would not expect her to conform to their standards, since they themselves had disregarded custom to be with each other. Perhaps she would be allowed to go her own way, to strike out with their blessing. After all, they had six other children doing them proud in every way. But this was too much to hope for. It would take many more generations of evolution for T-Papa and Camille to reach a state where they could accept Grace. She knew this instinctively. Their youngest and darkest child, she was a both a comfort and a challenge. Grace reminded Camille of the family she'd left to marry T-Papa, the family she still missed daily, thirty-two years and eight children later. Grace reminded T-Papa of the family he'd betrayed. Both her parents loved her greatly, but their love was laced with guilt and limited by culture. Grace was too much for them.

Even so, she considered herself lucky. She had seen enough of her color-struck Burbank cousins to realize that she was fortunate to belong to more enlightened folks. Her parents were not afraid of darkness per se. They were afraid of what the darkness held. For Grace, it held the universe. It was to these inner variations that she attributed her cramps. Inside her abdomen stirred many shades of longing her parents could not fathom.

The beach was a great place to let the mind wander. Grace sent her thoughts far away from home and family. She watched them as they blithely made their way out to sea. The realization of her confinement, like a woman of Leviticus cast out of camp, brought salt water to her eyes. She yearned for Exodus and the days of deliverance. A Red Sea could be crossed if you believed it could. Grace did not believe; this was her problem. She was as rooted to the temporal as a starfish to a rock. Her mind could only wander so far.

She decided to cut her hair.

Radical, self-inflicted change, that's what was needed. Her family wouldn't recognize her. Yes, hair must be the first to go.

So unnecessary to her growth, so inimical to her desires, hair was the thing that kept her mindful of her captivity. She must cast it aside for a lighter cloak, yank herself up by the roots. She would take her hair to task, making it pay for her years of misery with these good people who would subsume her. This simple paring down of substance would deliver a complicated message of defiance and betrayal. It would force her family to realize she did not belong to them. She would never be like them. Since she was afraid to confront them with this knowledge, she would confront them with her hair.

It was important to the teenage Grace that she cut her own hair, instead of going to the beauty parlor where the rest of the family went. The beauticians were proper New Orleans maidens; they had never done her hair the way she wanted. To ensure the maximum shock value she'd have to cut it herself. She wanted a sacrificial style, one that would suit a personality on the brink of self-immolation. Her family would refuse to be seen with her. And she'd save one tuft for Elena, whom she had only recently come to love.

Presently, Grace was joined on her blanket by one of her girl cousins from Burbank. This girl had always humiliated Grace by flipping her hair from side to side while she talked, knowing full well that Grace could do no such tricks. Her name was Genevieve, but she insisted on the French pronunciation. Genevieve was a study in self-aggrandizement. From inside her denim beach bag, she took a small pink bottle and began to wipe a little brush across her fingernails. She was fat and pretty, but her nails reminded Grace of a dog's toes. The minute Genevieve opened her mouth, Grace knew she was in trouble. Talking to her was a trap. She was family CIA. Every family has them. They don't carry bugging devices, but their ears stand up like a Doberman's. And Genevieve's eyes were always jumping up and down, even as they held you steady.

"I'm not going into the water," she announced. "It'll ruin my *do*."

Hair was the pride of Creoles like Genevieve. White hair was flimsy, Black hair was bulky. Creole hair was silky, wavy, curly, bouncy hair that could swing both ways. The luckiest ones had strands so thick you could braid them like Lakota, curl them like Jews, or straighten them like other Negroes. The homeliest Creoles with forgiving hair could pass the "comb test" for entry into exclusive parties that the comeliest Negroes could never attend. Unlike their Negro brethren, Creoles could gain admission almost anywhere, so long as their hair conformed. They could puff it up and run with the Black Power crowd or slick it down and blend with the Mediterraneans. They could take their hair on interviews and win White-only jobs. To the densest Creole it was clear: Opportunity followed Hair. If their hair was pulled in school, if they were teased because of it, they suffered only proud tears, never wishing to change one lock of it. Lucky for them, they lived in America, where Whites wanted to be Black and Blacks wanted to be White. Creoles took this to mean that everybody's deepest aspiration was to be them. Genevieve was convinced of it.

"I had to pay thirty dollars to get this perm, but it was worth it. See that boy over there? He has a crush on me. Lots of boys do, but I can't be bothered with most of them. He tried to kiss me once. I think he's peculiar. He missed my mouth."

Grace followed the dog's toe to its pointed conclusion. At the end of the line stood Rouby, the patron saint of the Broussard car. Sleek and handsome in his red flowered shorts, he watched the other boys play football but did not join in.

"Creole boys are prudes. I won't date any of them. They don't know how to kiss." Genevieve lay back seductively, half on the blanket, half off. She signaled to Rouby by wiggling her foot and rotating her knee. He blushed and looked away.

"Do you like Creole boys?"

Grace considered the boy in question. He was Creole enough. She'd seen a lot of him because he liked to hang around her father's workbench. He lived in Leimert Park, went to a public high school, and was a member of the neighborhood swim team. Grace thought he was spectacular. He had the biggest ears she had ever seen, with a nose and mouth to match. His brown skin was taut and tan. His green eyes were big and lively.

"That one really likes you. I can tell," Genevieve sneered, throwing back her hair. "His ears are too big."

The fact that Rouby might "like" her had never occurred to Grace. That any boy would look at her with a pinch of desire seemed altogether misguided. Rouby had always been kind to her. If she didn't "like" him, chances are she wouldn't like any of his number. Grace examined her heart and found it unmoved. She met Genevieve's jumping eyes and shrugged.

"Don't you like boys? My mother says going to a girls' school warps a person. I don't know how you can stand it!"

Grace certainly felt warped, but she didn't attribute this feeling to her girls' school. Our Lady of Fatima was actually the only place where she felt just fine. Not only could she "stand it" there, she frequently wished she could borrow a sleeping bag and camp out in its poorly lit halls. Whenever Grace felt like running away from home, she could only imagine running as far as the good Sisters of Mercy. Joining them would have been an option worth serious consideration if she had believed a word they said about God. Sister Victorine had let it be known that, in her opinion, Grace Broussard had a "vocation." Grace figured Sister was lying on account of vocations being down. She didn't want to marry anyone, especially not Jesus, who was bound to be even more demanding than a Creole boy. As far as she knew, He didn't have any designs on her, either. As she lay there on her blanket, unnerved by Genevieve's nervy question, her mind lay with Elena.

"I don't think you like boys." This time, Genevieve announced it for all the world to hear. Since all the world was playing football, eating, laughing loudly, or chasing each other, no one batted an eye.

However, Rouby was a world unto himself, and his ears were mighty large. He looked from Grace to Genevieve and back to Grace again, his huge mouth hanging open. If Grace had been Yvette, she would have been pink by now. As it was, she turned several shades of crimson, leapt to her feet, and hurled the only curse at her disposal. "Shut up," she said to Genevieve and headed for the water.

At first plunge, she felt cold and brittle. The drop in temperature seemed especially sharp due to her loss of blood. Grace persevered. She dipped her body down and let the water carry her. She fell upon its shoulders and rested in its arms. The zeal of the summer sea filled all her heart's crevices. Its salt purified her blood and took away her sins.

Grace was sailing out to sea without oar or rudder. She was going wherever the water would take her. If it was along the road to heaven, she was going there. More likely, it was to the floodgates of hell. Strange men leered at her with fiery eyes. Beach devils, they were, but no matter. The water itself was holy, consecrated by the sun, which performed sacred rites at eventide. She needed only the clouds to guide her. Thankfully, there were a few thin troubadours lining the summer sky. From what she could tell, they were heading for Hawaii. She would call her folks when she got there.

In the meantime, her folks were calling to her from the thirsty water's edge. A small crowd had gathered around Camille, who stood roaring her daughter's name. Genevieve was busy pointing for the benefit of new arrivals. T-Papa came pacing, his hat in his hand. Beyond the bouncing waves Grace could hear none of this commotion, but she could tell they were afraid because they looked so angry.

Though she probably should have been, Grace was not afraid. She had seen her death, and she knew it would not be by drowning. She lived by drowning, by sinking deep into her heart and letting the waves overcome her. She survived every day by drowning out her parents, drowning out her teachers, drowning out the Church. She was not afraid of drowning, which had become for her a necessary thing. She knew she would not die this way. She would die trying to walk on water. She would suffocate trying to live up to her parents' expectations. The perfect report card, the perfect disposition, the perfectly set table, the perfectly respectable job, the perfect Creole husband—none of these would ever be hers, but the striving for them would be enough to kill her. In her pursuit of Creole perfection, Grace would forget to look where she was going and stumble over the cliff's edge. It would be a sudden death; she would hit the air running, no parachute, no liquid below, only hard, hard land. Her family would know her to be an impostor by the unsaintly way she would die.

To Grace's horror, walking on water was a feat her brothers and sisters performed on command. It was the least expected of a Broussard. Casting out demons, multiplying loaves and fishes, raising the dead—these were tricks her parents managed as a matter of course. The only thing separating the Broussards from their rightful place in the Bible was a few unfortunate centuries.

But Grace was not kin to Jesus. She was not even one of the

twelve. Trying to walk on water would only land her in deep trouble. Her talent lay in sinking, in delving beneath the spirit to caress the demon flesh. Hers was a talent the family did not prize. They sought to rise above the tide. Grace wanted the tide to carry her away. To mingle with life in the depths was her unending need. For this she would suffer, for this she would bleed, for this she would eventually die.

On the shore, her family grew smaller and smaller. Turning around to look at them, Grace was struck by the beauty of their waning voices. They were reaching for her with spiked tentacles, chasing her with their hooked tongues. Camille, who had cast out her umbilical cord, was straining like a fisherman with seaweed on his line. She was gesturing in stereo, a score of frantic cousins praying at her elbows. Children jumped and wailed and sucked their thumbs. Yvette waved a pair of Bermuda shorts. No one thought to contact the White lifeguards a hundred yards away, who were occupied with what looked to be an actual drowning but which was, in fact, a training exercise. Instead, T-Papa rushed into the water, flailing about until his trousers filled with sand. Camille sent her sons to marshal him in. "Lord today! Now we gonna have to rescue you too!"

The Broussards had never seen a Fellini film, so it was possible for them to carry on this way without feeling the least bit self-conscious. To Grace, they looked ridiculous. Camille's scarf became the babushka of a European peasant desperately trying to save her children from war and famine. Grace had read *Mother Courage* in her World Literature class, and she knew a parody when she saw one.

Being the cause of all this drama did not disturb her in the least. It's hard to stage drama when you're the youngest child of a large family. Everything has already been done before, two or

three times. Venial sins garner no notice at all. To get the
family's attention, you have to transgress a commandment. The
more mortal, the more effective. This desperate act of Grace's
was not only mortal, it was new. No one had ever tried to drown
before. The youngest child took great pleasure in rousing her
family's love of near tragedy. But she herself was not worried.
She knew their prayers would save her. Besides, Grace could
swim.

Elena had taught her. On secret trips to the beach in the
back of Felipe's pickup truck, they had held hands and let the
road bump them into each other. Felipe was Elena's brother and
the best Mexican swimmer at Bishop McGreevy High School.
Ocean swimming was his favorite pastime and, according to
Elena, he sometimes came at night and swam without his trunks.

The Hurtados had a sense of danger that excited Grace. Her
own family was so constrained in comparison. They blamed
their need for caution on the world in which they lived. But
Elena's family inhabited the same scary world, and they ran toward it instead of letting it chase them. The fact that they would
die one day did nothing to dissuade them.

Grace dreamed of swimming nude. At night in her flowered
gown, she roamed the bed with visions of abandon. It was impossible for her to know that others in the house on Compton
Avenue were having the same kind of robust nocturnal fanta-
sies. Their dreams were confined to their sleep and did not spill
over into the daylight as Grace's were prone to do. And the
other Broussards didn't know how to swim; they didn't know
how to drown. In these two things, Grace was completely alone.

As summer approached, Elena had led Grace further and
further into the Fluid Mysteries. She taught her how to stroke
and breathe, how not to fight, how to roll with the waves. Each

time they inched toward the water, Grace felt her own tides surging. She couldn't name the feeling, but she knew it was something powerful, and she didn't want to lose it.

She was afraid her mother would see her desire and force her to relinquish it. After each ocean outing, Grace struggled to rid her body of every grain of passion before she reached her mother's door. Once, when Camille discovered sand on the porch, Grace lied about its origin, claiming she had acquired it from the park, playing with Elena's nephew.

"What park?" her mother wanted to know.

"Sugar Ray Robinson."

"You know better than to go there! It's dangerous. You're not to go there anymore. Do you hear me?"

"But Felipe was with us."

"What's Felipe going to do? If Felipe doesn't have any better sense than to take you to the park, he's not much protection, now, is he?"

"What do we need protection for? It was broad daylight. Nothing's going to happen in broad daylight."

Camille was not used to Broussard children who "talked back." Somewhere between her first child and her last child, she had lost her knack for effortless intimidation.

"I don't want you talking back to me. Somebody got shot at just the other day in broad daylight outside the liquor store."

Grace persisted. "That was at the liquor store. I'm not going to get shot at."

"How do you know?"

Getting "shot at" was the guiding fear of the Broussards. They knew well the hatred that consumed many of their brethren, and because of the way they looked, they feared becoming mistaken targets of this hatred. They feared the day when their darker neighbors, who were used to dying untimely deaths, would wrest their little colony from White domination. On that day, questionables such as themselves were unlikely to be real popular. Maybe they'd have time to run to relatives in the suburbs. Or maybe they would join the revolution. As Creoles, they had options. Since Grace did not look like most of the other Broussards, she didn't share their fear of being taken for White. If it came to revolution, she knew which side to join behind the barricades.

It was the same side with Elena.

Drifting out to sea, Grace imagined Elena's arms around her as the earth dropped out from under her. She was barely in over her head. While her family on shore pictured her as 20,000 leagues under the sea, Grace gauged she was only about seven feet deep. They had no way of knowing this and she wasn't about to tell them. Her legs were strong and her arms were able. She would wander a little bit farther before turning and venturing back. Going back would be her act of courage. She didn't look forward to the welcoming party, which was growing more hysterical by the minute.

A red-waisted figure ran headlong into the waves, a blur of flowered trunks. Grace watched as Rouby approached with the elegance of a wild dolphin. It took him all of two minutes to reach her. A silent cheer went up from the shore. Rouby bobbed up and down, grinning. He didn't touch Grace but regarded her with a mixture of wonder and delight.

"They sent me to keep you company."

"I thought they were calling the Coast Guard."

"I'm supposed to let you know that you're in grave danger."

"I'll be in grave danger when I go back."

"You ain't never lied!"

"Oh, tell them to just leave me alone! It's impossible to get any privacy in this family."

"Come on. Let's swim to where we can stand and talk. Follow me across this way. You can ride on my shoulders."

Grace could see no harm in obliging. She draped her arms around her cousin's neck and let him lead her east. They stood where the waves were breaking, and laughed as the water tossed them about. Grace felt disturbingly calm. She gave a playful squeal when the ocean tried to swallow her. "Surrender!" was her battle cry.

Watching this strange cousin of his, Rouby became suddenly serious. Though she was with him, she seemed utterly alone, completely contained. He held her in his eyes and found that she was beautiful. He wished he could tell her so.

The crowd on the shore was growing impatient. Some had already left to "see about the beans." Camille and Yvette were locked arm in arm, two women on a war poster. T-Papa was rumbling with fatherly oaths, his hat cupped over his mouth. His sons and their wives whispered amongst themselves. The football boys tossed insults at the sea and at each other. Old people started the slow walk back. Children collected shells. Genevieve was nowhere to be found.

"Well, do you like boys or don't you?" Rouby's voice was insistent, his eyes hopeful.

Liking boys had never occurred to Grace. She had five brothers, all of whom she was deeply devoted to and each of whom she disliked immensely. There were always boys around the house — her brothers' friends, her father's apprentices, boys who were charming, silly, and disagreeable. What was there to like about them? She had gone to school with boys until she was thirteen, when she had graduated to Our Lady of Fatima Girls' High School. There she had met Elena. She wondered if Rouby would like Elena. Did it matter if girls liked boys? Grace struggled to find an answer. Elena was still a secret in the back of her throat.

"I like boys," offered Rouby.

This seemed right to Grace, genuine, fitting, proper. He was a boy, he should like boys. She felt at ease with Rouby. Now she understood why. He was different, like her. She let her back sink into his chest and felt his arms glide beneath her breasts. The water swirled around her legs and dipped between her thighs. She could feel the clumsy pad, bloated and bulging, as he lifted her with his knee.

By the time they reached the shore, the rescue party had dwindled to three. Yvette glared at Grace in disbelief. Camille turned from her, embarrassed. Grace realized her bra was showing. It was T-Papa who spoke.

"You losing your mind, 'tite fille?" He motioned to Rouby, who disappeared. Yvette led her mother away. Grace stood shivering, unable to speak. She had caused her family grief, which had not been her intention. She had only wished to get away from them. But this was not possible. Grace could not meet her father's eyes.

He wrapped his towel around her. It was wet. She didn't mind. He began to walk along the shore. She followed behind him, stooping to collect a piece of brown glass. His words caught her as she rose.

"You went out too far."

Grace let every word sink into her soul. When she was a young child, "too far" was next door. A little bit older and "too far" was around the corner. The important thing was never to go out of the family's sight. Camille could take in a lot from the porch, and Grace was not to stray outside the territory marked by her mother's vision. As she matured, she was allowed to spend time with trusted others away from her family. Usually, these "others" were relatives or people from church.

Once, Grace had followed some Baptist playmates into forbidden realms. Almost immediately, some older boys appeared

and took away their bicycles. Grace cried and was given her
bicycle back. She pedaled home as fast as she could, reassured of
her mother's wisdom.

By the time she entered high school, "too far" was anywhere
without permission. Permission could be given out over the
phone, but usually a dispensation was required at least a week in
advance. If she was going to be more than ten minutes late
returning home, Camille required a phone call. (Camille refused
to worry needlessly for more than ten minutes at a time.) Any
activity that couldn't be done in two hours didn't need to be
done at all. No place was worth going if you couldn't go accompanied by a small, officially sanctioned mob. As Grace understood it, she was never to experience herself as a solitary soul.
"Too far" and "alone" were synonymous.

"What you go so far out for?" T-Papa was looking at her as
though she had suddenly become a stranger.

"I wanted to see what was out there."

"Ain't nothing but water out there. You can see that from
the shore. What's out there you need to see?"

"I wanted to see the shore."

T-Papa squinted in an effort to understand. He looked at
Grace for a long time. They continued on in silence. When he
spoke again, his tone was one of pained concern.

"You'll drown if you go out too far."

"It wasn't that far."

"It was far away from the rest of us."

Grace had wanted to be far away. Now she wanted to be
close. At sixteen years old, she did not know how to be either.
She slid her thumb over the glass in her hand. From her throat
came bottled tears.

"We never go anywhere! Just back and forth to Louisiana.
Or to the beach once a year."

"Where you want to go, 'tite fille?"

"I want to go somewhere with my friends. Not just with my family all the time."

"Where you want to go?"

"Anywhere!"

"Now, you know you can't just go anywhere. It's not safe."

"I want to invite my friends to come with me, then."

"Come with you where?"

"Here."

"What friends you want to bring with you here?"

Grace didn't know what to say. Her father didn't know about her friends. He didn't know about her life. Her dreams were those of a teenage girl. They were not meaningful to him. It was this last realization that shattered her. She couldn't say a thing.

"Why you so anxious to get away from us? You should spend more time with your family. Pretty soon, you'll be grown and gone and married. And then you'll miss these old people."

Grace knew he wasn't right, but she cried anyway.

T-Papa looked hurt. "You shouldn't have gone so far out."

Grace was not yet contrite. If this was far, then she wanted to go to the ends of the earth. She gripped the glass until her palm ached. She wanted her father to know her.

"You don't understand. I'm different from you. I'm different from everybody!"

"Different how?"

Grace didn't know how to explain herself. Couldn't he see she was different? Wasn't it obvious? She had to find a way to show him.

They were headed back to camp, back to the waiting family, back to the roasting food and the smoking gossip and the fiery shame. Grace looked out at the water where she had left herself. She shook with muffled sobs.

"What's the matter, 'tite fille?"

"I'm not your little girl!" she cried. "Stop calling me that!"

"You're acting like a little girl. As long as you're under my roof, I'll call you what I please."

Grace wasn't listening. She turned her back and walked away. She would have nothing to do with this tyrant. She would cast him off like the seaweed clinging to her foot. If only they weren't tangled together in one great heap of Broussard algae!

In less than a moment, T-Papa was at her side. He grabbed her arm, his body trembling. "Don't you walk away from me, girl!"

"Let me go! You don't own me."

"You and every hair on your head. You ain't grown, yet, 'tite fille."

Using the glass as a jagged comb, Grace grabbed a clump of curls and yanked it from her head. T-Papa looked on in horror. He sat down. Eyes glazed, struggling to breathe, hand at his throat, he was unable to speak.

Grace stared at him. Frozen to the sand, she could not warm herself. She stood bereft, bedraggled. Dangling from her fingers were a few wet strands.

T-Papa turned and started toward the fire. In everything, he was a determined man. Somehow he had failed. The look in Grace's eyes frightened him. It was a look of passionate non-compliance. His fervent love betrayed, T-Papa moved slowly toward the ebbing tide of nourishment and laughter where Camille had his burger waiting.

Burning, sizzling, raw. A frozen heap of salt. From the shore of her soul, Grace watched herself drowning in wave after wave of Broussard blood.

3

The House on Compton Avenue

Midday, Christmas, 1978

Appearance is everything. The Broussards would put up with unsightliness so long as they didn't have to look at it. If it was something within them they didn't want to see, they would go to great lengths to tear it limb from limb before it had a chance to rear its ugly head. Most of their moral energy was expended trying to make things disappear. Weakness, desire, poverty, death—eventually, everything becomes apparent. Smoke inside of mountains, bodies hidden by the sea. Weeds appear and reappear, blossoms only once. Ghosts only appear to people who see them.

H e followed her home.
T-Papa may have been out of body, but he still cast a heavy shadow. Long after abandoning the beach, Grace could feel waves of sorrow lapping at her sanity. When Yvette returned to the hospital about three that afternoon, Grace was left alone in the house. She could hear its eaves and shutters breathing her dismay.

She prepared to go after her father tooth and nail. Drown him out with Christmas carols played at ungodly volumes. How dare he try to rule her from the grave! Lose him in the red and green sparkles of stale butter cookies, blind him with the pert lights of a captive tree. Her life belonged to her, not to him, not to her family. She had paid for it with furious tears shed late at night in fits of shame. No further gumbo ransom was required. Her father's ghost would never wrest from her this final act of obedience.

Everywhere Grace went, T-Papa pursued her with his absence. Walls strained for want of his voice, floorboards cried out for his footsteps. Whole rooms were damp with missing him. From the linen closet, from the oven, from the breadbox, he crooned to her. His ramblings on fidelity caused her to forfeit dinner, forget manners, forgo rest. With him she could not reason. He insisted on proffering his opinions, unwanted though they were. She tried fending him off with pungent thoughts, bowls of irreverence stacked upon plates of insolence. He would not budge.

Grace hadn't told anyone of his visit. She didn't want to lend him that weight. As far as the Broussards were concerned, being visited by the dead was an honor. Any sighting of the late great patriarch was bound to lead to a flurry of prayers, enough to swell his already prodigious head. If he could work three miracles and wait fifty years, he'd be a candidate for sainthood. Grace hoped she'd be dead by then.

Somehow, coming to terms with her parents' deaths was harder than contemplating her own. The future had no end to it, but the past was forever slipping away. One day, it would be gone altogether. One day, even Camille would die. Her gumbo would be no more. This thought plunged Grace into throes of compassion. All of a sudden, she knew what her father must feel. To be forever deprived of her mother's gumbo? She flinched at the thought of refusing one bowl. And what must it be like for Camille? To live without the love of her life?

Grace thought of life without Elena. Oh, how she would hate that! No eyes boring through her soul, no legs struggling against her for warmth. They had loved each other for four vulnerable years. What would it be like to love someone for forty? Grace could not imagine it. To love someone that long and lose your "loved one" in the end. Grace hated the thought of being left.

What was it like to be the leaver? That was the feeling Grace wanted to have. Leavers went on to the next adventure. Leavers were busy, occupied with their leaving. They didn't wait for succor that would never come. Waiting was the worst. Time has contempt for people who wait, but time is kind to the leavers. They don't stand in windows, hoping for a sign. Leavers don't pine. Grace wondered what life was like on the inflicting side of sorrow.

These thoughts left her too dizzy to stand. T-Papa had sapped her strength, deprived her of balance. The afternoon sun made her shiver. Grace lay down to nap.

In her dreams, she was being chased by a White man. A big hulking fellow with arms distended, lips flapping, a punishing prison guard of a brute. The house shook with his thundering exhortations. *Heave ho! Man overboard!* He was trying to tell her something, but the language was one she did not understand. Grace recognized the White man. He was her father.

Your Daddy is White. "He is not!" she had protested, defending T-Papa to the whole first grade. *Grace's daddy is an old White man.* It made for a nice taunt, succinct but untrue.

Your Daddy is White. Well, now he was. Thinner than white, ashen, translucent.

T-Papa had the temerity to die at a time when Grace had stopped sticking up for him, a time when she was ashamed of him. She had drawn no comfort from the fact that most of her teenage friends were ashamed of their parents for one reason or another. From what she could gather, their shame had to do with unreasonable demands and embarrassing behavior on the part of their elders. But Grace was not ashamed of her father's character. She was embarrassed by his color.

T-Papa was a white Creole. Grace was a black Creole. She identified as Black. He identified as Creole or Colored. Since "Negro" had never really caught on in his part of the world, "Black" didn't stand a chance.

Most Creoles considered it high tragedy that when Louisiana was acquired from the French in 1804, their people had been forced to register as Negroes. It was indeed tragedy, but of a much lower kind than they could imagine. Under the French, Creoles had been given privileges most Negroes could not expect. With Napoleon's sale to the Americans, they began to feel like the bastards they really were. They struggled to retain their status. They clung to their food, their language, their music, their sense of themselves as a select group rather than an outcast one. "Creole" was their race. "Black" was an insult hurled by hooligans without regard for manners or sentiment. "Negro" was the proper term, but too easily corrupted by the slightest southern accent. The state marked their every turn by stamping this identity on birth and death certificates, marriage and driver's licenses. A Negro had been born, a Negro had married, a Negro was driving the car in which a Negro had died after being run off the road by a person who was not a Negro.

To Creoles, "Black" and "White" demonstrated the American penchant for reducing life to its most shallow, trivial form.

In Louisiana, as in the whole of the United States, these identities were forced on people of every heritage and hue, and the names took on a power of their own. Entire civilizations had been obliterated by these terms—Black, White, Red, Yellow, Brown. The result was a country of people who didn't know who they were or where they came from. But being Southerners and Creoles, the Broussards barely considered themselves Americans at all, thus avoiding the daunting confusion that paralyzed many of their neighbors.

The first time Grace was called a "nigger," she flinched. She'd heard that word bandied about by her brothers and their friends. It rolled off their tongues like a sanctified curse but, to Grace, no amount of sugar could redeem it. At the beach, she had seen it carved into park benches, often in the plural form, accompanied by suggestions like "Go Home" and "Die." Once, when she wandered as far as the rocks, she met with the invective, "No Niggers Allowed." That sign had stopped her in her tracks, just as it was meant to do. She did not think of herself as a "nigger," but she knew she had wandered much too far, crossed into a land where other people did. None of these signs was intended solely or specifically for her, no matter how deeply they knifed her. The first knife that was meant for Grace alone was flung by another Creole.

It was a Saturday in early 1969. Yvette had been invited to a party, a baby shower for a girl she knew from high school. Grace had not yet been born when Yvette was in high school. She didn't know Yvette's friends from long ago unless they still lived in Watts, and most of them did not. (If they hadn't moved by the time of the Riots, they had fled shortly thereafter.) This particular woman's family had moved to Culver City long before the old neighborhood had gone up in flames. She had married an accountant from Cuba. Yvette had been in their wedding, and it had not escaped her notice that the darkest person in church that day was a statue of St. Paul.

The shower was being held at her sister-in-law's home in Santa Monica. Yvette called and asked if she could bring her little sister. The boys were off playing basketball, T-Papa was on retreat, and Camille was making dinner for the priests. Yvette dressed Grace in a yellow frock with a white apron and affixed two bows to her hair. The Valiant was relatively new then, and Grace loved to ride in the front. They stopped at a gas station to fill the tank and get directions to this foreign land.

They started two hours early, as Yvette was afraid of the freeway. The trip down Olympic Boulevard was interesting for a ten-year-old. Grace didn't mind being taken along, and Yvette seemed glad for the company. They arrived in a cheery state, forty-five minutes early. The house was a California stucco with a red tiled roof. It was the most beautiful house Grace had ever seen up close. Yvette thought they should ring the bell and see if the hosts needed help setting up. The doorbell was soft and melodious. They stood on the porch for a long time. The porch had been painted red. They could hear voices inside, attempting to hush themselves. Yvette looked at the address again; it matched the invitation. She rang the bell one last time. "Tell them to go away." The door opened abruptly.

"Oh, Yvette!" exclaimed the expectant mother's sister, "I didn't recognize you. We thought it was somebody collecting something. From one of those weird church groups." She looked down at Grace, who was pulling on one of her bows.

"Who is it?" called a voice from the kitchen.

"It's Yvette, Mama. Yvette Broussard. Remember?"

"Who's that nigger she brought with her?"

Yvette's hands rushed to gather Grace into her fold. It was

too late. Grace had heard the hated word. She knew who it referred to. She would not soon forget it. Flushed with embarrassment and sullied with shame, the Broussard sisters turned away
from the stucco house with its red tiled roof and chiming doorbell. No such embarrassment or shame was felt within the
house. The car was silent all the way home.

The memory of that day caused Grace to recoil. Skin color
was the one thing the Broussards never talked about. Grace
thought about it all the time. Skin color was everywhere. You
couldn't go out the door without hearing reference to it. The
girls she had hung with in high school were all darker than she
was—even Elena had the same dark eyes and hair and brown
skin as Grace.

These were the people Grace thought of as hers. They were
different from her people's people, the ones who crowded the
house every Sunday. Grace's people were not part of the family
gatherings. They were not family.

Grace awoke from her nap groggy, perturbed. A noise in the
hall made her jump from bed. She shuddered with the knowledge that the house was empty save for her and her father's
ghost. Slowly, gingerly, she moved toward the noise. Lingering
in the hall closet was the figure from her dreams. She could feel
his presence. She could hear him breathing.

Grace ran to the kitchen and grabbed the salt. She raced
around the house tossing salt in every crevice and in all the open
spaces. "Out! Out!" she cried, sweeping and scattering the salt
at his feet. She staggered onto the great porch of the house on
Compton Avenue, flinging handfuls of salt in all directions.

Mr. Pep just happened to be out on his porch when some
salt caught him on the ear. "All right, all right. Pretty Miss
Grace, all right?" He was drunk. "Who you trying to dispel,
Miss Grace?"

Grace coughed in reply.

Pretty Miss Alma was sitting up next to her husband, sober as ever. "Is that my Grace? Come over here and give Auntie Alma a Christmas kiss."

Through watery eyes, Grace made out her neighbors' forms. They were a sorry sight—Mr. Pep, with his scraggly beard and rotting teeth, Pretty Miss Alma, with her bones jutting out, all of her joints like elbows. She was skinny beyond belief. She looked like one of those people the nuns were always collecting mission money for. Grace wondered if the nuns' money ever reached people like Mr. Pep and Miss Alma, who sat way below the poverty line on their porch on Compton Avenue. They lived right down the street from St. Martin de Porres (where some of the poorest people in the city regularly donated to the missions) but Grace didn't think they had ever been inside. They weren't Catholic, they weren't anything. "Keep the faith," Miss Alma used to say to her. "Somebody's got to."

Grace liked Pretty Miss Alma despite her afflictions, or maybe because of them. It was her cynicism that Grace found most attractive. In 1969, when Tom Bradley was making his bid to become L.A.'s first Black mayor, Camille had taken Grace with her when she canvassed the neighborhood. Grace liked canvassing. She enjoyed protecting her mother from stray dogs, seeing more of the neighborhood than she was customarily allowed to see, and being invited into people's houses for peach cobbler and iced tea. She and her mother would spend long days going door-to-door, drumming up enthusiasm and getting out the vote. Most people were already convinced that Mayor Bradley would mean good things for Watts and Black Los Angeles. And even if they weren't sure about Bradley, they had a healthy disdain for Mayor Yorty. In 1969, many people in Watts and all over America still believed in their power to change things. King was gone, the War on Poverty was lost, Nixon was President, but the fight was not over. Not yet. Every once in awhile, Camille and Grace would come across a throwback Negro who still reckoned that only the White Man could successfully run a city, bank, or business, but those folks were getting rarer and rarer. By 1969, most of them had the good sense to keep their tongues still.

Well, on this particular day, mother and daughter were tired as they returned to their block. They could see Miss Alma standing on her front porch, hands on what remained of her once ample hips. "Pretty Miss Alma, can we count on your vote?" Camille sang to her neighbor as they came up the drive.

Pretty Miss Alma turned her pose to face them. There was no smile in her voice, only a steady gaze that bid them answer. "Miss Alma's running. Who's voting for she?"

Camille couldn't say.

That was a full four years after the Riots had turned Pretty Miss Alma off politics and life in general. Actually, it wasn't the rioting, which she had found exciting in an illicit sort of way. The Riots had made her feel powerful and proud of the people of Watts. They were protesting, they were serving notice. It was "the fire next time," the one God had ordered for all unreformed sinners, and America was the worst kind of sinner. One hundred years after the Emancipation, Pretty Miss Alma still was not free. No, it wasn't the Riots that had brought her down. It was the aftermath of burnt-out buildings and charred hopes which made her lose her appetite.

According to Camille, Miss Alma never touched a bottle except for those blazing nights of summer '65. Rumor had it that she'd been amongst the looters who'd torched the corner liquor store (long the nemesis of all right-thinking neighbors.) For many weeks after pouring vodka on the flames, she'd been wild with a sense of accomplishment. But just as suddenly as it had arrived, her enthusiasm had left her. The signs were in her body. Her beautiful rolls of flesh had all broiled away until she'd reached her present state of emaciation, from which she had nothing more to lose.

Before the Riots, Mr. Pep had been a gardener. He had driven his truck long distances to work in the gardens of Beverly Hills. After the Riots, there was no work for him. No work anywhere. He still had a few rosebushes that he doted on. Camille paid him $20 a month to look after her flowers, which grew fine on their own but better when Mr. Pep talked to them.

Neither Mr. Pep nor Pretty Miss Alma had ever been invited to a Broussard family dinner. Mr. Pep occasionally came in for a plate of something. Miss Alma wasn't prone to cook, seeing as she wasn't prone to eat. Mr. Pep was a fine cook, but he couldn't rival Camille. Her black-eyed peas were his favorites, but he had never eaten them at her dining room table. Miss Alma had never eaten them at all. Even in the days when she was eating, she didn't eat Camille's food. She didn't trust Camille and her family. She didn't trust them living next door. Why hadn't they moved like the other Creoles? If she had been as light-skinned and as stuck up as they were, she would have been gone from Watts long ago. They were peculiar folk, not exactly poor in the way other people were. She didn't wish to share their food.

Pretty Miss Alma and Mr. Pep had no children. They'd never actually been in love, but they'd always been "in good company." They fit together; he had no first name and she had no last. Mr. Pep loved children, he loved people in general, and talked to them freely whenever they happened by. Miss Alma did not care for people. She only cared for Mr. Pep, who she liked because he referred to all women as Pretty Miss and she could trust that he would always do so. She didn't like children because she'd been one, and there was no fondness in the memory. The Broussard children, in particular, bothered her with their clannish ways. All except Grace, who she liked in spite of herself. She liked Grace because Grace was bad at pretending. Pretty Miss Alma had watched Grace struggle with this liability every day since she was born. It was a struggle made beautiful in the older woman's eyes.

"What's the matter, my Grace? Come speak to your Auntie Alma. Those people over there giving Grace a hard time? They ain't mean nothing by it. Bring Missy over here where somebody know she."

Grace was spinning as she made her way across the little patch of brown grass, salt in hand. She felt desolate, estranged. She struggled to keep her neighbors in focus. Pretty Miss Alma waited.

"Merry Christmas," Grace sang flatly, shoving the salt into her pocket.

"Is it that now, then? You sure you want to spend it talking to the infidels?"

"Speak for yourself, Pretty Miss. Mr. Pep is one of the true believers! If Christ hadn't been born, I wouldn't be sitting here right now."

"How you figure, old man?"

"No Christian to run the Indians off this land, no Christian to bring me here as slave, no Christian to act all Christian to me when all they want is my money. It's Christians sat me on this throne, I tell you! Without them kind, Mr. Pep would not be sitting up here broke."

"You'd be sitting in Africa broke."

"Surrounded by my beautiful wives. Man never broke when he surrounded by all these pretty misses. He a lucky man! And how is my Pretty Miss Camille?"

"She's still in the hospital."

"What? On Christmas Day! And you not there with her?"

"I was there this morning. Yvette's there now."

"Pretty Miss Yvette! And I wondered how come I didn't see your brothers' cars. They must be at the hospital too."

"Yes, sir. That's where they all are."

"They left you here to watch the house. Mr. Henri never wanted to leave his house unattended, ain't that right? Whenever he took you all to Louisiana, he'd come over here with fifty dollars. 'Now, Mr. Pep, you watch my house,' he'd say. I sure miss me some Mr. Henri! I used to call him Mr. Ornery." Pep let out a long laugh.

His laughter startled Grace. No one ever spoke of her father in such human terms. *Henri.* That was his name, after all. She was so unused to hearing it spoken that, for a moment, she thought she missed him as well.

"Oh, Mr. Henri, he was a good man in spite of hisself. He used to call me Felix, the wonderful cat. I used to call him Casper, the friendly ghost."

At this last comment, Grace began to cough, then to hack. Pep came over and hit her on the back but she waved him away. She was sucking air in and coughing it out like a dying person. Her eyes were red and watery. "What got you by the throat, my Grace?" Pretty Miss Alma wanted to know.

"It's nothing," Grace took deep breaths.

"Auntie Alma feels my Grace's tears. You tell she what bring them down."

"Pretty Miss Grace sure is looking fine," piped up Mr. Pep. "Ain't nothing wrong with Pretty Miss Grace!"

"Hush now, man. Don't you have something to do with yourself?"

"I'm fixing to sell me some blood."

"Nobody wants your blood on Christmas Day."

"Sure they do! I could do with a cup of Miss Camille's gumbo to get up my strength, sure could."

"You better git before I beat you, old man. Thinking about your stomach at a time like this! Can't you see my Grace here got she feeling hurt?"

Grace stared at them. "It's nothing, really," she ventured.

"Don't waste that lie on Miss Alma, baby. You think she blind? You tell Auntie Alma what's troubling you."

"Everything, Miss Alma. Everything and nothing."

"I see what you mean. Nothing but everything. Sometimes, my Grace, you can't take care of every little thing along the way. You just have to take care of that one big thing. You know what Miss Alma mean?"

Grace bowed her head and bit her bottom lip. Miss Alma drew her close.

"Stand up straight now, baby. Why you all bent and hobbled down?"

Appearance often suggests a deeper reality. Grace looked lopsided because she was. Her burdens were not distributed evenly. All her efforts to convey strength and balance were frustrated by an innermost sense of lopsidedness. This teetering was owing not to any structural concerns but to some serious moral leanings. As much as she tried to appear upright and composed, her posture gave her away.

"You come on in and tell she about it. Miss Alma'll see if she can't work some juju on it." She held Grace by the waist as they made their way inside. The house was filled with colored glass and shells, some of which the child Grace had hunted for on the beach as a present for her neighbor. Miss Alma led her to a small table situated in front of the living room window. They left Mr. Pep laughing to himself on the porch.

Grace didn't know what to say. Miss Alma was rumored to have powers, but no Broussard had ever availed herself of them. Other neighbors visited from time to time and left money in a pickle jar. Mr. Pep would not touch this money, no matter how desperate he was. He called it her "transportation money." Nobody but Miss Alma knew what that meant. Grace was leery of Miss Alma's powers. She wondered if it was too late to make a discreet exit. "I don't have any money," she said by way of departure.

"Now, don't go insulting Miss Alma. Do you think Miss Alma would take money from a child? Come on over here and sit down. Bring that money by later..." Miss Alma chuckled, "when the child is all growed up."

Grace thanked her and sat down. The table was covered with sunflower seeds and candle stubs. Miss Alma struck a match and lit some wax.

"Now, Miss Alma going to tell Grace she problem. Shake that head if Miss Alma got it right." She placed her hand on the back of Grace's neck.

Grace nodded.

"You've had a little disturbance."

Grace bobbed her head.

"A disturbance emotional and spiritual in nature which took on a physical manifestation and became a vexation."

Grace continued to nod, though she was having trouble following Miss Alma's train of thought.

"It's somebody in your family, girl."

Nod.

"Somebody away?"

Double nod.

"Somebody you miss."

Nod and frown.

"Somebody miss you."

Full nod and sigh.

"Is this somebody in the land of the living?"

Wagging of the head, enormous eyes.

"Have Miss Grace received a visit?"

Frantic nodding.

"I see. What have she tried?"

"I tried salt."

"Salt only works on the living. The dead are trickier."

"Oh, Miss Alma, what did I do to cause him to haunt me?"

"Miss Alma don't see the past. Miss Alma only see the future. It may be what Miss Grace haven't yet done."

"Tell me. Tell me and I'll do it."

"Has Miss Grace told that old man to be on his way?"

"Yes!"

"What did she say?"

"I told him to go to hell!"

"Hell only holds sway for the living. What else she say?"

"I told him to stop following me."

"And what him do?"

"He followed me!"

"Typical. Thickheaded them ghosts. Can't pussyfoot around with they, no! You got to kill they with unkindness. Repeat after Miss Alma: This a warning to all unwanted guests, uninvited visitors, and lowdown haints: Be gone, burnished flesh! Die and let live!"

Grace tried to repeat Miss Alma's words but they didn't roll off her tongue in the same fearsome way. She was afraid T-Papa would laugh at her. "Do I have to use those exact words?"

"Miss Grace say whatever she want. So long as it's mean enough for a thickheaded ghost to get the point."

With that, Pretty Miss Alma bolted to her feet. Her skinny

body began to oscillate and a tremulous voice emanated from her throat. "Miss Alma calls Mister Casper out his name. Be gone, tired haint! This girl did not ask you to come. She want you to leave she be. Miss Alma take this girl under she wing. Don't be messing with she girl. Miss Alma say once, Miss Alma say deuce, Miss Alma say trey times, 'Get thee from my sight!'" She slumped back into her chair and passed out.

Grace stared at the slumbering figure before her. She did not see a reason to rouse her. Instead, she searched the room for paper. The corner of a racing form would have to do. With the head of a spent match, she wrote out an IOU and deposited it in the pickle jar. Before leaving, she bent and kissed the parched fingers dangling from Miss Alma's hands. For most of the time Grace had known her, Miss Alma had been blind. Glaucoma had taken her vision, but she could still "see" things. Some people said it was the things she saw that had blinded her.

Grace said goodbye to Mr. Pep and raced down the driveway to her own back yard. If she was going to duke it out with her father's ghost, she didn't want it to happen on the street. She waited on the back steps. If she listened closely enough, she could hear the chickens of her childhood scurrying across the yard. From the shed, she could hear the grinding of a saw. In the early afternoon glare, she noticed that the shed was beginning to lean a little. Leaning up against it, arms crossed, was T-Papa.

"Trying to put me in my grave!" T-Papa looked upset. He appeared to Grace as a young man in ill-fitting overalls, but there was no mistaking his voice. It gave her a start. "Is that what you want then, little girl?"

"I don't care where you go. Just leave me alone!"

"You want to bury your Papa once and for all? You want to even get rid of his memory?"

"Die and let live!"

"What language you talking?"

"Stop following me!" She batted the air around her head as if to ward off a persistent fly.

"Can't a man visit his own home?"

"It's not your home anymore. It belongs to us now."

"It'll always be my home. Long as I'm alive!"

"You're not alive. You're dead. D-E-A-D!"

"I ain't dead in your heart."

"Yes, you are. I don't want nothing to do with you."

"You take that back. You talking all crazy, now!"

"I mean it."

"You don't mean nothing."

"I said it, didn't I?"

"People say things they regret."

"Well, I say things I mean."

"You can't look me in the eye and be so cruel."

"I don't want no White man following me around."

"What did you say, little girl?"

"I said I don't want no White man following me!"

T-Papa's eyebrows arched and fell. He rubbed his hand over his face and pinched the crook of his nose. "You think you can just call me anything? You think I don't have no feelings?" Camille had always said her husband was "better as a young man." Something about this young man made Grace know this was true. His feelings hung from him like his clothes. He turned his back to her. "I'll never leave you" was all he said, and then he was walking away from her. He kept on walking until he was old and Grace could see the sloped shoulders and halting gait of his last trip to the beach.

He had been the world to her. However alone she might be again, she would never be as lost as the day he left her. His death hit her with such a sorrow, she had to turn away from it. She had

called to him many times since then. When she was at her most
distraught, in vain, she had called him back to her. What was the
sound of his death? The absence of hammering, sawing, filing.
No one else laughed with his tongue between his teeth—that
was strictly her father. Because she'd been born when he was
forty-eight, he treated this last of his children with the affection
of a grandfather. He'd bounced her on his knee far longer than
any of the other babies and lifted her to the sky long after she
was "too heavy." He'd seen his other children through their
childhoods, through their graduations and marriages and, one
of them, through a war. She wanted him to see her through.
Whenever the night had tormented her, she'd crawled in on his
side. He'd always been there to shelter her. Who could she ask to
shelter her from his death?

Grace was tired of her father being dead. If he were alive, she
could choose to ignore him. Dead, he menaced her thoughts
with a sorrow so great she had no choice but to fear him. Why
hadn't he answered her before, in those terrible first months
after his death when she'd been expected to carry on as though
the sun had not fallen from the sky? He only came now that she
was determined not to need him.

"Get thee from my sight!" Grace whirled around the yard
waving a crow's feather. She refused to feel shame for what she
had done. Pretty Miss Alma had instructed her and she had
followed those instructions to their desired conclusion. As a
sealant, she echoed Miss Alma's words, "Be gone, tired haint."

Mr. Juge stood watching from five yards away. He was sure
he had just witnessed a modified *voudou* ritual, complete with
juju and trance. He knew the Broussards to be trinket Catholics,
but he never reckoned them practitioners of the one true faith.
He approached the girl cautiously, not wanting to upset her
ritual. Hat in hand, he ventured a smoky whisper, "Ma'm'selle,

can old Juge be of some assistance?" Grace jumped at the sound of him, pointing her feather in warning.

Alas, it was only old Mr. Juge. She mumbled a greeting.

"And a Merry Christmas to you, Ma'm'selle. A lovely winter's day, if I do say so myself." Grace looked at him as though he were speaking in tongues. Juge continued, "Forgive me for intruding, Miss Grace, but your sister suggested I call on you. When I remarked to her that I intended to visit your mother in hospital today, she asked if I might pass by the house and see if you desired to accompany me."

Grace didn't know what to say. The nerve of Yvette, who surely knew she would have no desire to accompany Mr. Juge anywhere, least of all to the hospital! The family would all be there making merry like Christmas and secretly worrying that this operation marked the beginning of Camille's decline. Perhaps Grace should go. She did have a pressing need to escape the house. For her mother's sake, she would go.

Her mother's surgery had sent Grace on a downward spiral. She was frayed, uprooted, an emotional vagabond. The sight of Camille prostrate and wombless was terrifying, almost as terrifying as T-Papa's dying had been. Grace had never seen her mother down. Being the youngest, she had never even seen her pregnant. Change had come like a bandit, stealing the ground from under her feet. The possibility of return had been removed with Camille's womb. For the second time in her life, Grace had been cut loose.

She pictured Camille dwarfed in her hospital bed. How did people do without things like wombs and breasts and kidneys? On the outside Camille had not changed, but she was lying in bed, unable to cook, unable to drive, unable to laugh. Grace was rocked to her foundation. Her original home had been demolished. She had only known one other home—the house on

Compton Avenue, which she was now preparing to leave. She wanted to move — all over creation, if need be — but she wanted to be able to come home again. She wanted to change, but she wanted home and Camille to stay the same.

"I'll wait if you'd like to get ready." Mr. Juge seemed prepared to spend the afternoon.

"Well, that's mighty kind of you, Mr. Juge." Grace always started talking funny when she got around old-time Louisiana people. In Los Angeles, it seemed impossible to get away from them. They were forever coming round and ingratiating themselves. Before you knew it, they'd be sitting at your table downing the last little bit of sherry, devouring the final slice of pecan pie, and prying from you all the gossip they could hold. "Kindly wait right here," Grace continued "I'll only be a moment."

"Delighted. Delighted. My pleasure." Mr. Juge clasped his hands behind his back and strode about the yard.

Grace flung open the back door and slipped in through the service porch. She repaired to the bathroom where she searched the cabinets and drawers for her father. He was not there. The shaving drawer was exactly as he'd left it. Camille had not disturbed one of his things. With both hands Grace clutched his razor. The blades were as sharp as the day he died. She dared herself to use them. No, that was not the effect she wanted. After all, she would have to live with herself no matter where she ended up. She put the razor down and grabbed her comb instead. After a quarter hour of picking, Grace was confident of her unsightliness. On her way out the door, she remembered the toys.

Mr. Juge was waiting in his carriage. Grace quickened her gait. She had always wanted to ride in a '54 Chevy. Upon recognizing her underneath her parachute of a hairdo, Mr. Juge alighted from the coach and relieved Grace of the bag she was carrying. He held the back door open for her. She bowed her head so as not to dent her *do*. The car smelled of gardenias. There were doilies on the top of the seats. Riding high upon those enormous cushions, Grace watched the only manmade house she had ever known disappear out the back window. And T-Papa along with it.

4

The Hospital Room

Christmas Dinner, 1978

Striking just the right balance between engaging and imposing was the goal of every Broussard. They believed in making their presence felt in the world. Skinniness was frowned upon, as was leanness of heart. Nothing was worse than going unnoticed. Presence was a quality to be cultivated, albeit an elusive one. By contrast, absence was a tangible thing, easily achieved. Absence is felt. Its hunger looms large in the lives of children, and all who have ever been left.

L ord today! If you children don't settle down," Camille shouted at her grandchildren who were terrorizing the women on the ward with Christmas carols, "I'm going to ask Santa to take your presents back!" Camille was downed, but she wasn't dethroned. Father Sullivan had postponed his vacation to come by with the Eucharist, and she wanted some due respect given. With one stroke of her mighty voice, she scattered the children like pigeons.

Yvette, who had been hovering by her mother's bedside like the bird of doom, was busy leading no one but herself in the five

sorrowful mysteries of the rosary. Camille kept trying to point
out that she wasn't dead yet and didn't need to be rosaried all
the way there. Under constant assault from the patient, Yvette
thought it best to continue her droning in the hallway. As it
would happen, she was putting the final "Glory Be" on her
beads when Grace approached carrying a bag of toys.

Yvette took one look at the new visitor, who was decked out
in a black rayon shirt and brush denim pants, and her eyes grew
bulbous. She opened her mouth to speak, but Grace's finger
pressed against her lips, blocking the words. "Don't talk," advised the younger sister. "It's not polite to state the obvious."

"And the Holy Spirit, Amen," replied Yvette. "Your hair..."

"You're being impolite, Yvette. How's Mama?"

"I feel so sorry for Mama. Internal bleeding is a terrible
thing." Yvette began to cry. She was suffering from prolonged
hospital visitation syndrome, an acute case of the kind most
often seen at County.

Grace sought to comfort her. "If anyone can take it, Mama
can."

"I don't know why they let residents operate on such important patients."

"They probably didn't know who she was."

"Poor Mama. She'll just die if she has to be in the hospital
one more day!"

"No, she won't. Just stop it."

"I wonder what it feels like to know that a part of you is
gone forever."

"Jesus, Yvette, snap out of it!" This, said a touch too loud,
brought unwanted attention from the patient herself. "Who's
that making all that noise in the hall? Is that you, Grace?"

Grace collected herself to enter the chamber. Peeking in the

door, she spotted her brothers Anthony and Louis, Louis's wife
Deborah, all of their children and some of Raymond's too. But
who were those other folks? Camille's room was positively
brimming with well-wishers; Grace could barely see her mother
for all the bodies. These were the same people who wouldn't
venture south of the San Fernando Valley Mason-Dixon line
under normal circumstances but who somehow made their way
to County Hospital on Christmas Day to gawk at the afflicted.
And what timing they had! Each of them was cradling a huge
plate of a Christmas dinner which had been transported to the
hospital by Camille's feckless daughters-in-law.

Grace attempted a retreat back to the hall the minute she
spotted her Burbank cousins, who had taken all the available
chairs. Too late. Genevieve had noticed her.

"Grace? Is that you? We were just talking about you.
Weren't we, Miss Camille? Whatever have you done to your
hair? I'm surprised I recognized you."

Grace ran the gauntlet of relatives surrounding her mother's
bed, kissing and Merry Christmasing as she went. Grandchildren were circling the lair, anxious for the gifts Santa had
entrusted to Auntie Grace but which she, in fact, had forgotten
to wrap. As she made her way to Camille's sweaty cheek, Grace
was careful to lead into the embrace with her good hair side.

Camille turned on her daughter. "How can you come in
here on the day Christ was born looking like something the cat
dragged in?" The Burbank cousins found this remark to be
extremely witty, seeing as how it was made by a sick person.
Grace blanched.

"I think it looks lovely," Yvette lied copiously. "Grace has
a style of her own. This family simply can't appreciate it."

"It's called *out of style.*" Anthony offered the perspective of
one who sat stuffed in a corner.

"And that outfit!" Camille continued. "You look like you're going to the rodeo." Grace had never been to the rodeo but she wished she were there now. Better yet, she desired to be *in* the rodeo, wielding a lasso large enough to rope her entire extended family and tie them to an anthill.

"How did you get here?" Camille wanted to know. "Yvette told me you weren't coming."

"Mr. Juge gave me a ride."

"Urbain Juge? He's not here, is he?"

"He's parking."

"Lord today! That man is the Angel of Death. Why would you bring him to a place where there are sick people?"

"Mama! What a horrible thing to say!" Yvette did not like to hear people badmouthed. Everyone else laughed.

The cousins only remained for seven more tortuous minutes, but to Grace these seemed an epoch. Wasn't there a meter limiting unwanted visitors to three minutes loading and unloading? Had she been foolish enough to think she might piece together a few moments of privacy with the woman who birthed her? Total privacy could not be had on such a day in such a place. Visitors, patients, and hospital personnel practically collided in their desperation to get out alive. It was regrettable that none of the conscientious Broussard relatives had the cash required to do the decent thing and transfer Camille to a private hospital. If any of them did have the dough, they weren't letting on. Families like theirs could be utterly decent given the proper leadership, but with the leadership prone, decency went to the dogs. Grace was glad the dogs were leaving. Yvette saw them to the gate.

After saying her fond goodbyes, Camille turned her attention back to making Grace miserable. "What are you moping about? All I asked you to do was wrap the kids' presents. You'd think I'd asked you to storm the Bastille."

"I'm having a bad day."

"A Wednesday's child," confirmed Camille. "Full of woe. I had a child for every day of the week."

This was a tale that Camille liked to perpetrate on gullible admirers. Father Sullivan listened dutifully, chuckling in all the right places, nodding his modest amens whenever she hit a bump of recognition. Anthony was a Saturday's child, he could see that. Hard-working young man like Anthony had to be a Saturday's child, all right. And Marc, fair of face, indeed... definitely not a Saturday's child. Yvette, she was the Sabbath's own, now wasn't she? Couldn't keep that girl out of church, no ma'am. Yes, Joseph had far to go, but so did a lot of people. Grace could barely stand to be within earshot of such inconsequence. She was relieved when Mr. Juge stepped into the breach.

"My dear Miss Camille, it's so nice to see you looking yourself again." He tipped his hat elaborately.

"Hello, Urbain. Did you see me looking like someone else?"

Mr. Juge chuckled warmly before turning grim. "I must say I was most sorry to hear of your misfortune. I've been keeping you in my prayers, I have."

Camille was cognizant of the fact that sick people don't need just anybody praying for them, and she tried to convey this information without being rude. "Well, that's mighty thoughtful of you, Urbain. But you can stop praying now because I'm about to be released."

"Well, then, it is a merry Christmas indeed!" He littered the room with handshakes and kisses. "My, my, but the Broussards have been plenty blessed, but haven't they now, Father?"

Father Sullivan concurred. Camille rolled her eyes. Mr. Juge was the kind of Southern gentleman who made her itch all over—one of those stately, dapper, molasses men who marry syrupy women. She willed him from the room.

"Miss Camille, I brought you some flowers."

"Why, Mr. Juge, where did you get such lovely gardenias this time of year?" Deborah was impressed.

"I went out of my way, Miss Deborah. Nothing is too good for your mother-in-law."

Camille frowned at the flowers. "Deborah, put these in some water. Merry Christmas to you, Urbain. Come on, Father. I'm ready to partake."

Mr. Juge heeded the warning. "No need for me to take up any more of your time. You rest up now and have yourself a merry little Christmas surrounded by all these beautiful children of yours. I can see Father Sullivan is waiting to administer Our Lord." He kissed Camille's hand and turned to depart.

"I'll see Mr. Juge out." Yvette, who had just returned from seeing out another unwelcomed party, turned again and led the intruder away.

With that, Camille closed her eyes, clasped her hands, and assumed the expression of a penitent. Father Sullivan murmured something that began with "on Christmas Day, the Son of God became flesh" and ended with "receive the Body of Christ." He then dispensed the holy wafer. If it weren't for the Pope, Camille could have administered it herself and cut out the middleman altogether. She was gracious nonetheless and thanked Father for sacrificing his Christmas to be with her. Given that she was the rectory cook, Father had every reason to employ whatever feeble powers he held to bring about her speedy recovery. Camille relished being missed in such a primal way; she enjoyed knowing that her bread was more potent than his. She had to take such acknowledgments whenever she could get them, since she wasn't likely to receive a cash bonus, Christmas or no.

As Yvette hadn't come back yet from seeing the last guest out, Camille called to Grace, who was crouched on the floor

with her sister-in-law wrapping toys in paper recycled from earlier gifts. "Grace, please see Father Sullivan out." Grace rose on
command.

"Wait a minute, girl. Have you been to church today?"

"No, ma'am." The Ten Point Plan was really taking off
now. No Mass on Christmas Day? Camille would be furious,
incredulous. Grace waited for wrath to rain down upon her.

"Thank God you didn't go to church looking like that!"
Camille exclaimed and ordered Father Sullivan to give Grace
the Eucharist. Father searched his case, produced a few crumbs
and pieced them together to form a modified "Body of Christ."
Grace gave it a lame "Amen."

"Thank you for coming, Father. It's hard not being in a
Catholic hospital." Camille said this loud enough for her sons
to hear. That their mother was in County was a source of great
shame for the Broussard children. County was a teaching hospital, and Camille blamed this fact for her excessive loss of blood
during surgery. Every Broussard child winced to hear of her dis-
pleasure. When T-Papa was alive, the Broussards had always
been in the care of the nuns. Now that he was gone, Camille
couldn't keep up with the insurance payments. Because she
worked less than twenty hours a week the Archdiocese's insurance refused to cover her. Of the three in the house only Yvette
had insurance, and because her employer happened to be the
same as her mother's, her policy didn't extend to other family
members. The doctor had promised Camille she'd be out by
Christmas. She was still in, and he was nowhere to be found.

Grace tried to show Father out, but on the way to the door
he accepted Louis's offer of some Christmas punch laced with
Trinidadian rum. Father was soon happily lapping up a supper
consisting of Deborah's dry turkey, Yvette's soggy dressing, and
Vanessa's low-calorie sweet potato pie.

Camille began to hand out her presents to the assembled grandchildren. Yvette had not yet returned and Camille wondered aloud where she might be. Amid hugs and cries of "thank you, Mémère," a nurse cruised by to take a blood pressure reading. "This lady needs rest," she ordered and, one by one, the remaining Broussard families paid homage by way of departure.

Grace hung on the outskirts of the action. She was desperate to be with Elena. This Christmas Day was a dreary affair. Elena had gone skiing with her bourgeois atheist housemate who liked to tease Grace about her unscientific approach to life. Grace gladly suffered the holiday in town rather than risk the humiliation of learning to ski. But as she bid farewell to her brothers and their families, it pained her to be the only one present who was seemingly unattached.

Grace was suddenly alone with her mother. Camille was tired, she could see that, tired and old. She'd gone gray around the edges. In the hospital for almost a week, she'd been unable to dye her hair.

For the first time all day the area was free of clamor, save for the happy sounds of Father Sullivan slurping his pie. Camille patted the mattress for Grace to sit down. Here was Grace's chance to speak, but no words would come. Camille fingered her daughter's hair and cried gently, two acts which Grace suspected of being related. She didn't know what to do.

While Grace was perched on the bed like a pigeon, her mother lay next to her unable to speak. Camille missed her husband and she missed her womb. Menopause had not particularly bothered her, but when the blood had returned to taunt her, she resented it. As with all things beneath her, she chose to ignore it until months later when she was faced with a hysterectomy. Neither menopause nor widowhood had brought it home to her like this surgery: she would bear no more children.

No miracle births, no old people's blessings, no freak accidents. Now, even if she could manage some unexpected guests, she would have no place to house them. They would be buns in search of an oven. She reached over and gave Grace's doughy body a squeeze.

Camille was worried about her youngest. She'd been worried about her for a long time—ever since Grace was twelve—and on a daily basis since the Beach Trip of 1975. T-Papa's death had eclipsed this lesser, vaguer concern, but now that he'd been cold in the ground for three years running and life had gone on, despite the predictions, Camille found her mind idling on the stranger at her side.

Grace sensed her mother's misgivings. She was indeed a stranger, but this was not a new development. She had been born a stranger, and it had only taken her family twenty years to recognize the gravity of this fact. While they'd been guarding their secrets in strict privacy and grim loyalty, a stranger walked amongst them recording their dishonors and dishonoring their ways. Night after night she had supped with them, prattled with them, prayed with them. Soon she would leave them wondering who it was they were losing. This thought made her sigh long and hard.

The sigh arrested Camille's tears and caused her to perk up considerably. "Why so gloomy on Christmas Day?" she inquired of her daughter.

Grace could not say.

"Don't waste any worry on me, baby. I'm going to be fine."

This declaration made Grace doubtful. "You promise?" she hugged her mother close.

Father Sullivan, not known to be a shrewd observer of human relations, recognized this as a sensitive moment and

pronounced a meek blessing before angling his way out of the
room. Camille and Grace both laughed at his ineptitude. It was
in that moment of levity that Grace longed to tell Camille of
T-Papa's visits. She tried to think of a way that would be casual,
nonchalant. Before she could compose herself, Camille had
moved on to something else.

"Baby, you have to make me a promise, too."

"What, Mama?"

"You have to go back to school."

In one fell swoop, Camille had derailed any hopes of further
intimacy. Grace was annoyed. Talking to Camille was like driving with Yvette—she was always taking detours and never to
the places Grace wanted to go.

"You should have tried for a university. Junior college
won't get you anywhere these days."

Now Camille was on to a sore spot—Grace's dropping out
of El Camino. After graduating from Our Lady of Fatima, Grace
had decided to attend a junior college instead of a university as
her parents had suggested. She had been content to play Ping-
Pong for her six months at El Camino, drifting in and out of
Spanish classes before drifting away altogether to take the job at
the Louisiana Fish Market. Camille referred to her job as "that
little dead-fin job."

Grace couldn't understand why college was such a big deal.
Neither T-Papa nor Camille had gone to college; they hadn't
needed to. All of the older Broussard boys had followed family
tradition and gone into the trades. Joseph had joined the Army.
Only Marc and, now, Yvette had pursued an education. The
way the Broussards figured, college wasn't necessary unless you
didn't have a talent or unless the profession you wanted required a proof of purchase certificate. If you were going to go to

college at all, you might as well go all the way, attend a respectable four-year institution, come out with honors, and do your family proud. That's what Marc had done.

"Why don't you go to Marc's school?"

"I'm not Marc."

Marc was an architect with a degree from the University of Southern California. The first Broussard to go to college, he had been the beneficiary of an era of new thinking about Negroes. Marc had graduated high school the year Grace entered kindergarten, the year President Kennedy was killed. After Kennedy's death, Civil Rights had really taken off as a concept and Marc had cashed in. Because he had a lot of practical experience working summers in construction with Uncle Claude, architecture school proved easier for him than for his white classmates. It was hard for Marc not to gloat. Nobody was going to keep him out of any union, the way they had excluded his father. He wouldn't need their lousy union. Every time opportunity knocked, he would answer the door dressed to kill.

"Well, I'm not saying you have to be like Marc, but it wouldn't hurt to have a little bit of ambition. Isn't that where your little friend goes to school?"

"Who?"

"That little Mexican girl. Doesn't she go to USC?"

"There are lots of Mexicans at USC."

"You know which one I mean. What's she studying?"

"Political science."

"Political science? What's she going to do with that? Lead a revolution?"

"Maybe."

"You stay away from those revolutionaries."

"Then why go to college? That's where they all hang out."

"Well, whatever you do, don't get stuck in a job with no advancement like Yvette did. You'll be going to school when you should be retiring."

At seventeen, Yvette had thought she wanted to be a secretary, the career she prepared for in high school. She liked working with paper. But after nineteen years of menial labor, small talk, and low pay, she decided to become a teacher, a career that also involved little money, lots of paperwork, and small minds, this time gazing up at her instead of down. For this she needed college, so off to Cal State L.A. she went at the age of thirty-six. At present she was in her first year of teaching third grade at St. Martin de Porres School down the street from her parents' house. Her challenging new job hadn't stopped her from pursuing continuing education classes in the hopes of one day becoming a vice principal. True to the family teachings, Yvette was never too old to "better" herself, a joy which her younger sister had not yet come to know.

"I'll go back to school when I have the money."

"What do you do with your money? All this time you've been working, I haven't seen a penny of it. Lord knows you don't spend it at the beauty parlor."

"I'm saving it."

"For what? Might as well spend it on school. Tuition is only going up. You're lucky you don't have any living expenses. What are you going to do if something happens to me?"

Grace slipped off the bed and stood at her mother's side. She thought about breaking her news to Camille. If her mother was truly concerned about her, perhaps she would react with pride on learning of her daughter's plans. Unfortunately, Grace didn't have time to test this hypothesis because when she got up, she left a little puddle of sand behind her.

"What's all this sand everywhere?" Camille exclaimed. "Have you been to the beach? In the middle of winter? I leave and you all lose your minds!"

"That's enough talking, now." Yvette danced through the door like a Rockette. Grace was grateful that, this once, her sister was on cue.

"Where have you been?" Camille wanted to know.

"You get some sleep now, Mama. It's time to get well so we can take you home. We'll talk about my whereabouts another day." Yvette patted Camille on the head and gave her a kiss on the cheek.

Grace prepared to go. "Come give me a kiss," Camille ordered. "And this time, act like you mean it."

"See you soon, Mama," Grace caressed the familiar forehead with her lips.

"How did we get to talking about all these things?" Camille was fading. "I wanted to talk about your hair." She looked at her daughter through bleary eyes. "What were you thinking?" Before Grace could answer, Camille was sound asleep.

Grace was preoccupied all the way home, her mind agitated and overstuffed. It was hard to concentrate in Yvette's car. Yvette filled the air with a constant prattle and, like all the Broussard cars, hers was laden with distracting icons. While her decorations had a decidedly religious flavor to them, her brothers' cars and trucks were populated by the bouncing balls and bobbing dolls of various sports deities. Camille had a car but, like her, it was in the shop. All its medals and holy cards had not kept it from needing a brake job. Grace didn't understand how people could drive with so many trinkets blocking their vision. She was easily the best Broussard driver and the only one without a car. When she did get her own car, she would keep it free

of decorations, just in case she wanted to think and drive at the
same time.

Because Grace refused to talk to her, Yvette resorted to
"reparation driving." Yvette was a member of the Sacred Heart
Auto League, and her Plymouth Valiant was adorned with
membership cards stretching back to the early 60s. In order to
keep her membership current, Yvette sent an annual donation
and signed a pledge to "drive prayerfully." Grace knew lots of
folks who belonged to the League, but Yvette was the only person she knew who actually recited the Driver's Prayer before
setting off. Abbreviated though her version was, it still irked
Grace to no end. *God our Father, you led Abraham from his
home and guarded him in all his wanderings. You guided him
safely to the destination you had chosen for him. Guide us to
our destination for today and may it bring us one day closer to
our final destination with you.*

Grace objected strongly to this last line, which she felt needlessly flirted with highway statistics. Furthermore, she had a
healthy distrust of reparation drivers, "generous souls who seek
to give the Sacred Heart more love, over and above, thereby
making up in some small way for the inconsideration and reck-
lessness of careless drivers." T-Papa had practiced reparation
driving, and Grace had every reason to believe his account was
still owing. Prayer alone could never compensate for the fear he
had inspired as the Broussards went careening down the road.
Grace focused now on the towering Jesus serenely displaying his
Sacred Heart (shrouded in a crown of thorns, surrounded by a
halo of light, and topped by a cross in flames) as two cars and a
semi-truck prayerfully drove by.

The Sacred Heart was a most captivating image, and the
house on Compton Avenue featured several depictions of the

sacred hearts of Jesus and Mary. Sometimes, when Grace saw the words "sacred heart," she mistakenly read them as "scared heart" or "scarred heart." During intermittent flurries of heresy and Weltschmerz, she imagined her own heart engulfed in flames and thorns.

It was 8:30 by the time the sisters arrived home. The Christmas tree lights were flashing senselessly in the living room window. The house was quiet, empty. Not like any other Christmas, this. Yvette went to bed early, saying she needed to dream. Grace stayed up with her thoughts.

She had banished him and now she missed him. Those things she said to him, they were cruel, wicked things. She regretted them. That he was no longer in her heart—what could be further from the truth? Her heart was full with him, with the father she had known and the one she hadn't. The man who appeared to her was an apparition, a pretense. He was not her real father, only her father's messenger. Why should she regret what she said to a ghost? And what was she going to do about it now? Telephone and apologize? He had taken his leave, that was the important thing. She faced him down and he retreated. At last, it was safe to miss T-Papa. He was finally gone.

Dust mop in hand, Grace let go of her tears and unburdened the house of salt and sand.

Part Two

New Year's Eve, 1978

I t was New Year's Eve and the saddest day of the year, the day that held the least promise and the most regret. T-Papa was not the only person Grace missed. She missed her friends from school and the neighborhood—the double-dutch-jumping girls whose fun was now lost to her. They were gone to boys and she was no longer in their circle. Some of them were mothers. Grace felt jealous when she saw them with their babies. Their lives seemed full of purpose. Whatever their resolutions, they could count on the new year bringing them connection and change. She could count on neither.

Grace was determined to start the Buick. For weeks after his death, T-Papa's large American car had rested in front of the house on Compton Avenue. The Broussards had intended to junk it, but Grace refused. Who could have guessed that a sensitive girl like Grace would want to drive an old battleship like the Buick, held together as it was by rubber bands and paper clips? The other Broussards wouldn't touch it for fear it might fall apart. It wasn't long before thieves took the initiative and stripped the beast of its garments. Hubcaps were the first to go, followed by battery, visors, mirror, and back seat. Before they could dissect the carcass, Anthony and Mr. Pep had pushed it to the back yard. There it lay in state for more than three years.

Grace worked to revive the thing. To be dead and gone like an old year—this is what she could not accept. Like Yvette, she needed something to hold on to—a handkerchief, a sock—something permanent. Things can survive frail life. Some, like love, are virtually indestructible. So it was with the Buick.

5

The Buick

Sunday, December 31, 1978

There is no accounting for loneliness. It can seize the guest of honor in the midst of a celebration or throttle the candidate surrounded by supporters. Children are lonely for grandparents who died before they were born. Fields are lonely for flowers. All beings seek to be adored. The Broussards were no different. More than anything, they wanted to be able to make hearts stir. No one is dead who is alive in the heart. Souls that are lost and forgotten come alive to the touch. In the gentle stroke of a cheek, prayers for companionship are answered.

Yvette could barely hear her mother above the sputtering of the engine.

"Is Grace out of her mind?" At eight o'clock in the morning on the last day of the year, dust and declarations assaulted house and yard. Mother and younger sister both struggled to rev their respective engines. From the sound of things, one of them was making progress.

"She's in the back yard," Yvette called from the kitchen.

"Why's she out there so early in the morning?"

"She's trying to get Daddy's car started."

"I know that! But why does she have to make all that racket at this hour? Is she crazy?"

Camille had gotten more sleep in the hospital. At home, Yvette prayed all night and Grace fretted all morning. Men passed on the street drunk and talking loud. Grandchildren came to visit and ran wild in the yard. By her own reckoning, Camille had left and the house had gone to hell. Apparently, she had crashed the party by coming home. More loving attention could be had from underpaid strangers than from her inconsiderate kin.

It was enough to make her want to check in to a hotel. All her shouting for peace and quiet was really taking its toll. She was cold most of the time and had great difficulty walking. Her shoulder and abdomen were in constant pain. With four weeks of no heavy lifting and no driving, she couldn't go to work, which meant she didn't get a paycheck. The church collection taken up in her honor had amounted to all of $38.72. The hotel would have to be a cheap one.

Camille had never been barren before, but she was barren now. She lay in her king-size bed, a starfish in a bed of sand. Right after T-Papa died, Yvette had come and slept next to her. Yvette was so small and her body so light that she hardly gave off any heat. Her presence had only made T-Papa's absence larger. Camille had sent her away. With no man's hands on her belly and no one to lie heavily beside her, she had felt empty down to her womb. Now her sorrow had no place to go. It bunched up around her eyes and rolled down her cheeks.

This time of year always brought an overwhelming sense of loss. Camille didn't like to get out of bed until she was certain she had conquered it. With her body still aching from the surgery only eight days before, there was no reason to get out of bed at all. Yvette would waltz in soon enough, attending to her mother's every need, including her need for gossip. They would wonder aloud about Grace. What an excessive desire for privacy that child seemed to have! What a peculiar sense of self!

Grace, for the moment, was indifferent to her restive, mirthless mother. For five days now—the entire time Camille had been home—Grace had been locked in combat with the Buick. When she first dared to open the hood, she was horrified at the ancient pieces of gum and rusty bobby pins that held the car together. T-Papa had been a gifted cabinetmaker, but he made a lousy mechanic. Rouby took Grace to get a new battery and showed her how to connect it, but even he couldn't make the Buick run. "They must have messed up your starter when they broke in and took the visors," he concluded. Grace wasn't satisfied with this explanation and plugged along on her own.

Camille and her brothers offered nothing but ridicule. Yvette offered condolences. It seemed the Sacred Heart Auto League didn't concern itself with repairs, and the saints proved to be no help at all. Only T-Papa took Grace seriously. Now that he had crossed over, she confirmed his passage by praying to him. The results were astounding.

He guided her to clean the dashboard, then directed her eyes to the gasoline gauge and, finally, to the tank itself. Grace was delighted to find it empty. Due to its stolen battery and consequent lack of juice, no one had noticed that the Buick was out of gas. In this moment of simple revelation, Grace was mindful of T-Papa's premature passing. His car had run out of gas at the same time he had.

Mr. Pep escorted Grace down to the station at dawn. Five dollars worth of regular and the car coughed and hissed, gagged and spit as Grace cheered it on. For the first time, she could actually envision herself moving out. She wouldn't need Felipe's truck, after all. The Buick was plenty big enough to transport her meager belongings. She was on her way. Grace had wheels!

The importance of wheels cannot be overestimated in a place like Los Angeles; being without them was like being without a camel on the high Sahara. Grace had been stranded more than once waiting for a bus that never came. Now she could forget about the bus altogether. Ecstatic, she gave her bus pass to Mr. Pep.

Everything about Grace's existence was about to grow larger. This house, this yard, this room where she had spent virtually every night of her childhood would be traded for another room across town. In that room would be a bed, a bed she would share with Elena. They would lie down in sin and rise up in splendor. Grace would dress differently in that room — in full sun with the windows open. Her clothes would be light and airy.

She stormed the kitchen, waving her hands in a victory sign.

"Don't tell me you got that car started?" Yvette met her at the door.

"I told you I would," Grace boasted, washing her hands.

"You're not actually going anywhere in it, are you?"

"Just as soon as I can." Grace coated a slab of bread with butter. "I'm out of here!"

Yvette was jealous. Grace was a jot too gleeful. "Go and turn that thing off. It's polluting the whole neighborhood."

"It's got to warm up." Grace strutted towards the door.

Yvette, who had already started preparing the hoghead cheese for New Year's day, gave a sideways glance and shook her head. "Where do you think you're going looking like that?"

"To work."

"You might want to turn your shirt around and put on some socks that match."

"Oops! I dressed in the dark."

"Good morning, America! Must we begin every year with the same woeful disorder? Do you even have your license?"

"Oh yeah..." Grace cuffed herself on the forehead.

"You look like some fallen disco queen. Does Sylvester have a sister?"

"I don't know. Gotta go!"

"Don't they ever close that store? Who has to work on New Year's Eve?"

"I do."

Grace worked in the Fox Hills Mall. Her job was the centerpiece of her Plan. She quit the Louisiana Fish Market and hired on at the department store just in time for the Christmas rush. The Fish Market people were upset with her—they didn't understand how a cousin could desert them with only a week's notice—but Grace explained that she was planning to go back to school and the 10% discount on clothes (there was no such discount on fish) would be of use to her. While she might return to college eventually, for now her 10% discount would go towards a red dress that would never see the halls of academe. The money she was making working overtime would help finance her move, and she could earn it without being subject to the watchful eyes of relatives and fish.

The Mall was located just down the road and across the street from the cemetery. Grace could usually get a ride to work, as someone was always going to the cemetery. Camille and Yvette went on Wednesdays, Aunt Julie went on Fridays, Louis sometimes took his children to play there on Saturdays. If she didn't mind the company of a hapless widower, Mr. Juge went all the time.

When she couldn't get a ride, Grace didn't mind traveling

two hours to Fox Hills for earnings of $2.85 an hour. She wasn't
wild about the work, but she relished the sojourn. The bus—
oafish, sluggish animal that it was—provided her with interesting scenery and time to herself. And she liked the fact that the
albatross took her to another side of town where her people had
more clout, where they were busy being dentists and judges and
pharmacists. The Black folks of Fox Hills were doing things.
They could afford to shop in the new mall. She liked being
around them.

Shopping had gained in popularity since the advent of
Grace's job. More and more store-bought clothes began showing up on Broussard bodies. Yvette had gone so far as to get a
new swimsuit for the annual beach trip. The Broadway Fox
Hills was making the Broussards heady with desire. Camille
wanted a new sofa; the one in the living room was a generation
older than Grace. With no T-Papa to make her new furniture,
Camille was finding that she needed all kinds of things—
nightstands, bookcases, end tables. Anthony had offered to
make her a new set of kitchen chairs, but she wanted them
"store-bought."

Since T-Papa's death, Camille had begun to discover previ-
ously uncharted worlds. She read about sales in the paper and
demanded that Grace survey the merchandise to make sure "it
was worth it." Once, she gave Grace ten dollars to purchase a
$9.99 lamp, only to find the one in the store was smaller than
the one in the paper.

Grace worked in China. Every day she set places at tables
and waited for someone to appreciate them. Grace was not interested in china. Trivets meant nothing to her. Cloth napkins
with matching rings were not the least bit exciting. For all she
cared, ceramic gravy boats could sail off to sea. She was allergic

to linen, and bridal registries fatigued her. Silverware, flat-
ware — it was all the same to Grace. Mostly, she worried about
dropping the crystal.

China was a slow department. It wasn't just that weddings
were down; divorces were up and people didn't want to buy
china for newlyweds who might not be together six months
from now. News of the decline in weddings hadn't reached the
Broussard clan, and this was the worst thing about working at
Fox Hills. Any odd customer was likely to be one of Grace's
more prosperous cousins. She would then be obliged to trade
gossip, which she hated more than setting tables.

On her morning and afternoon breaks, she visited other
more interesting departments. She dreamed of dressing Elena in
pearl earrings and French cologne. In accordance with her Ten
Point Plan, Grace would bring her lover home to dinner, prefer-
ably next week. So she marched over to Petites on one of her
breaks and put a red dress on layaway. It was a snug little knit
number with a vinyl belt. With her 10% discount, Grace could
purchase it out of her next paycheck. She would surprise Elena
and have it gift-wrapped.

Grace had just located her license under a stack of old love
notes when she heard Camille calling from her sickbed,
"Where's Grace? Tell her to come here."

"Grace!" Yvette relayed from the kitchen. "Mama's looking
for you."

"I'm on my way to work!"

"Stop in and see what she wants."

"You come here, Grace! I've got some work for you to do."

"Mama, I have to go." Grace entered her mother's bedroom
tying a scarf around her neck. "I'm going to be late."

"You should comb your hair."

"I combed it."

"Then uncomb it! I know you're not going to work looking like that, and you can't be going anywhere in that deathtrap of a car. You're an accident waiting to happen."

"Nothing's going to happen to me."

"How can you see with all that hair? What if a wind comes up? What about peripheral vision?"

"Mama, I have to go. The store will be opening soon."

"You can't have a career selling plates."

"It's not a career. It's a job."

"Why do you want to spend your holiday with strangers?"

"I get paid for it, Mama."

"You don't need money. I give you food and shelter!"

"I need other things."

"What other things? What else is there?"

"Something of my own?"

"Your generation is so selfish, always wanting more, more! Since when did money become more important than family?"

"Money is necessary to life."

"Well, family is the mother of life. Money is an invention. Are you avoiding us?" Camille looked hurt.

"I'm not avoiding anything."

"Well, come home as soon as you can."

"I will."

"New Year's is a holy day."

"I know."

"When are you planning to go to Mass?"

"Soon." Grace hated lying to her mother. It was futile, anyway. "I've got to run or the car is going to die on me."

"You can't drive a heap of scrap metal!"

"Plenty of people do."

"You don't see any Broussards driving cars like that."

"No, not since he died."

"Young lady, don't you dare blaspheme your father!"

"I'm not blaspheming, Mama. Daddy was a mortal."

"Your father was a saint!" Camille burst into tears. She looked pitiful. Grace was instantly contrite. She looked around the room at all the shrines and memorabilia. The entire room was an altar to T-Papa.

"Will you be back by dark?" her mother wanted to know.

"What happens at dark?"

"The guns."

"Oh." Grace hated to be reminded. Her spirits sank.

"Well, maybe you could go over to Linens and take a look at those pillows that are on sale. I could use a new pillow. This one's not very comfortable."

Guilt always worked on Grace, guilt and the possibility of being found out. Camille would know if she didn't comply—her spies would tell her. Spies were everywhere in the Broussard clan, poised to report any and all transgressions to headquarters. Grace hadn't sinned in years, but she had done the penance of a medieval village.

Camille was well aware of her daughter's tendency to feel guilty and pressed it to advantage. The arch of an eyebrow, a drop in tone intimidated Grace. She didn't stop there. "If you have to go to that miserable little job, you can at least carry some flowers to your father's grave. Hand me my purse."

Holy Rosary looked cheap in its after-Christmas clothes—fallen trees, smashed tinsel, a memorial to a party that no one had survived. Remnants of the holiday spirit littered the ground with loss. Life stirred intermittently like wind chimes at an abandoned house. A few birds, mechanical and otherwise, squeaked their irksome melodies. The grass reeked of dew and tears.

When Grace arrived, the gates were just opening. The Buick had lurched and lunged all the way there. By the time she arrived, Grace looked as worn out as everything else in the place. Nevertheless, she entered singing, "I got wheels, you got wheels, all God's chirren got wheels!" She consciously strove to fill her lungs with some of the only fresh air in the county. She sang all the way to the flower shop.

The flower shop was situated next to the mausoleum, at the opposite end of the cemetery from T-Papa's grave. All kinds of stars were buried in the mausoleum, and the flower shop was conveniently located next to them. As many times as she'd been to the cemetery, Grace had never been inside the mausoleum. She couldn't fathom anybody, celebrity or not, resting in peace on a shelf. After being advised every Ash Wednesday of her childhood to "*Remember man that you are dust and unto dust you shall return*," the mausoleum looked altogether too clean. She steered the Buick to the flower shop side and dismounted without turning it off.

Grace pulled the shop door so hard it rattled, causing the proprietor to jump.

"Well, hello there, morning glory. Like I always say, 'Early body gets the worms.'"

Kaz Matsumoto was a cemetery fixture. For him, life was a poorly performed interlude between birth and death punctuated, as it were, by flowers. A native of Hawaii, for the sake of conversation he dressed in tacky flowered shirts purchased at second-hand stores in L.A. He described what he did for a living as "hanging out in the most peaceful spot this side of Molokai." Grace considered him a little too cheery. His flowers were not particularly vibrant and his jokes were worse than a dentist's.

"Haven't seen you since the Stone Age. Got tired of communing with us deadbeats, huh?"

"Hey, Mr. Matsu. Long time."

"When you were little, you used to haunt this place. I hardly recognize you without your white sheet."

"I traded it in."

"For a bright green Buick, I see. Whose car is that you're driving? It looks like it's seen better days."

"It's my car."

"May it live long and prosper!"

"Got any flowers besides these?"

"What's wrong with these?"

"They're barely breathing!"

"Consider their destination…"

"Come on, Mr. Matsu. You think my mother sends me to the cemetery to buy dead flowers? Don't you ever throw anything away?"

"Perish the thought! One person's trash is another one's treasure. Say, how's your mom, anyway? Haven't seen her since her surgery."

"She's well enough to order me around."

"Ah, she's recovering. An excellent sign! You tell her Mr. Matsu said everybody's been asking about her, them that's still got the breath of life and them that's breathed their last."

"How about those yellow irises?"

"You don't want those."

"Why not?"

"They're on their way to rigor mortis."

"How about a discount?"

"Or this lively bunch of roses. Only $3.50."

"Three dollars."

"Life is cheap."

"That's my final offer."

"Look at these colors! Enough to wake the dead."

"Got anything to keep them asleep?"

"Eternal insomnia, a terrible thing. Only $3.25 for you."

"Your flowers are too expensive."

"Too expensive? What price Life? Don't answer that. I'll give you the mums for $2.25. Gift-wrapped?"

"A bow would be nice."

"One bow for the mum. Coming up!"

Grace watched as he wrapped. She wondered if Mr. Matsu had family buried here and if he ever took flowers to them.

"Here you go, kiddo. Be careful out there. You wouldn't want to step on anybody's toes."

Grace handed him the money.

"See you soon, sweet petune."

"Only in death, baby's breath." She pocketed the change and took her leave shrouded by his pleasant laughter.

The Buick waited dutifully, smoking up the atmosphere for miles around. Grace had always been embarrassed by her father's car, but today it had taken on a curious appeal. She patted the dashboard before taking off. With the shift into drive, it lunged forward, heaving and sighing all the way to the Redemption. Once there, she thought it best to turn the motor off and give it a rest.

The fact that T-Papa was now resting where he belonged was little comfort to Grace, who had met his reappearance with all the dread of an atheist and none of the surprise. Her apprehensions mounted as her feet hit the ground. What if he was waiting for her, perched on the mound in his Sunday best, napkin waiting and spoon in hand? She would toss the flowers on the grave and hightail it out of there.

Grace found the grave looking submissive enough. The mums from the week before were holding up nicely, and there was no sign of the old man. She pushed the new flowers into the canister, intending to leave now that duty was done.

It was then that she noticed a figure deep in prayer. Grace

tottered backwards, but she caught herself. It was not her father. Too small to be him, and wearing a veil. Was it a relative? A spy? Where had this person come from, so fast, in the time it took her to jam the flowers, in the seconds her back was turned? Grace reckoned that the figure belonged to the plot next door, which stood out from the holiday clutter, decorated by a single straw hand-broom tied with a velvet bow. Old man Panganiban had been eighty-two when he died. Like the Widow Broussard, the Widow Panganiban was awaiting her turn on the stone. She was Consuela, born in 1914, twenty years younger than her husband. Grace did not know if this was her. She had no desire to find out.

The woman looked up. She smiled at Grace. Could Grace leave without saying a prayer? The neighbors were watching. She straightened the chrysanthemums, spruced up the stone, tried to look like a devoted daughter. The veiled one spoke.

"You make this grave so pretty. All the time flowers."

"Thank you. But it's my mother who…"

"Such a big love! Was it your husband?"

"My husband? It was my…"

"It's good to marry an old man. He's already sure of himself. Maybe, he has his own business. He can support you."

"I'm not married."

"You're young. You can remarry."

"I've never been mar…"

"I'm too old to marry. What for? My relatives are saying always, 'You're young. You should marry again.' But I say, 'What for? My husband left me money. Do you think he doesn't provide for me?'"

"No. I mean, yes. Why not?"

"Older men take care of you. I always tell my granddaughters, 'Marry an old man,' but they marry whoever they want.

One year later, they are getting divorced. It's not good to have too many husbands. You don't know who to be buried with."

Mr. and Mrs. Panganiban had been married for forty-five years. They had three children, all girls. These girls, in turn, had seven children, all girls. One of these girls had just given birth to a boy, who'd been named Prudencio after his great-grandfather.

Prudencio Panganiban had been a barber, and every Christmas his wife brought him a new broom. With the money from his insurance she had opened a bowling alley. She handed Grace a coupon for the Saturday night "Rock and Bowl" special. Grace didn't want any coupons. She didn't want any advice either, but the widow insisted on giving her some. In addition to being ferociously Catholic (not even Camille could be found in a veil), Mrs. Panganiban had studied at the cliché school of English. Her husband clipped hair, she clipped sentences.

"You only live once," the widow began. "Don't take life…"

"Too seriously."

"For granted."

"Of course. Don't take life for granted," Grace felt like she was the challenger in a game show. However, something about the widow put her at ease. From a stranger she could accept the counsel she would never tolerate from her family.

"You don't know what you have…"

"Until it's gone."

"Good. I'd give anything…"

"To do it all over again."

"To have him back."

"Oh." Grace's score was slipping.

"I never got to tell him…"

"How much I loved him?"

"You only live…"

"Until you die." She could hear buzzers sounding.

"Once."

"Sorry."

"Death puts everything…"

"To shame."

"In perspective!"

"We can never know…"

"The hour."

"It's important to keep the family…"

"In perspective."

"Together. Marry an old…"

"Man."

"Very good."

"What do I win?"

"Eternity."

"Is that all?"

"What do you want?"

"An apartment."

"Your generation, no ambition! Come, pray with me." She held out her hand. Grace took it and knelt down. It was the warmest grasp she had ever known. There, on her knees next to her father's grave, she felt a strange sense of communion.

"Eternal rest grant unto him, O Lord…"

"And let perpetual light…" Grace closed her eyes.

"May his soul and all the souls of the faithful departed…"

"Through the mercy of God…"

Mrs. Panganiban was fading. Grace felt her hand slipping. A gentle wind caressed her cheek. "Rest in peace." The stranger was no more. Grace opened her eyes and leapt to her feet. Heart thrashing about her chest, knees locked beneath her, Grace was stung. How dare he! Hiding in the shell of an aged widow woman! Rage surfaced like flotsam. He had drawn her out into the open and left her dangling in prayer. For the third time in a week, she had fallen into his clutches with nothing to protect her.

Grace needed a mirror. Ghosts don't like to see their reflections. Or was that vampires? Did it matter? T-Papa was sucking her blood, to be sure. Suppose his reflection turned out to be more of an aphrodisiac than a repellent? Chains, that's what she needed. Ghosts fear the sound of scraping. Or was it the sound of bells ringing?

Grace might have to beseech the saints, after all. She couldn't call upon the ancestors. The wrong one might answer. She needed to exorcise her father from her life. Scaring him wouldn't cut it. Friendly ghosts you can scare, not the ghost of a wronged parent. Grace prepared for battle. T-Papa was a wily opponent. He didn't play fair. He didn't respond to polite entreaties. He didn't respond to insults. She needed something more potent, something downright deadly. She needed gumbo.

With half a broken ornament she set about collecting ingredients. Grace would make him a gumbo, all right, a gumbo he would choke on! A clump of grass here, a potato bug there, some stale water. Dilapidated pieces of tinsel, two dead leaves, a broken sprig of holly. Fingernails. Gravel. A ground poinsettia petal. Mud. A few twigs. It looked like the real stuff. Now, to get him to eat it!

Grace placed her bitter stew on top of T-Papa's grave, right where she imagined his belly to be. She thought she saw it moving up and down in rhythm with his breathing. He knew how to unnerve a girl.

Shakily, she began a roving incantation. "Lord of fire, Lord of dust, bring to rest your faithful servant, lost upon this lonely earth. Hear my desperate plea!" Her chin quivered as she spoke. She wasn't sure to whom she was praying or if anybody was listening and would intercede on her behalf.

Grace decided to appeal directly to her tormentor. "*Mangé, mangé*," she sang. "*Bon mangé, mon 'ti papa.*" T-Papa had always loved a "*bon mangé.*" While Grace implored her father to "eat up," she regarded her creation with distaste. Maybe, she should move it closer to his mouth. How did the dead consume? Was it an intravenous kind of thing, or did they use their fangs? Grace waited for her father to take the bait.

She traced his name with her foot. "Broussard"—that was the name he'd given her, the yoke that hung around her neck. The "Grace" had come from her mother. "My saving Grace," Camille insisted. "Your Daddy wanted to name you Michelle." Michelle was the name of the baby who had died. "Too weak to live" was all Grace had ever heard about her. Grace often felt "too weak to live," and she wondered if she'd gotten some of the same genes that Michelle had. At least, Camille had insisted she get her own name. Camille sometimes visited Michelle in the Holy Innocents section of the cemetery where she had lain since 1945. Grace wondered if her father ever made it over there. He already had one daughter who would never leave him. Why did he need another one? Grace kicked dust over his name.

The first tear that fell was an insolent tear. It burned her cheek and seared her tongue. She was tired of living this half-life. She felt obscure to herself, distant, as though she were watching someone else muddle through her days. When Grace could forget who she was and what she owed to the world and to her family—the only place she could forget was in Elena's bed—she trembled with life. But these moments were rare. Most of the time she was lonely. Tears rolled off her chin. She added them to the stew.

Minutes had passed, but the fool's gumbo was not diminished. Grace had hoped it would seep from the cup to T-Papa's waiting gullet, but he had not partaken. She needed something to entice him. What could serve as a lure for a man struck down before he was ready? Leavers hate to be left. By what cruel ruse did she find herself inside these gates paying homage to the Fourth Commandment? She was supposed to be hunting apartments with Elena.

T-Papa, she knew, was laughing at her. No doubt he considered this a victory of sorts. Again she had broken her vow. Grace had sworn off cemeteries the day they buried her father. No plot of ground, however hallowed, could hold a life so grand. His death had been an act of betrayal. How could she reward such treachery? Yet here she had trampled her vow on Christmas Day, shamed into that pilgrimage by an ailing mother. And now, less than a week later, she was making a second journey to forage for the lost father. What was her excuse this time? She smashed the ornament and its contents before kicking it down the hill. The gardeners would get it on their next round.

On her way back to the car, Grace was seized by a sudden gust of sympathy for her father. No doubt he was lonely too. Planted in a glorious garden surrounded by relatives and friends, T-Papa was longing still. He was not the invincible one they made him out to be.

Grace remembered the first time she realized that her father was mortal, the day of the Accident. A decade before, in this same car barreling down the interstate, she had come face to face with her fears of being orphaned. She survived the crash fine, but it was the aftermath that gave her such a fright, when she feared she would never see T-Papa again. That fear seemed silly to her now.

Grace climbed into the Buick. She held the wheel for a moment before turning the key. The Buick gave a short cry, then fell back into silence. Grace pumped the gas, coaxed the key, slapped the wheel. The car died over and over, a noisy death of bucking and belching.

At first, Grace refused to relinquish the wheel. Finally she surrendered in tears of frustration. The Buick was dead, deader than anyone in this place. Head bowed, fist to the heavens, Grace pounded the dash. One way or another, T-Papa had her for all time. Why had she ever despaired of losing him?

6

The Accident

Holy Thursday, April 3, 1969

Holy Thursday was presented in Catholic schools as Jesus's last good supper with his buddies. Three-D paintings and velvet rugs commemorating that great event were sold year-round on street corners in L.A. Grace preferred to think of Holy Thursday as the night when Jesus prayed and got no deliverance, the night one of his closest friends betrayed him, the night he was led away. It was in the spring of 1969 that she first came to think of it this way, when she first learned to distinguish embarrassment from shame and humiliation.

Embarrassment was the routine fear of every Broussard, what they dreaded individually and collectively, what they were each loath to experience but all eager to foist upon each other. A Broussard who made a slip of the tongue, the foot, or the mind could count on being the center of a story told into perpetuity. In this way, embarrassment was akin to immortality. If someone else could die for your sins, then all the better. Embarrassment was to be avoided whenever possible.

Shame was something altogether different. Shame could not be avoided. It had to do with who you were. Embarrassment you caused yourself and, in that sense, you were in control. Shame fell upon you like a heavy tree. Embarrassment hurt your feelings; shame paralyzed them. Embarrassment would dress you down; shame would lay you out. Shame was not something the Broussards talked about. Off in a corner, they waited it out, people with hives who hoped nobody would notice. The Broussards did not wish shame upon anybody, not even upon each other.

As bad as shame was, it shrank in front of humiliation. Short of death by torture, being humiliated in front of one's fellows was the worst that could happen to you. If shown a photo history of World War II, Broussard eyes would fix upon the photo of an elderly Jewish man being forced to clean the boots of a laughing Brown Shirt or a shorn French woman carrying her German-fathered baby before a jeering crowd. They had no trouble superimposing their own fears onto these photos. Countless generations of Broussards had experienced humiliation—at the hands of Southern sheriffs, Southern hounds, and Catholic nuns. While most of them survived it, they did not always survive it well. The Broussards could stand being down; they could not stand being reduced. As far as they were concerned, one could be happily poor, merrily wrong, ecstatically humble. Being made to bow was the intolerable ordeal, the ultimate sin against dignity.

Dignity was everywhere in the Negro South. It was with the silent, simmering men who stood, hats off, heads bowed, as the bodies of their brethren were carried off to early graves. It was with the women who bore the weight of Southern manhood,

backs straight, minds bent on every type of treason. It was with
the children who would not "lower themselves" to answer calls
of contempt. Negroes thought dignity, walked dignity, dressed it
when they could. Deprived of rights, deprived of riches, they
would not soon be parted from their dignity. When they feigned
abasement, it was for the benefit of White people. The costliest
pain was the pain resulting from a loss of dignity.

Grace crossed reluctantly into Texas, its nine hundred miles
languishing before her like a tired, dirty carpet. Wedged against
the door under steamy adult flesh, it was all she could do not to
bolt from the car and fling her ten-year-old body at New
Mexico's feet. Through the drowsy eyes of Texas, New Mexico
became a fading Nirvana, and Louisiana looked like the Promised Land. Somewhere in the Great Beyond lay California, but
this knowledge was small comfort. To a restless child, eager to
tussle with her cousins in the shade of great oak trees, the Texas
landscape held all the interest of a paper bag. Paint it, cut it, fold
it, adorn it with cotton balls and glitter, it was still only worth a
half hour's attention. But Texas would take a whole day. Grace
feared she would die there.

*The pain was getting worse. It swirled around her stomach
and enveloped her bottom. It wasn't what she had eaten because
she hadn't eaten anything. Grace was too nauseated to eat. Her
mother told her she was carsick—if she went to sleep, it would
pass. But this feeling was different from carsickness. It felt like it
must feel to be dying. So she was very quiet because she didn't
want anyone to know she was dying. She wanted to die quietly.
Without causing a fuss.*

Grace had no reason to doubt that the family's two-year-old
Buick could double as a hearse. It was the biggest car the
Broussards had ever owned and, quite possibly, the biggest car
the world had ever known. Grace was sure it could hold her

casket, the pallbearers, the flowers, and the whole grieving family as well. Its comfortable limit was 1,840 pounds and, what with the suitcases, T-Papa, Camille, Anthony, Joseph, Yvette, and Grace, it was already pushing 1,480. On the return drive, after everyone had spent a week gorging themselves, they would tip the scales all the way home, stuffed with catfish and embalmed in hot sauce. One thing Grace knew for sure: even if she died in Texas, she didn't want Texas to bury her.

Camille was upset to be on the road on Holy Thursday. She had wanted to leave that Monday, but T-Papa was finishing the rectory's new dining room table, which took him all of Monday and most of Tuesday. They left at 3:00 Wednesday morning, speeding through California before coming to a halt halfway through Arizona. The men passed the wheel amongst themselves, seldom stopping the car. Camille had made them promise they would have her at her mother's house well before 3:00 Good Friday afternoon, the time at which the Lord had given up his spirit. It wouldn't do to be traveling at a time when the world was standing still.

Grace couldn't wait to set her eyes on Louisiana, to smell the greens of her Grandma Chenier's kitchen, which would be cooking no matter what time of day or night they arrived. Her mother's people were always perfectly welcoming but in a perpetual state of uproar. Her father's people, on the other hand, were not inclined toward agitation, but neither were they inclined toward affection. The differences between the families could be summed up by the way the grandmothers wore their hair. Grandma Chenier let her silver hair stand on end, straight back behind her like a bramble bush. Nannan Broussard dyed her hair and tied it in a knot. It was the absence of the knot that was bound to make this trip more agreeable. It had been buried with her two winters before.

T-Papa had driven back for the funeral, accompanied in mourning by his eldest son, Raymond. Raymond was the only L.A. grandchild to whom Nannan was even slightly sympathetic. Being both male and light, he was the only one who met both of her prerequisites for respect. He and his father made the arduous journey in two days and a night, racing through Texas in the spanking new Buick (bought with cash the day before).

The funeral had been held up for them, and the wake for Nannan was still going on when they arrived. They kissed her on both cheeks, which was no less satisfying than kissing her when she was alive. She had never returned a kiss in anyone's memory. Still, T-Papa was sad, as a son should be, and Raymond cried for reasons unknown. The actual ceremony was an elaborate affair, complete with the first limousine procession ever to be seen in Grimelle. It motored in from Baton Rouge and picked Nannan up from the back bedroom. On the way up the drive they got stuck in the mud, and Uncle Adolphe's tractor had to tow them out. People said privately "that's what you get" for trying to be so pretentious but, since the procession had been Nannan's last pretentious request, her family really didn't have a choice. To this day, T-Papa became solemn whenever his mother was mentioned. Grace knew she ought to feel sad, but her sorrow was as distant as her dead grandmother's affection.

T-Papa was never supposed to have married Camille, because she was one of the Chenier girls. Both the Broussards and the Cheniers remembered slavery. Camille's great-grandmother had journeyed from the cane fields of Haiti to the cane fields of Louisiana two generations after the Haitian slaves had killed their masters, seized their freedom, and gained the enmity of their neighbors. She had been a slight, silky woman who had borne her children of rape and watched them die of rage. The Cheniers remembered her singing. The Broussards remembered no singers, only the tuneless ancestors who had once owned slaves and were unsound enough to brag about it. They had almost owned the Cheniers.

The Cheniers could not be owned. They were much too exuberant. A one-horse family of farmers, they never had any leftover money but always had plenty of leftover food. They cooked as though they were feeding the masses, canned as if preparing for famine, and ate with the verve of swamp mosquitoes. There were an awful lot of them, but not enough to justify a daily Mardi Gras. Cheniers had a tendency to get carried away with everything; this enthusiasm was expressed in their food, their number, and their sizes. In every crowd, the one who laughed too often and too loudly was bound to be a Chenier.

They had none of the self-control of the Broussards, who regarded all Cheniers with cultivated distaste. Broussards thought of themselves as Louisiana royalty, which made the Cheniers laugh hardest of all. Didn't they die like Cheniers? Weren't they buried in the same brown earth? And born of women in the back rooms of houses that rose and sank with their mothers' breathing? Didn't they cry to find themselves here, just like Chenier babies did? Who cares what they did between the birthing and the burying? Wasn't it all just passing time?

To Broussards, time was important. This was because they were so busy improving themselves, an occupation that would stand them in good stead once segregation was outlawed. They were carpenters and cabinetmakers, trades that would lead future generations into the lucrative California construction business. Broussard women were not sent out to work; their daughters were sent to school. Family members who were not predisposed by gender to hammer and saw were predisposed to stir and stitch. Every job was done to perfection. They were a family bursting with skill and aching with pride. It was impossible not to resent them daily.

They had their hands in everything. When someone passed away, Broussard men gathered in the front yard to fashion a coffin while the deceased waited lamely in a Broussard bed in the back of a house that the Broussards had built. Broussard women helped dress the body, as they dressed the brides and the baptismal babies, in gauze and lace and cotton. No one looked to the Broussards for daily bread—they were not known to share their catfish—but when they wished to advertise their superiority, the spreads could be lavish. Extravagance was their specialty. To marry a Broussard was to marry a Brahmin.

When Henri Joseph Broussard, Jr. made known his intentions to wed Camille Marie Chenier, his mother took to her bed for two months. This did not deter the young couple, as theirs was a union of the heart. In family lore, their subsequent migration to Los Angeles had been fueled by the Depression. In truth, they had been frozen out. Nannan could not be expected to love a colored grandchild. She had died without doing so.

To the Cheniers, the match was laughably bad. Who did Camille Marie think she was, marrying a Broussard? Didn't she know he was bred to look down on her and all of her people? He would want her to bend to his will, to give up not only her name but her claim to herself as well. She would forget she was a Chenier. (The fact that she never did was merely a testament to the Chenier stamina.) They cried when she left for L.A., certain she was being carried to her ruin but unable to disapprove because her ruin seemed so glamorous. All but the most generous Cheniers believed T-Papa was no good for Camille up until the day he died, at which point they decided he was a saint.

Now that Nannan Broussard was gone, Grace looked forward to spending more time with her mother's family. She always had to pay homage to the Broussards, to sit on home-made stiff-backed chairs and listen to their accomplishments. No such posturing was required by the Cheniers, who would delight in Grace's black beret, and in Joseph's and Anthony's "big hair" and the cake cutters protruding from their back pockets. Militant high fashion had yet to reach the Louisiana countryside, and the L.A. Broussards were proud to introduce it.

Grace, for her part, would fall right in with the stuffing of crawfish heads. She would let herself be measured for a new dress and learn again how to thread a needle. ("What y'all be doing in California that this girl don't know how to thread a needle?") These "girl things" were plenty fine, but playing with the boys was what Grace really looked forward to. With the Cheniers, she could get dirty and not have it seen as a reflection on the state of her soul. Grace was not afraid in Louisiana the way she was in L.A. At least, she was not afraid of the same things. She did not worry about crime and police brutality. She worried about faux pas and manners.

One of her boy cousins had promised to take Grace fishing. This cousin's name was Paul. He was the same age as Grace but very small. He liked to read and dreamed of moving to a big city like New Orleans, which he had visited only once. Grace told him all about the city where she lived and suggested that he come for a visit. Later she regretted the invitation. Would a boy from the country feel safe in L.A.? She wasn't sure. He seemed too lovely for the city.

In the year since the L.A. family had last been in Grimelle, their world had changed a dozen times. It had been a year of Panthers and nationalists and takeovers on college campuses. King was dead. Whole cities had erupted in furious grief. Olympic champions had raised their fists to the American flag. Mayor Daley had ordered the Chicago police to "shoot to kill" demonstrators outside the Democratic National Convention. Sirhan Sirhan was on trial for assassinating Bobby Kennedy at L.A.'s Ambassador Hotel. (According to Uncle Claude, the Ambassador had been a grand hotel, but Grace would always associate it with death.) Tom Bradley had won the Democratic primary for Mayor of L.A. by garnering the support of many Whites who, according to the press, believed that "only a black man could keep the blacks in line." Nixon had won the presidency, and Camille wanted to know what sins the country was paying for through that wretched little man.

Change had barely touched Grimelle, which could have been any village in the world. One cousin had gone to Vietnam, first crossing the border into Mississippi, which could be just as dangerous. His mother was threatening to ship him some Louisiana blood sausage, some *boudin*, though his siblings argued he was probably seeing enough blood as it was. Instead, they had sent him prayers. The city Broussards looked forward to the stability of their country homeland. They longed to be surrounded by barefoot children, slumbering trees, and chickens running in the dirt. No matter how much the world changed, "home" always stayed the same.

So did Texas. The immutable, impenetrable state had not changed one iota since Grace had last seen it. The Texas sun coaxed the sweat from her hair and the Texas rain made her tremble. Without a doubt, the Longhorn State constituted the most grueling stretch of the Broussards' yearly sojourn. Chinese checkers and backgammon did little to draw the mind away from the interstate.

Whole boxes of Ritz Crackers and jars of Cheez Whiz could be consumed without the slightest change of scenery. No amount of Vanilla Wafers could make the Lone Star state go by any faster. And what was there to imagine with cattle auctions playing on the radio? Grace stared absently at the horizon. This must be the way astronauts felt after too much space. Somewhere out there, Lady Bird Johnson was planting her wildflowers. Grace wished they could stop by and visit her. Instead, she passed the time counting armadillos by the side of the road. The rolling wheels coupled with the rolling sky combined with her rolling stomach to make for underground seismic activity deep in the pit of her. She burrowed into the cushion and waited for an end to life or an end to Texas, whichever came first.

The pain only grew worse. It was not constant but fell in sheets. Grace would wriggle with it when it came. And when it was gone, she would know she had swindled death. Death and Texas. She could not let herself succumb.

"If you could live in any of the fifty states, where would it be?" Yvette was entertaining the car with food for thought.

"Florida."

"Anthony would live in Florida. That's nice. Where would you live, Joseph?"

"I don't want to play this game."

"Very well. Joseph would live in the State of Confusion."

"I ain't confused. I don't want to play."

"The State of Discontent."

"Yvette, leave Joseph alone. He doesn't want to play."

"Very well, Daddy. Anthony, what draws you to Florida?"

"Florida? Why would anybody want to live in Florida?

"Joseph, we must not disparage another's remarks. If Anthony says he wants to live in Florida, it's his decision."

"What does Florida have that California ain't got?"

"Alligators."

" 'Ain't got' is not proper English."

"What are you doing, Yvette, practicing to be a schoolteacher? Just lay off of me!"

"A voice from the Valley of the Discontent."

"Shut up."

"I will do no such thing!"

"Yvette, stop teasing your brother. He needs to get some sleep so he can help with the driving."

"Very well, then. Go to sleep, Joseph."

"Somebody tell her to be quiet. If she's going to talk all the way through Texas, I'll kill myself."

"Joseph, I don't want to hear any talk like that."

"Mama, do I have to sit next to her?"

"Yvette's a born teacher. The oldest always is. She's been teaching you since you was babies."

"Thank you, Mama. Maybe I should become a teacher."

"Maybe you shouldn't."

"Joseph, that's enough!"

"I think he ought to be expelled from class."

"I think you ought to be expelled from this car. Left by the side of the road…"

"Didn't Daddy tell y'all to quit that squabbling? It's annoying as hell!"

"We cross the Texas line and Anthony starts saying y'all."

"It makes me feel good to say y'all. I like the way it rolls off my tongue."

"Buddy, don't curse in the car."

"Hell's not cursing. And my name's Anthony, not Buddy."

"That's what your Nannan called you."

"That's cause she couldn't remember my name."

"It's always that way with the middle child. People fuss over the oldest and the youngest. Middle children get lost."

"Middle children should kill themselves."

"Joseph!"

"Why do you children have to be so violent?"

"You children? That was Joseph!"

"I don't want to hear that kind of talk in this car. From anybody! I only see one child in this car, and she's got more sense than all y'all combined."

"Did you hear that, Grace? Mama says you're the most grown-up person here. What do you think about that?"

Grace didn't want to think about anything. Her mind was on autopilot. She would just let it glide until somewhere around Houston. Then she would see if there was anything left to salvage. Her fellow passengers were becoming unbearable, but if she focused on this fact, she was bound to lose the few wits she had left.

Everybody had something to do but her. T-Papa drove. Anthony awaited his turn at the wheel, peeling oranges and passing slices to his father. He had only come on this trip in the hopes of courting. Not having found much luck amongst the Creole girls in Los Angeles, he was hoping to impress one of his Grimelle cousins with his big city ways. Joseph had left off thinking about girls and was reading Eldridge Cleaver's *Soul on Ice*. Yvette, because she was the skinniest, was placed in the back seat between Camille's bulk and Joseph's brawn. Still, she managed to crochet. Camille distributed food. Grace did nothing but look out the window. Since there was nothing to see, this was a non-activity. Hemmed in on either side—on one side by her mother, on the other by the door—her mind didn't have the room it needed to move around. Because she was a child, she wasn't allotted a space of her own but was encouraged to find in Camille an indentation large enough to house herself.

The pain was getting to her now. She felt it stabbing at her side. Her body gave way and sagged into the seat. There was a pain that came from thinking too much, from trying to put things together that didn't want to go together. Trying to

*reconcile the body to the mind was the most painful kind of
thinking. The mind seemed to need things that the body didn't
want, things like guilt and shame and regret. Grace was aware
that her body was changing, but she couldn't account for its
rapid deterioration since leaving California's doorstep. She
knew that young people died. Children had died in the Holo-
caust. A child she knew had died of leukemia. But she always
thought people died when they were stopped—death stopped
them, didn't it?—not on their way somewhere. Grace pressed
her eyes shut and held her breath and wished for a little death.
Not a complete one, but a respite. A temporary stunning of the
lower half of her body. More than St. Joseph's aspirin, more
than ginger ale, she needed something to stop the pain. She tried
not to think about it.*

"Grace sure is awful quiet. There must be something wrong
with her."

"She's thinking about her boyfriend."

"What boyfriend?"

"Cousin Paaaaaaul…"

"He's not my boyfriend!"

"Grace likes Cousin Pa-aul. Don't you?"

"Better than I like any of you!"

"Oooooooooooohhhhh!"

"Stop picking on Grace. Can't a person be alone with her
thoughts? Grace, where would you like to live?"

Adults were simple creatures. They were amused by the
thinnest of diversions. Grace's mind required more stimulation.
She settled into her corner and started counting billboards.

"Grace is ignoring us."

"That sounds like a good idea. I could use a few miles of
silence." T-Papa had spoken and the car grew quiet. This produced an atmosphere that Grace found to be more fertile. If she

couldn't summon a thought, she could always draw on her memories. They were good for a few idle miles. She settled on her memories of Nannan Broussard. That her beloved Daddy could have sprung from this woman's stomach... A gruesome idea.

The only sounds in the car were Yvette humming to the rhythm of her crochet needles and Anthony thumping the armrest. Before long, the humming died down and the car fell asleep.

Grace could not sleep. The pain was snaking through her abdomen, feeding on her nerves. She curled inside herself and tried to find a way out. Addled by the rocking of the car and the snoring of her mother, she became a wad of tension. She joined her hands in prayer and jammed them into her lap. The pain shot down to her toes. She didn't want to wake Camille to tell her about it. It was better to beseech Mary. Everything was pressing in on her. The car, her mother, Texas. The sun threatened to melt her away. With no relief in sight, Grace pressed her knees tighter, tucked her bottom under, burrowed further into the seat. Somehow, it helped to take a handful of herself. She gripped soft flesh, moving her prying hands in a wave-like motion. She tried to make her legs touch, but her hands precluded that, wedged as they were in the center of things. This became a kind of game, quite unlike Chinese checkers or backgammon. Grace was teasing, tempting herself. She felt a vibrato stirring between her thighs. The tremor climbed up her arm and shook her brain, sending a trill running down her legs. Her heart dropped to her loins, and no amount of pressure would still its beat. First a murmur, then a raging torrent. It had not been her intention to cause herself pleasure. She had done so by accident. Curled in supplication, bowed in worship, Grace had felt a pure unbound craving for herself. The pain went away. Her mind was at ease. It was like dying.

When Grace awoke she was hot and hungry. She woke to the sound of Yvette complaining.

"It's been hours since we last stopped. Can't we at least pull over and freshen ourselves?"

"It's all this stopping that makes us go so slow. It'll be June by the time we get there."

"Now, Daddy, don't exaggerate. Isn't it time to fill up the gas tank? For heaven's sake, someone besides me must need to go to the bathroom."

"I need to go."

"You see? Grace needs to go to the bathroom too."

They stopped at a gas station just outside of Ozona. The passengers roused themselves and sprang into action. While the listless attendant filled the tank, Joseph checked the oil, Camille emptied the trash, and T-Papa and Anthony effected a switch of drivers. Yvette and Grace headed for the tiny restroom on the far side of the building. A metal indoor outhouse, it hadn't been cleaned in recent history. They would have to "hold it" until they could stop again, a solution that would not thrill T-Papa. Grace prayed the next station would be cleaner, since she was not prepared to "hold it" all the way to Grimelle. They repacked themselves into the Buick, everyone stoic about the challenge that lay ahead except for a grumpy Grace, who was nestled next to Camille like a burr. Anthony took the wheel as they headed back to the highway.

The pain had subsided but Grace was still aware of the pleasure. She remembered her little death, which had settled like a warm fog over her body. Grace cradled her secret. She had been surprised to wake up and still be in Texas. She had half expected to find herself in heaven.

Grace noticed the speeding Chevy just as it was bearing down on her. A moment faster and it would have hit the exact

spot where she was sitting. Instead, it pierced the side of the
trunk with a loud bang. As soon as the Broussards realized what
was happening, a horrible scrambling began. "Is everyone
okay? Where's Grace?"

Mashed against the door, Grace could hear her family
calling to her. But a heavy weight had fallen on her, and she
couldn't move or answer. It wasn't the weight of steel or glass
or fear. It was the warm, pleasant weight of Camille. Slowly the
weight shifted, and mother and daughter embraced.

"Are you all right, baby?"

Grace nodded her head. "I couldn't hold it," she whispered,
and tears poured from her eyes.

Camille held her tight and offered a prayer of gratitude.
"That's all right, baby. That's all right."

T-Papa was out of the car and on his feet. Anthony and
Joseph emerged next. Their hair had grown even higher with the
shock of it all. Yvette helped her mother carry Grace to the roadside. Nobody was hurt, but all of them were scared. This was,
after all, Texas.

In the middle of the road stood the boy. He couldn't have
been more than thirteen, and he wasn't much taller than Grace.
"He doesn't even have hair on his face," snapped Camille. The
Broussard men approached their foe. When they drew near him,
the boy tilted his head and smiled sweetly. He had a toothpick in
his mouth.

"Name's Homer. Pleased to meet y'all," he nodded.

"I don't know, Homer. Seems like we could have met a
better way," answered Joseph. "You was going mighty fast."

Homer looked chagrined by this observation. "I reckon I
was going the speed limit," he testified.

Joseph was undaunted. "You was going the limit all right.
Just not the legal one."

At this, he felt a sharp grip on his upper arm. It was his
father, tugging him aside. "Watch the way you talk to him," he
cautioned under his breath.

"Why? He's just a boy," snarled Joseph.

"Yes, but you don't know whose boy he is," explained his
father. "This is the South."

"Christ, it's 1969!" the younger Broussard stormed. "The
South can go to hell."

Not missing a beat, Homer followed, "Y'all ain't from
around here, is you? I seen your plates."

T-Papa shot back, "We're from Lou'siana. Straight across
the border. I been driving since before your daddy was born."

Homer seemed offended by the reference to his daddy. "You
ain't been driving in Texas," he swelled. "We got different rules
around here."

"You got a license?"

"Don't need one. I got Texas plates." He went and sat on
the side of the road, opposite the women. He was picking his
teeth and waiting.

A tow truck appeared out of nowhere and, on its heels, a
deputy sheriff. Homer sprang to life at the sight of them. The
tow truck driver immediately began strapping up the Buick.
When T-Papa protested, he was told to be quiet. The sheriff con-
versed with Homer while the Broussards stared in silence.
Homer was gesturing to beat the band. "If you know what's
good for you, you'll run along, now," the sheriff said. Homer
jumped into his Chevy and sped away.

The sheriff turned his attention to T-Papa. "From California, are you? Well, I don't know how they do things in California, but in Texas we don't turn into oncoming traffic."

Anthony stepped forward. "It was me driving."

"Stay right there, young man. I'll decide who was driving."

"Yes, sir," answered T-Papa to the back of Anthony's neck.

"Yes, *sir*," Anthony repeated under his breath.

"Where are your keys?" the sheriff barked. Anthony handed them over.

The sheriff turned his attention to T-Papa. "Let me see your license. You too, boys."

He perused T-Papa's license like it was some kind of foreign currency.

"Henry Bruzzard. This your family?"

"Yes, sir."

The sheriff looked at them and snickered. He turned and said something to the tow truck driver. "Lookit this whide nigruh wid is cullah fambly" was what it sounded like to Grace, a language she couldn't make out. Both men laughed, and she knew by their laughter that what was said was meant to hurt. She saw her father stiffen and turn pale.

"And just what was y'all doing around here?"

"We stopped for some gas. We was just passing through."

"Any of you boys carrying any weapons?"

"No, sir!"

"All right. You don't have to make a fuss about it. But if y'all are carrying something, you best hand it to me right now." Nobody moved.

The sheriff had his hand on his gun. He surveyed the licenses some more, talked things over with the tow truck driver, moved his boot around in the dirt. "I'll have to take you boys with me. Otis, you take the gals."

Camille began to protest, "The gas station's right here."

The sheriff ignored her and addressed T-Papa. "You boys pile on in the car." Camille began to say something, but T-Papa flashed a look that silenced her. The Broussard men squeezed themselves into the back seat of the sheriff's car. They didn't need handcuffs since none of them could move in any direction. The sheriff used his gun to motion to the tow truck driver, who was rounding up "the gals." After making sure his prisoners were "secure and comfortable," the sheriff climbed into his car, placing the pistol on the seat next to him. He waited for the tow truck driver to finish loading up before speeding off with his "cargo."

Grace squeezed into the middle of the tow truck's cab, flanked by Yvette and Camille, who were tight with worry. The tow truck driver smelled like gasoline. He looked like he'd washed his hair in it. Camille was wearing a dress. So was Yvette. They were proper Negro women. The driver said he liked their dresses. He drove fast and howled. He seemed excited about something. They hoped it wasn't them. Camille took out her rosary and began caressing its powerful beads. Grace held on to one end of it. Yvette murmured "Hail Marys" into the dashboard. This made Otis howl louder.

What was the worst this White man could visit upon them? They knew what it was, and it wasn't murder. It was what had been visited upon their foremothers, a brutality known to all conquered peoples. To this brutality the Broussards owed their very existence. It was something they never talked about, some-thing they feared with all their beings, something they would survive. Every day they were aware of the history which made this ride so precarious. In the considered opinion of many Southern gentlemen, women who looked like them existed for one thing only. They rambled on in silence.

"Coming in with a carload of coloreds." The message on the scanner was unmistakable. Camille let forth a gasp, and her hand involuntarily rose to cover her mouth. Up until that moment, she had known they would be all right. Now she was not so sure. Her beloved husband and sons had been reduced to "a carload of coloreds." She wished she had forced the boys to cut their hair. As she pictured them careening down a back-woods Texas road, she fancied it might have made a difference. The tow truck driver said nothing. No doubt the message was familiar to him. He slapped the steering wheel. Camille didn't hear what came after that.

By this time, Yvette was sobbing into a crocheted hankie. Camille lifted her chin with the back of her hand. Grace shivered on her mother's lap. She could feel a warm stream trickling down her thighs, but she couldn't stem its flow. Camille held her tighter. Yvette sobbed louder. The tow truck driver cursed.

They were traveling deep into enemy territory. In L.A., enemy territory was Lynwood, "the beautiful Caucasian city." Or Orange County with its reactionaries. Or Whittier, where Nixon was from. Here, enemy territory was anywhere off the Interstate. A few years before, they had stopped at an Arizona Denny's and watched as the hostess greeted a would-be diner with the words, "We don't serve no Injuns." They left before she came around to them.

The tow truck came to a halt in a muddy bed of gravel. The driver jumped out and began unhooking the Buick. The Broussard women felt sick to their souls. The far side of the moon would have looked more inviting.

A wooden garage sat directly in front of them. It looked to have been painted gray some decades before. Half of its planks were missing. The same could be said of its proprietor.

"What have we here, Otis?" He surveyed the wreckage. "Good job. Good job." He slapped the back of the Buick. "Fine. Mighty fine." He leered at Yvette. Camille scowled back.

"Is she your girl, this one? How'd she get to be so bright? Her Daddy white?"

"If he was white, he wouldn't be in jail. Now, would he?"

"Are you contradicting me, gal? You must be one of them civil rights niggers, always marching and rioting and trying to start trouble. Y'all need to go back where you came from."

"California?"

"Don't get fresh with me, gal. You ain't in California now."

"I'm from Lou'siana," said Camille. "Texas don't scare me none." This statement was not true. Texas terrified Camille, as did parts of her home state and every other place she'd ever been. But she looked him right in the eye when she said it. And he backed off.

"One of them Lou'siana coloreds," he spat. "All high and mighty! Well, around here, you nothin' but a nigger, gal. Don't you forget it."

Around here, she had no rights and would get no privileges—Camille didn't have to be reminded of that. In 1969, people like the Broussards were mostly illegal. The only way for them to exist was illegitimately. Black and White were prohibited to marry, forbidden to sleep together. And while this illicit coupling happened all the time, it was scorned in the eyes of the law unless it was the rape of a Black woman by a White man. The country simply did not recognize a racial intersection. Pure White was viewed as one end of a spectrum whose opposite consisted of pure Black and all of its shades. There was no middle. And, in this little corner of Texas, there was no place for Black Pride in any shade.

Still, Camille had to try. She had to make him think she would be more trouble than she was worth. Nobody would harm her children, not without a fight in the dirt, if need be. "You got a restroom my girls can use?" Grace's nose was running and her clothes were soiled. Together with Yvette, whose bottom lip was bleeding from where she had practically bitten through it, they made a powerful case for leniency.

The proprietor motioned to the rear. "Restroom?" he sneered. "Hey, Otis! This nigger trash wants to know if we got a restroom." He laughed and spat on the ground.

Yvette knew to avoid the outhouse. She led Grace behind the garage while Camille stood guard out front. If they all got busy taking care of each other, the time would go by quickly. This was the lie they told themselves. Behind the garage was a water pump. Yvette didn't say a word as she undid Grace's pants. She pumped some water and wiped Grace's legs with the crocheted square. It was then that Yvette noticed that her sister was bleeding. She ran to get Camille.

Camille gasped at the news but remained calm. Upon reflection, she was not surprised that the events of the day had called forth Grace's blood. Sudden adversity will make an adult out of any child who is already at the threshold. And Grace had always been a special child. If anybody within her sight was suffering, she suffered too. Camille pressed Grace to her and held her tight.

Grace wasn't expecting her period so soon. Yvette told her it was coming but said it wouldn't arrive until Grace was ready for it. As usual, Yvette had lied. Anne Frank hadn't gotten her period until she was fourteen. Grace thought about Anne in her little attic, all crowded with no privacy. Anne had an older sister too. Grace thought about Anne and her sister as her own mother and sister labored to clean her up and comfort her. She was afraid she would never see her home again. And what about her father and brothers? Where had they been taken? Grace felt sorry for what her family was suffering. She sensed that they were embarrassed, and she worried that she was the cause.

The problem with embarrassment is that, unlike shame, it is a public event, necessarily involving other people. Phrases like "you're not going to embarrass me" rang in Broussard ears from childhood to the end of life when, confined to hospital beds, they struggled not to embarrass their nurses. What Grace had done in the car she had done in secret, but the intensity of her pleasure made it unmistakably evil. What followed was calamity. Had she caused the accidents—the one with the Chevy and the one in her panties? She worried that her body had conspired with Texas to humiliate her family. She had seen the Chevy coming but hadn't screamed a word of warning. She had felt her own dampness, held on to it in her dreams. For these and other crimes, she believed herself to be guilty beyond redemption.

At seven o'clock, Grace began to shake with fear. It was dark, and the Broussard men had not appeared. Camille and Yvette continued to whisper countless rosaries—the Stations of the Cross and novenas to St. Bridget. At first it had been comforting, mesmerizing, stupefying. Now it was like being at a wake. For Grace, everything was suddenly as clear as a corpse's eyes. They were going to die in Texas.

The pain was hard to conceive, harder to bear. It masked the sorrow that swallowed the hope which fondled the dreams of a ten-year-old girl. Grace didn't know where she stood, where she had landed, what would become of her. But one thing was sure. The pain was what connected her to generations of her family, and she could only banish it at great risk to herself.

Camille squinted in concentration. A car was coming up the road. She could hear it from a long way off. It deposited the Broussard men, haggard but unharmed, before tearing off into the night.

Nobody said a thing. T-Papa saw the spots of blood and urine on Grace's dress and stiffened like a zombie. *"C'est pas que tu pensé,"* whispered Camille. *It's not what you think.* The patriarch gathered his family, paid the little money he had left to ransom the car, and drove down the gravel road back to Interstate 10. Camille sat in front this time, her hand resting on

Grace's knee. They drove without stopping. Easter was almost upon them. In no time, the Lord would be rising. They would miss the Good Friday services and Cousin Titine's screechy rendition of "Were You There?" They would never talk about the Accident, and it would pass into history. In Grace's mind, it would become part of all the evil that is done but never spoken of. There was no eloquence in humiliation.

Joseph had left off *Soul on Ice* and was reading Dr. King's "Letter from a Birmingham Jail." To allay the deadening tension in the car, he read aloud. It was this battle cry for human dignity that finally pushed T-Papa into an emotional ditch from which he could not immediately extract himself. He pulled over to the side of the road and cried.

The pain was very bad now. It was everywhere in that tank of a car, encircling them and stealing their breath. Grace knew it would pass. There was nothing she could do but wait. She looked out the window at Texas. And saw herself in the glass.

7

The Date

New Year's Eve, 1978

The Broussards didn't have sex per se. They had dating and dancing. They had marriages, miscarriages, and children. They had menopause, impotence, and sterility, but sex was not amongst their possessions. Sex was cheap, public entertainment, and the Broussards were private people. They knew something of love, but they did not share what they knew with outsiders. Love was something personal, altogether unlike sex, which could be shared with absolute strangers. Romantic love was a privilege, a grave and perilous promise, a treaty whispered in the dark. It had nothing to do with sex, which was a sin.

E lena mounted the steps two by two, and the staircase moved with her. The Fox Hills Broadway was packed with after-Christmas sales fanatics and Scrooges who had come to return all their gifts. Eyes cast far afield, thoughts fleet and guarded, Grace's young lover parted the crowds like a seasoned New Yorker. It was not the first time she had had to chase Grace down and hold her to her word. In fact, every time they were scheduled to look for an apartment, Grace found a way to foil their plans. Not this time. Elena stepped with authority.

Grace beheld her lover. From pillar to post, Elena was stunning. The sight of her filled Grace with a gentle ardor, the kind that comes from watching a child sleep. Elena alighted from the escalator and flowed through Linens. She was heading for China. Grace joined the crowds converging on the sales tables to fight over frayed napkins and flawed crystal. She tried not to crumple the red dress, which was slung under her arm in a green Christmas bag. The thought of Elena twisting in that dress sent shivers down Grace's back. As her lover paused to survey the scene, Grace pulled up behind her.

"*¿Necesitas ayuda, linda?*"

Hair swinging behind her, lips resisting a smile, Elena spun on her toes like a matador. She was a dancer. She had this dancing way of talking, of gliding in and out of conversation without losing her balance.

"Why didn't you tell me you were working today? Look at your hair! I call your house and your mother tells me she doesn't even know what time you're getting off. We were supposed to look at apartments, remember? What's in the bag? I made an appointment. How about my party? Did you forget about me, *amiguita*? I don't have all day to wait for you. When do you get out of here, anyway?"

"Now."

"*¿Mande?*"

"*Ahorita. Estoy lista. Me da mucho gusto verte, mi amor.*"

"*¡No des lata, Grace!* Don't drag out your tired little Spanish because you know I'm mad at you. It don't give me *mucho gusto* to see you. *Mucha lucha*, maybe. *¡Me caes gorda!*"

Elena could trade insults with the best of them. Grace's feelings were frequently bruised but never bloodied by her. Elena

was a "homegirl" from "the hood," a "sister." Grace, who re-
coiled from the touch of friends and relatives alike, found it easy
to touch and be touched by Elena. She let her take her hand and
guide her through the greedy throngs.

"Where do you think you're going, Miss Broussard?"

Racine Estes was the floor supervisor. Tall and gloomy, she
was not a person to be trifled with. Around her minimal waist
there was always a belt, looped twice. Grace surmised Miss
Estes might have been a nun in another life, in which case the
belt would have come in handy. Even now, Grace never doubted
that the belt could be made to unwind itself in the blink of an
eye. Had she been this woman's child instead of her underling,
Grace would have dropped Elena's hand and taken off down the
escalator in an attempt to avoid a whipping. As it was, she
dropped Elena's hand anyway, but met her accuser's glare with
a flicker of her own.

"Hello, Miss Estes. How are you?"

"What are you doing?"

"I'm taking my lunch break."

"Lunch? You just got here!"

"I can't help it. My car broke down. I have to go and deal
with it."

Elena looked on incredulously. Miss Estes was undaunted.
"Be back in an hour or you answer to me." Grace's nostrils
flared. She could feel the red dress pulsating in her hand.

"I don't believe you, *loca*. How are you going to pay your
rent if you get yourself fired? 'My car broke down.' What car?
You're such a bad liar. I told this guy we'd be there at 12:30. It's
already 12:55. So, what you got in the bag, huh? Is it for me?
Come on. I have a feeling this is going to be the place."

The apartment was sunny, spacious, and clean. The one
problem was its location directly behind Inglewood High
School. Grace could imagine AWOL students bailing over the

stucco walls and smoking on her doorstep. The apartment building itself had several advantages. It was too ugly to attract burglars, and Grace felt confident that the shocking pink doors and orange shag carpets would be enough to repel her relatives.

The landlord was a Mr. Winston. Diminutive in build, he appeared to be led around by a cigarette. "You're not going to bring a bunch of boys up in here, are you?" He eyed the pair suspiciously.

"No, sir." Grace let Elena do the talking.

"Which one of you wants to rent?"

"Both of us."

"This is a one-bedroom. It's not big enough for two people."

"It's huge! You could fit a family of twelve in here." Elena loved to flirt.

"I don't want no more than the two of you, got that? And no pets either!"

"Got it! No boys, no pets, just the two of us." Elena was a charmer. Mr. Winston was warming to her.

"That's right. You girls got jobs?"

"Yes, sir. I'm a student and…"

"That ain't no job."

"I also work twenty hours a week at a print shop."

"You legal?"

"Of course I'm legal! Are you legal?"

"You got your card?"

"What is this, South Africa? You ain't seen me on any wanted posters, have you? Gringos!"

"Hey, don't be calling me no gringo. I just don't want no trouble, that's all."

"I work. I go to school. I have a card. What else do you want to know?"

"What about your friend?"

"She works too."

"Does she talk?"

Grace cut her eyes at Mr. Winston, who was starting to sound like a relative.

"I work at the Broadway Fox Hills."

"Is that a fact? My niece is a supervisor over there. Rae Estes. Been with them since they opened. You know her?"

"I think so." Grace pictured Miss Estes's avenging eyes.

"I'll have to ask her about you. What's your name?"

"Grace."

"All right, then. You can have the place."

"For free?" Elena was pushing their luck.

"Two-fifty a month. First, last, and $50 security."

"When can we move in?"

"As soon as your checks clear."

"Cool."

"Maybe we should talk it over first." Grace's voice startled all three of them.

"You girls want the place or don't you?"

The fact that Racine Estes might get secondhand knowledge of her personal life terrified Grace. Until now, the ramifications of moving in with Elena had only seemed to involve her family. Suppose people at work knew? Suppose random students at Inglewood High saw the way she and Elena looked at each other and instantly knew they were sharing love in a one-bed apartment? Grace hadn't considered any of this when she agreed to move in with Elena. She had only considered her mother's opposition, her sister's bewilderment, her brothers' limitless cynicism.

"Of course we do. I'll bring the money to you later."

"Be here by six. Or I'll rent it out from under you."

"You'd do that, too, wouldn't you? Catch you later."

"Okay. *Mañana*—I mean, *hasta luego*."

Elena slammed the car door and jerked on the seat belt. "*¡Dios mio!* Do you want to live with me or not? So the carpet's hideous and the landlord smells like cigarettes. He's going to die soon anyway. Maybe he'll leave us the place. What am I going to do with you, Grace? You don't say anything. You're wearing that crazy scarf? You think we're going to find something this nice for cheaper? Who do you think's going to want you with that hairdo?"

Grace sat in the passenger's seat twisting her curls. She didn't know if she could stand to be around Elena on a daily basis. True, the place was large for a one-bedroom, but a palace with eighty rooms would have been less scary. Maybe they should look for a duplex. Grace suggested this to her lover.

"A duplex? What's the point of that? I could just get my own place. If you don't want to live with me, just say so. Are you afraid of living in sin? Is the Pope going to live with us too?"

"I want to live with you."

"Say, 'I want to live with you in sin without the Pope.' See, you can't say it. *¡Dios mio, cariña*, it's 1979! When are you going to give up that family of yours and get a life of your own? You're driving me to drink."

"I do want to live with you. Just not in that place, okay?"

"Turn on some music, would you?"

Grace chewed her lip. "What do you want to hear?"

"Anything. Anything but church music!" They drove on in silence. Elena switched lanes while Grace switched stations. She really did want to live in sin. In her heart of hearts she wanted nothing more than to wake up to Elena's husky breath on her shoulder. She just needed to sleep on it, that's all. The Pope had nothing to do with it.

"Let's go someplace where we can talk."

"Don't you have to get back to work?"

"It hasn't been an hour yet."

"Where do you want to go?"

They were passing Holy Rosary. "The cemetery's nice and quiet," Grace suggested. Elena turned her Mustang around and swung it through the imposing gates.

Grace directed while Elena drove, one hand on the wheel, the other on the stick. Grace rested her hand on Elena's, fingers braided through fingers. They stretched and pulled in a silent tug of war of sighs and gasps and winces. Thumbs rubbing, pinching flesh. Elena was getting in the groove, driving like a mobster. Grace squeezed her lover's fingers. She knew the taste of them. She could feel the tension of the gears popping into place, the tension running up Elena's arm into her waiting shoulder. If she was doomed to die a sinner, she would take Elena with her. Grace shivered with love.

There was something vaguely sacrilegious about this visit. Why had she wanted to bring Elena here? To show her the Broussards in all their glory? To let her girlfriend know exactly what she was getting into, that the home they would share might be the first of many plots they would occupy together? Or had she come to make her father jealous, to tease him with their presence and see how he reacted? So far, he was lying low. But Grace didn't trust him. He was not one to pass up provocation. She had come bearing no gifts, saying no prayers, carrying no flowers. She was there in the company of her love. T-Papa would surely be offended.

Or maybe it was only Elena who would be offended. What had Grace hoped to show her friend by bringing her to this place of death? What new intimacy did she hope to find?

Grace rarely came to sex naked. True, she had lain bare before Elena on many occasions. Like a sweep of grass, she had offered herself for tending. But physical nakedness was one thing. Grace could take off her clothes without revealing a thing.

After her father's death, she had learned how to wrap herself in a shroud that no tenderness could penetrate. To a sixteen-year-old girl, sex had seemed like the most promising of adventures. But bliss was granted only when she approached sex with abandon. Most of the time, Grace approached sex with zeal, but that was different. For her, it was a lot like singing with someone. It could be a harmonious experience or it could be painful and disjointed. It didn't have to be revealing.

Death, not sex, was the most intimate of experiences, the most vulnerable. Vulnerable was what took your breath away. Death did this as a rule; sex only sometimes. A towering person like T-Papa, reduced to a breathless body. A hearty connoisseur of gumbo eating his grass from the roots up. By sharing his death with Elena, Grace hoped to cement the bond between them. By bringing her love to the cemetery, she hoped to show her father that nothing was inviolate.

Elena had never known anyone dead, at least nobody close to her. She had come to T-Papa's funeral along with many other classmates and all of Grace's teachers. They had cried to see Grace cry. It had been a haunting experience, the entire Broussard family streaming down the aisle consumed by grief. The sight of them made Elena shy. When she tried to talk to Grace afterwards, all they could do was cry together. Elena had never felt so alone as during the time of Grace's mourning. T-Papa's death had been a family affair. She had not been included.

It felt strange to be included now, on this unexpected outing to Holy Rosary. The Broussards struck Elena as slightly odd. They talked about the past as if it were right there before them, all the while ignoring the pressing realities of the day. Grace's

seething discontent had Elena worried. Hadn't the Broussards
noticed it? They talked about the Pope as if he were their house
guest but failed to relate to the sinner in their midst.

Grace instructed Elena to park outside the grotto. The day
was cool and cloudy. Elena stepped gingerly from the car into
the mouth of the fake cave. They lit a candle and held hands.

Grace kissed Elena's shoulder. She had adored this girl ever
since Geometry class, where they had surveyed each other's
curves and studied each other's angles. Grace would have felt
completely seduced by Elena if it weren't for the fact that she
herself had been the one to make the proposition. Grace had
slipped a note between the slits in Elena's locker: *siempre me da
mucho gusto verte.* "It always gives me pleasure to see you too,"
Elena had answered back, "so much I can hardly contain myself!" That had been all the encouragement either one of them
had needed.

Elena had had a girlfriend before Grace, an older girl who
had graduated when they were still sophomores. This girl had
showed Elena the safest place at Our Lady of Fatima to carry on
an affair, a place where nobody ever went unless they had to: the
school chapel. There, on the choir loft steps, Grace had first
kissed Elena's shoulder. She hadn't meant to. But just as Grace
had moved in for the kill, Elena had jerked her head away, leaving only a shoulder to meet those timid lips.

One summer night they had gone to see the grunion run
with Elena's brother Felipe. Before Grace knew it, they were
splashing naked in the waves, capturing the silvery fish only to
have them slip through their fingers. The few they managed to
hold on to were stuffed into Felipe's socks. That night had been
magic, alive with the sounds of an ancient lust. To Elena, sex
was like the grunion running. The catch was not nearly so exciting as the chase. Just when Grace thought she had her, Elena

would slip through her lips and make her give chase some more.

The grotto was moist and dark. Grace clasped Elena's hand and squeezed it. She liked the way this gesture caused her friend to smile. She found that if she ran her finger down Elena's spine, she could make her shiver. If she whispered in her ear, she could make her laugh. And if Grace kissed her shoulder, she could make her lover sigh.

The thing that interested Grace most about sex was cause and effect. You could run your finger down a lover's spine and cause the same effect every time until one day, without warning, the reaction wouldn't come. Was it the action itself that caused the reaction or a thought brought on by the action, a memory of some previous pleasure that had nothing to do with the current one? When the lover could no longer be counted on to conjure the same memory, did the action then cease to have the desired effect? Grace puzzled about these things. Questions like these made sex interesting, even when she wasn't directly engaged in it. She was constantly having to change approaches. Already, in four years, Elena and Grace had gone through too many motions to count. Grace had watched touch after touch become obsolete—the tickling of the foot, the stroking of the arm, the kiss behind the knee—only the ear seemed continually responsive. What a curious thing sex was! Grace imagined that cause and effect was even trickier to determine in sex between men and women. She was glad she didn't have to worry about this.

Elena, for her part, didn't seem bothered by worries of any kind. It's not that Elena didn't think as much as the person next to her, quite the contrary, she just didn't let her thoughts molest her. She did what came naturally, felt with her entire heart, and thought about the things that pleased her.

Grace kissed Elena's shoulder, but Elena was not stirred. None of her approaches seemed to be working. No matter how

Grace maneuvered, from the front, from the rear, from the side, Elena seemed immune to arousal. She simply did not find the cemetery sexy. Catholicism in general did nothing for her libido, and death in particular stymied it. She wasn't one of those "fast" girls who sinned and confessed every chance they got. Elena wasn't one of the faithful at all; she was one of the blessed. She had no creed, no tenets, no obtuse doctrines. She lived by her heart. And her heart did not like confusion.

Going to the cemetery had been Grace's idea. Against her better instincts, Elena had consented. Ever since they'd been talking about living together, Grace had been acting strangely. Her motives were more clandestine than ever, her mind a carousel of stampeding horses. Tired of trying to tame them, Elena decided to go along for the ride. Now that they were on hallowed ground, she realized she'd made a colossal mistake.

"I don't like it here," she complained to Grace.

"Just a few more minutes," Grace prodded.

Elena looked unnerved. Grace kissed Elena's shoulder. Elena gave way. She bit Grace's hand.

Grace was confounded by the surge of pleasure that washed over her whenever Elena bit her hand. If anyone else made this move, Grace would find it thoroughly unappealing. When Elena did it, it was simply riveting. Grace found her lover's ear and followed it like a map. She nibbled at the peninsula, circled the horn, blew mountain breezes across the dunes. Before she was done, she kissed the valley deep.

Elena was a moaner. Sex and moaning had become synonymous to Grace. She had no trouble conceptualizing sex between any two creatures capable of moaning. What one did with various organs was incidental. What one did with the vocal cords, now that was sex. It was fantastic how loud Elena could moan. On first hearing her, Grace had been startled. The first time they made love, she had been hesitant. But when she heard Elena moan, she recognized in that sound a land she wanted to visit again and again. It was a primal sound, the kind no Broussard had ever deigned to utter. It meant being lost to desire, a condition no Broussard ever suffered. Grace wanted to learn to replicate this sound, but she knew she would have to leave her parents to do it. Any sound that unrestrained within earshot of Compton Avenue would cause her family to call the police. Grace may have made the initial proposition, but it was Elena who had seduced her with her larynx.

When they were in high school at Our Lady of Fatima, Elena had been known for her big mouth. Up until Geometry class, Grace had never considered that they might be friends. Elena was too popular. Grace was well-liked, but she was weird. People tended to give her a wide berth. A nun who noticed this tendency suggested that Grace had been singled out by God for a vocation. Nobody ever talked to Elena about a vocation. Her spirit was too free. You could hear it in her mouth.

Besides making love, Elena liked to bake bread. She liked to cover her lover with dusty hands and knead while the lover kneaded. Once, when they were baking bread at the house Elena shared, a neighbor had come running over to see what was the matter. "I'm having cramps," Elena had apologized. "It always feels better to vocalize." Grace had stood there astounded, caught in the act, flour dusting the breasts of her T-shirt.

An otherworldly sound was now coming from the grotto. If this wasn't enough to rouse T-Papa and all his slumbering friends, Grace didn't know what could. They had been in the grotto a good five minutes, but so far there was no sign of her father. Grace was growing testy. T-Papa must mean to embarrass her. Demanding that she bring him food, forbidding her to leave the family, then not even bothering to watch her flout his rules. Grabbing Elena's hand, she headed for the car. She was putting on a show for the benefit of the devil; she meant to be seen. She would confront him where he lived.

This time, Grace drove. She pulled up behind her father's dormant car, which she had abandoned in disgust earlier that morning. Grace took Elena's face and kissed it. She worked in earnest to make something happen, not inside Elena but inside herself. She felt increasingly desperate and pointless. Inside her soul, a river of longing threatened to wash her away.

If only she could get lost in those lips. Elena's lips were warm. Even when it was cold outside, her lips were warm. Grace loved Elena's lips. She did not like to part with them. Now, in the car, she kept returning to Elena's waiting mouth. No chariot was needed to take Grace to heaven. Elena's lips were sufficient transport.

They dissolved into madness. Elena sank further into her seat. Grace followed. They could barely see, they were so far gone, practically under the dashboard. Grace wondered at the inert figure on the floor. Should she follow Elena down there or give her a hand up? Grace tried to follow but the steering wheel got in the way. How could Elena expect company if she kept diving so low? Grace was neither as small nor as skillful as her friend. She couldn't squeeze her passion into tight spaces and get out of them intact. She tapped Elena on the shoulder. "Come on. I've got to get back to work," she said.

Elena was irritated. "Aren't you going to show me where your father's buried?" She straightened her clothes.

They abandoned the car and set out on foot. It was a bit of a hike to the grave, prolonged by the fact that Grace was pretending not to remember exactly where it was. They were just about to give up the search when Elena noticed what looked like steam rising over a nearby slope. They headed for the summit.

Grace stared down at the stone. All around them, the air had turned to steam. Fog was rolling in from the ocean.

Elena drew Grace close to her. "Isn't it weird how people stay married forever? Until death do us part and all that stuff?"

Grace didn't think it was weird at all. She wished to grow senile with Elena. Since it wouldn't be possible for them to marry, their only option was to live in sin. By Grace's logic, if they were going to live in sin, they might as well do it to death. Suddenly, their relationship seemed old and wrinkled.

"What's that smell?" Elena brought her back.

"What smell?"

"It smells like that stuff you cook. Gumbo."

"What?"

"The fog. It smells like gumbo."

"No it doesn't."

"It must be really cold. I can see my breath."

"It must be your breath you're smelling, then."

"I don't eat gumbo."

Grace looked down at the grave. What she didn't see there spooked her to her bones. The date was missing. The birthdate was there, but T-Papa's death date was missing.

Her father was at large. Grace felt a small wind on her shoulder. At first it was chilly, but then it grew hotter. The breath of the dead is smoky.

They fled. Over the grass, holding hands as they went, tripping over stones, stepping into water canisters. The fog was growing denser and the sky was growing darker. Which way to the car? Elena wanted to retrace their steps, but Grace had no time for reason. She was being led in another direction, past the grotto, to the Chinese section. Elena was panting, trying to catch up with her. "Where are you going? The car's over there. What's the matter with you?"

Grace stopped to catch her breath. It was then, standing there heaving, hands on her knees, that she saw the food. On the Chinese graves, there was food. Eggs and oranges. It wasn't gumbo, but she got the message. Grace threw back her head and let out a moan, the likes of which Elena had never ever heard.

8

The Gunfire of the New Year

Nighttime, December 31, 1978

The Broussards were intimately acquainted with tragedy — not because they lived it but because they were its next-door neighbors. Tragedy was something that happened to other people, mostly to other poorer, darker people. Despite all their worrying about it, no Broussard ever got shot over a card game, no Broussard was ever beaten to death by the police, no Broussard was ever thrown out on the street with all their furniture. Their suffering was tolerable. Broussards did not sleep with tragedy. They said their prayers and went to bed and slept with an equanimity that is only possible for true believers.

E lena's house was a rambling wooden way station, host to numerous lowlifes, parasites, and passionate leftists. There were beds everywhere. Friends who were leaving their spouses asked to spend the night and ended up staying for months. Comrades who'd been kicked out of their own pads made it over to Normandie Avenue a few steps ahead of their creditors. Visitors from other cities and countries crashed on the living room floor. Elena's household didn't need to extend invitations to have a party. They just needed to find a time when everyone would be home.

Tonight the house was having an international dance party to ring in the new year, if not the revolution. Along with the usual disenchanted Americans (including at least one name from Nixon's enemies list), the guests included a family of Vietnamese refugees, a former prisoner of the Shah, a couple of radical French nuns, a Palestinian doctor, and a few Japanese Communists. Everybody was bringing five dollars and dancing to support the Sandinistas.

For the moment the house was quiet, a state in which Grace rarely found it. She would be glad when Elena didn't live there anymore. Grace couldn't see the use of living with so many other people if nobody answered the phone. The kitchen always carried the odor of the last thing that had burned. "Are you hungry, *preciosa?*" Elena sang to her.

"*Sí, tengo hombre.*"

"*Tengo hambre. 'Tengo hombre*' means 'I have man.' And we both know that isn't true. Want some chips? I keep telling these people not to leave things out on the counter. For proletarians, they sure waste a lot of food. What's the matter, *llorona?*"

"I hope I still have a job."

"Me, too. I can't afford to pay the rent by myself."

"Think she's going to dock my pay?"

"What did she say?"

"She said she'd deal with me later."

"Don't worry about it. Tomorrow's a new year."

Grace felt mortally lonely. She could hear her resolve being whittled away in the desperate sound of her chewing. "I don't want to lose you," she said.

"You're not going to lose me!"

"What if you die?"

"Die? I'm not going to die until sometime next century. And neither are you! So, forget about it. Just stay out of cemeteries."

Elena cradled Grace's head and kissed the back of her neck. "It's hard to lose somebody you love." She took Grace's hand and led her to the upstairs bedroom. Before long, Grace had dissolved into sleep, a whisper of "*Duerme, Negrita*" in her ears.

When she awoke, samba was coming from the record player and, from the kitchen, the smell of *mole*. The house was banging with the sound of men. Grace woke up afraid. She lay in the dark listening to the thrusts of the party. She thought about calling her family to assure them that she was all right, but she didn't want them to know where she was. She had to be home before the shooting began.

Getting shot at was definitely an option on New Year's Eve, so much so that Camille forbade either one of her daughters to venture out of the house. Grace tried to point out to her mother that stray bullets were just as likely to reach you *in* the house (while you might avoid the windows, they could always come through the roof), but Camille thought it was important not to court death. If a bullet penetrated the roof of your house, ricocheted off the altar and found you under the bed, yours would be an unexpected tragic kind of death for which you could not be held accountable. However, anyone foolish enough to step out into the streets of America when the National Rifle Association was holding its annual free-for-all and the liquor lobby was throwing its year-end fundraiser was asking for trouble. Spending the night on Normandie Avenue would be safer than dodging bullets all the way home. Grace would try to reason with her mother.

She sat up in bed. A stream of light from the house next door washed over one corner of the room. The air was grainy and cold, and her head was throbbing from a bad dream. Grace couldn't remember where she had put her clothes. She fumbled around for a minute before locating them on the floor. One of Elena's cats was sitting atop the heap. Grace pulled on her clothes, which were now covered in cat hair, and prepared to join the party.

The joy of the revelers assaulted her when she opened the bedroom door. The smell of marijuana wafted up the stairs. Grace made her way to the bathroom, where she washed her face and straightened her clothes. She couldn't remember which toothbrush was Elena's, so she squeezed some toothpaste onto her finger and rubbed it along the front of her mouth. There was nothing to be done for her hair.

Downstairs, bodies stomped and clapped to the beat. A long-legged man from Brazil was dancing *capoeira*, gliding through the air. Grace tried to avoid getting trampled. She started to make her way to the food but was intercepted by a group of merrymakers passing around a reefer and kissing the year goodbye.

She recognized Felipe, Elena's brother and her swimming instructor. He was sitting on the floor with his boots on the coffee table. "Hey, Grace, is that a new hairstyle? Come talk to me. What's on your mind?"

She didn't have anything on her mind but food. She said hello and tried to trip past him, but he pulled her to him, holding out a reefer the size of his fingernail.

Grace felt dizzy with hunger. Conversations swirled around her like flies. She batted away the joint and tried to follow what people were saying. The marijuana smokers were arguing about whether the strategic arms accord represented any real progress. Other talk was of the massacre at Jonestown, the assassinations of Mayor Moscone and Harvey Milk, the Briggs Initiative to outlaw gay teachers. Grace felt sick. She could hear Elena's laughter coming from the dance floor. The sound made her lonely. She pushed herself up from Felipe's lap and made her way to the food. Some soda sounded good, maybe some chicken *mole*.

A swinging ponytail got in the way of Grace's mission. She recognized Jerome, one of Elena's housemates. He was twirling a flash of red cloth. The crowd whistled as he dipped Elena low. In her hand, she held a hat full of dollar bills. She was wearing the red dress.

Grace spun around and headed for the door. She wanted no part of this party. Her head throbbed, her stomach growled, her heart hurt. At first, Elena hadn't noticed her, standing alone in the crowd of admirers. Circling in the red dress, hat in her outstretched hand, Elena could raise more money dancing than the Sandinistas might hope to make from any direct appeal. When she caught sight of Grace, her eyes lit up. She signaled her lover to join in, but Grace pushed through the screen door into the night air.

At one end of the porch, the Brazilian man stood wiping sweat from his brow. He gave Grace a curious look, began to say something, then thought better of it. "Cold out here," he smiled, stepping inside to rejoin the party. Grace was alone.

The porch was surrounded by laurel bushes, the lawn was overgrown. Grace couldn't see beyond the bushes. Moths rose to their deaths in the porchlight.

Standing in the light, Grace felt like a target. Passing cars reared up on hind legs, maniacal, menacing. Above her, the porch light flickered and died. She crept soundlessly into the darkness.

Grace knew this walkway, its dips and bumps, where it was likely to trip her. She had walked here many times from the Louisiana Fish Market on Jefferson, carrying a small white package under her arm. Up the steps to the ample porch, where Elena would be waiting to fry up the fish and electrify her lover.

There was no comfort for her in this house tonight. The noise, the smoke, the stomping feet made her long for the relative calm of the house on Compton Avenue. She was hungry. The days in her mother's house had an order to them. They started with grits and ended with cake. No one ever hungered there. Grace looked back at Elena's unsteady abode. Lodged in the doorway with a full plate of food was the ponytailed Jerome.

His lanky torso filled the frame. Torn dress shirt, corduroy pants faded at the knees and hanging low on his hips, burgundy loafers without socks, Jerome was the picture of pampered rebellion. Of all of Elena's housemates, he was Grace's least favorite. His father, an executive at a life insurance company, had cut Jerome's allowance to shreds when he learned that his son was subscribing to *Ms.* The old man had countered with a subscription to *Playboy*—a publication Jerome denounced in public but devoured on the sly. He was studying film at USC and had spent the previous summer in Castroville picking strawberries and shooting a documentary. As far as Grace could tell, he was in solidarity with anyone shorter than himself. She surveyed his face for suffering. It was a splendid face, kept eternally fresh by its own conceit. Grace was not in solidarity with any part of him.

"Want something to eat?" He offered his plate.

"What time is it?" She sat down on the bottom step.

"Eleven, eleven thirty. What's up?" He sat one step above her, bouncing the plate on his lap.

"I need to leave." Grace sounded wan, defeated.

"You have to stay till midnight."

"I can't. Can you take me home?"

Grace went in to find her sweater. As she was passing under

the mistletoe someone pressed against her, kissing wine into her mouth. The lips were delicious, but they did not touch her want. "*Feliz año nuevo*," Elena whispered. Grace felt tipsy from the spectacle of her life. The warmth of the wine made her stomach reel.

"I'm leaving." She looked at the red dress. Elena wore it well.

"*¿Porqué, amiga?* I tried to wake you two hours ago, but you were in a coma. The party's just beginning. Come. *¡Tienes que bailar!*"

"I don't want to dance. I have to go."

"Don't leave me, Grace."

"I'll call you tomorrow."

Jerome was waiting in his father's Porsche. Grace climbed in next to him, careful to keep her distance, grateful for bucket seats. They took off into the night.

Jerome drove with his plate on the dashboard, stealing bites whenever possible. When he wasn't eating, he told Grace about her life.

He knew all about Creoles. He had been to the top of the State House in Baton Rouge and dined in the French Quarter of New Orleans. He revered Tabasco sauce but thought gumbo was overrated. Bebop was better than Dixieland.

He knew all about Watts because he had leafleted the Watts Festival, but it had become "too commercial" for him. He had taken only a short tour of the Watts Towers because all that glass made him nervous.

Jerome didn't really understand how people could still be Catholic. After studying the Popes of the Middle Ages, he could clearly see that the whole religion was a sham. The missionaries had destroyed most of California and all of South America. One day, the native peoples would rise again. In the meantime, Black people in the diaspora should sue Europe for reparations and carve their own homeland out of the American South. Capitalism was in its death throes. The "Down with the Shah" graffiti was evidence. Nobody needed fifty pairs of shoes.

The Porsche roared up the Broussards' driveway. Grace said goodnight and disembarked.

It was chilly out but clear. Yvette had left the porch light on. Grace started up the steps when she heard a voice call to her.

"Who's there?" Miss Alma was sitting on her porch listening to the gunfire.

"It's just Grace, Miss Alma."

"Oh, Grace! How's my baby making out?"

"Just fine, Miss Alma."

"Is it pretty out?"

"Yes, ma'am. It's clear tonight. The stars are out."

"It smells clear. Auntie Alma can smell how fresh it is. But it's not safe. Time for Miss Grace to get inside."

"I wish I could sit out with you."

"Miss Alma wish you could too, baby. She just hates these fireworks. Those people around the corner are shooting off everything but a cannon. Miss Alma might have to take a bullet for somebody else. They can take out an old dried-up blind woman instead of one of these babies..."

"Don't say that, Miss Alma."

"Oh, baby, Alma seen the future and it don't look good. More of the same. More of the same." She slumped in her chair.

"Goodnight, Pretty Miss."

"Goodnight, my Grace. Happy New Year to all the Broussards."

It was not yet midnight and the Broussards were already sleeping. Grace contemplated her family, the ones she knew well and the ones she hardly knew. Tomorrow, they would all be coming over. Louis would bring his irritable children and skulking wife. Raymond's lively brood would scatter all the dust in the yard and accost all the furniture. Camille would be complaining ferociously and Yvette chattering endlessly. Marc always showed up late, for effect. He would drive up in his sporty little Stingray, Vanessa smiling at his side, both their hairdos blowing like mad. Grace loved her family. She loved them and she couldn't stand them.

All the house lights were out except one. Grace unlocked the door and slipped inside. Yvette's cabbage lingered in the kitchen like an unanswered prayer. The refrigerator hummed its disquieting tune. Grace paused in the dining room and listened to the sounds of the sleeping house. The living room clock ticked loudly. The floor complained as she tiptoed across it. Yvette snored softly in the next room. She would miss everything about this place.

A grunt from the couch gave Grace a start. She strained to see who was there. A form stirred in sleep. She approached it with caution. It looked to be one of her brothers. From the size of the bulk, she detected it was Louis. Why was he here? Was he guarding the house? Suddenly, Grace was afraid.

"Is that Grace?" Camille's voice lassoed her from the back room. Though faint and sleepy, it carried in its teeth the ire of a mother spurned.

Grace ventured into the holy chamber. "What happened to your car?" Camille was sitting up in bed, a prayer book resting on her breasts.

Grace sat in the chair opposite. "I had to abandon it."

"Why didn't you call? Didn't the store close early today? Where have you been all this time?"

Grace curled her bottom lip. "I'm tired, Mama. Can we talk about it later?"

Grace stood up slowly. She wanted to say something to re-assure her mother, but she couldn't find it in herself. Instead, she asked a question.

"What's Louis doing on the sofa?"

"Deborah kicked him out."

"For good?"

"She said she was going on a diet for the new year—that she needed to drop 230 pounds of dead weight. I reckon she'll take him back tomorrow."

"Happy New Year." Grace bent over and kissed her mother's cheek. Camille held her close with her rosary hand. "Next time, I want you to call me. Hear?"

Grace nodded and walked down the hall to her room. She fell into the bed without taking off her clothes. There was gun-fire coming from some enemy encampment not far away. It was right on top of them, all around them, the sound of neighbors shouting their contempt. This is how Beirut sounds, Grace thought before drifting off to sleep. The telephone woke her.

Elena's voice was frantic, frayed. Grace hardly recognized it. "I can't understand you," she kept repeating. She tried to whis-per but Camille was already up, easing herself down the hall to the bathroom.

"Who is it, Grace?"

"Don't worry, Mama. It's for me."

"It's too late to be getting phone calls."

"I know, Mama. It's just..." Grace couldn't hear herself think for Elena's meandering wail. "What *is* it? *¡Dígame!* I can't understand what you're saying."

"Felipe..."

"Where's Felipe? Put him on the phone." The phone was dropped. A strange voice picked it up.

"Allô, is it Grace?"

"Yes. Who's this?"

"This is Sœur Gislène. We are calling from the hospital."

"What hospital? Where?"

"Er, I don't know where exactly."

"What happened?"

"Elena's brother. He is shot."

"Felipe? Shot?"

"Yes, that's right. I am sorry, but my English…"

"Is he okay?"

"I think no. I am sorry."

"Oh, God, where are you? What hospital? Should I come?"

"No, it is not necessary. I think…"

"Where's Elena? Can you put her on the telephone?"

"Elena wants me to telephone you. She wants you to pray."

"There must be something I can do."

"Please pray. For her brother." The phone went dead.

Grace lay down. She pulled the covers over her head. "Please, Father, please. Don't take Felipe. Please, Lord. Don't forget your servant."

She breathed rapidly under the covers, staring blankly into the darkness. All night long, the guns kept up their elegies. She was terrified by the night—the night and the morning to come.

Part Three

The Epiphany, 1979

A child is born and in the birth of that child is the birth of divinity. Words are made flesh. A star appears in the east. The wise come bearing gifts. Gold, frankincense, and myrrh.

When children die, women keen. The veils of the temples are rent in two. Old men gather to weep. Tears of gold, frankincense, and myrrh.

Years go by. Others are born and others die. The new births never replace the old ones, and the new deaths never replace the old ones. Sorrows are heaped upon sorrows and joys upon joys until it is all too much to bear. Lives give way beneath the weight of lives that have gone before them.

Every day, divinity is born anew to those who can see it, revealing itself in the everyday epiphanies of those who mourn. *El día de los muertos*. In the Broussard house, every day was the day of the dead. All the saints and all the souls hovered about like ghostly piñatas. Grace was no longer sure if she wanted to escape her family or if she just wanted to escape the awful burden of love and death that they were so attached to. She longed for a release from death in all its manifestations.

9

The Lost Child

Saturday, January 6, 1979

If not for their belief in heaven, the Broussards would have been lost. Something had to be waiting for the good children of the earth. Something had to pay off for them. The end could not merely be brutal, painful, miserable, with no sequel to redeem it. Heaven must await the forsaken. If only Grace could have believed it, she wouldn't have felt so lost.

Grace's family was horrified to learn of Felipe's death, but no more horrified than they had been by all the deaths over all the years. Like most Angelenos, they had come to expect that a few of the bullets that filled their skies every New Year's Eve would pierce the bodies of innocents. Camille gave Grace the money to purchase a calla lily from Watanabe's Nursery. On the card she wrote, "They that sow in tears shall reap in joy. The Broussards." Grace went alone to the funeral.

Elena's eyes were ringed with sorrow, her lips were gnarled by it. When she saw Grace she screamed and cried and flew to her. "I keep looking for Felipe." Grace held her friend, saying

inadequate things like "it's okay" until Elena fell back into her
chair, overcome. It was startling, really, to be in this crowd of
wailing grief. Grace moved behind the circle of mourners.
Hands clasped, body still, she said nothing, thought nothing.

Mrs. Hurtado was shrouded in family. Cousins had come in
caravans from Oregon and Texas, grandparents and uncles had
taken the train from Mexico. Elena's father was seating them for
the burial service, his hands shaking as he ushered them along.
They had waited a week to bury Felipe, who was one of several
people killed that New Year's Eve in Los Angeles County.
Shortly after he left Elena's party, a bullet smashed through his
car window and hit him in the face. Throughout the services, the
casket remained closed. Someone had placed an enlarged photo
of the deceased on an easel behind the coffin. Felipe was pictured in swim trunks showing off a trophy, towel draped around
his neck, goggles wrapped around his wrist. Cousins collapsed
at the sight of him.

Grace had never witnessed such a public display of grief.
Her father's burial had not approached it. She was soon crying
into her hands. Someone reached over and pulled her close, and
there she was, clutching the fabric of a stranger's suit. She was
crying for all who had died—the grandmother she never liked,
the sister she never knew, the father she never mourned. Amid
the shrieking, sniffling, and questioning of the Almighty, Grace
felt a communion with all who grieve, especially Camille, who
was "starting another year without your father."

The priest made his sad pronouncements, but he could not
be heard above the voices soaked in sorrow, the joints cracking
under the injustice of it all. The Hurtado family had risen early
to bury Felipe. It was not yet ten o'clock, and the entire family

was half-crazed from keening. They were hard workers all, but this week of burying Felipe was the hardest work any of them had done.

Like Grace's relatives, many of Elena's cousins worked in construction. Once the body was blessed, they insisted it be lowered into the ground right then when they could see it. Elena's mother threw a handful of dirt into the hole that held her son and, over the protests of the official gravediggers, the Hurtado men began to heap earth upon him. The pallbearers, their white gloves soiled with dirt, worked until their ire was spent and Felipe's fate was sealed.

Elena threw herself on the mound and wept. She had lost weight. Her body looked frail and her hair was in disarray. An older sister moved to comfort her. Soon they were both on the ground, watering the soil with their tears.

Grace took out her father's hankie and blew her nose. She looked for someone to talk to in Elena's family, but she didn't really know any of the other Hurtados. Felipe had been her link. Over and over, she felt him pulling her down at the party. Over and over, she pushed him away. Her last words to him had been "No, thank you."

Some of Elena's other friends attended the funeral Mass, but only Grace had joined the procession to the cemetery. Yvette had offered to go with her, but Grace didn't want her sister to see her in distress. She was grateful for the use of Yvette's car. All the trinkets in it were comforting.

The burial ceremony came to an end and the Hurtado family was led back to the waiting limousines. Grace hugged Elena and promised to come by the house later. Even as she spoke the words, she knew them to be false. She would not come by. It was a day for family, and Grace was not family.

There was another reason she would not go to see Elena: Grace was struggling with the knowledge that all their plans had been for naught. Elena had decided to move back home.

The possibility of moving in with Elena had been the only thing that made living at home bearable. Now that Grace would have to go it alone, a tidal wave of loss threatened to engulf her. She felt herself losing ground.

Suicide did not seem an altogether evil thing. It was not unprecedented in the family. One of her relatives had leapt from a church steeple. Grace wasn't supposed to know this, but Yvette had let it slip on a night so sultry neither one of them could sleep. Yvette didn't realize what she had given her when she handed her this secret: suicide was not unthinkable for a Broussard.

Grace imagined throwing herself over a railing at the Fox Hills Mall right when it was swarming with relatives shopping for wedding gifts. Would they stop scavenging long enough to notice? What did she have to lose? She could become another family secret. Wasn't she one already? Who amongst the Broussards knew anything of her heart? Did they even understand whose funeral she was attending? She could stop by Playa del Rey, swim out to sea, wash up on a distant shore. When they found her, they could bring her back to Holy Rosary for burial.

Felipe was lying not far from T-Papa. Grace could see the hills of the Redemption a few hundred plots away. She would go to see her father. She would lay her problems squarely at his feet. She would beseech him to have mercy on her.

Grace commenced her trek to the grave, grief stuffed in her pockets, despair wedged up her sleeves. Before long, she was awash in self-pity. Where was God? Why had He forsaken His children? Where had He run? For all she knew, God did not exist. Since God could not be found, she sought His wily messenger.

It was because of people like T-Papa, who refused to take his place among the dead, that young people like Felipe were called to satisfy a merciful God. Had her father known that Felipe was in danger? Grace's Louisiana relatives held that someone who died on a Sunday (as T-Papa had) and was buried on a Sunday (as T-Papa was) would surely become an angel. Grace knew T-Papa was no angel, except perhaps the Angel of Death. For three years she had avoided her father. Now, in her inconsolable grief, she would confront him.

Musical theatre was the form of art which most closely approximated the Broussards' experience of life. Although not generally given to unprovoked singing and dancing, they tended to lead mundanely heroic lives interrupted by occasional outbursts of hysteria. In her fragile state, Grace succumbed.

"Chino!" she shouted. "Come and get me too!" Grace was reckless now, like Tony in *West Side Story* daring fate to do him in. She believed it was her fate to wrestle with the angel. Death would come as sure as disgrace, if she didn't meet T-Papa head on and wrestle him to the ground. Her soul would wither and die, her dreams would be extinguished.

Grace recalled Our Lady of Fatima's platonic production of *West Side Story*, which she had attended three times. She had even helped out once, when the girl who played Tony lost her voice during the final performance. Crouching behind a platform, Grace had wailed a version of "Tonight" perfected in the shower. Much to her delight, her effort had met with lavish applause instead of the usual requests for silence. Grace had been able to bring great feeling to the voice of Tony even though she considered his love to be extreme. She donned the same piercing anguish now in her attempt to rouse T-Papa, who didn't have a gun like Chino and wasn't looking to kill her but who was surely aiming to keep her down. "Come and get me, Chino!" she shouted.

The stones responded with grave indifference. No one was standing in judgment, though many were lying in wait. Did it matter what they thought of her? Only one. Suppose T-Papa didn't recognize himself in the character of Chino? Worse luck, suppose there was a real Chino, someone else's dearly departed who might mistakenly respond to her taunts? Grace decided it best to shut up. She huffed and puffed her way up the hill, recalling another character she had brought to life in kindergarten.

As she took the lonely hill, reliving her tiny moments of theatrical acclaim, Grace was grateful that in her stage experience someone else had always done the dying. Tears swept the audience whenever the hero was felled, never to rise again. Except to get up and take a bow. To get up and dress for the next performance. To get up and demand his gumbo.

A monstrous chill greeted Grace as she neared the hallowed spot. She bore down on her father's grave, pried the canister from the earth, and dumped out the silty water. Camille's mums were dead. Grace cried for her parents' lost love.

"We weren't ready for you to die," she howled. How to undo the past? How to undo love? Head bowed, spirit asunder, Grace surveyed the scene—rusty canister, dead mums, face swollen with grief.

There was something going on here that didn't include her, some circle of family fealty that involved marrying and having children who would marry and have children who would keep on marrying and having children until the end of time. If she did not marry, if she did not have children, who would Grace torment after her death? Every act, even the act of dying, was enlivened by the sense of being part of a tradition.

Grace was not part of this circle. She was not like Yvette. Though Yvette was childless, husbandless, ringless also, she was linked by all her efforts to be otherwise. Grace was a traitor with an artificial heart, a heart that preferred pleasure to her own flesh and blood.

Her father would have died if he suspected her of being a lesbian. He had died, hadn't he? His heart had given out while Grace and Elena were consecrating their love. Or had he died while they were still dancing, before they had fallen from the dance floor into one of the waiting beds? Grace worried after his death that she would never be able to touch Elena's body again. That had not been the case. She had needed Elena to get her through the languid nights of pain.

Grace prayed for strength. She prayed for deliverance. At times, a voice prayed along with her—the faint, distinct voice of a Creole lullaby. *Fe dodo, ti'tite.* Grace prayed herself into oblivion.

She awoke to a man standing over her. His boots were muddy, his beard uncut. A curious emissary, not the one she was expecting. It took her a moment to recognize him. "What are you doing here?" she yelled at her brother.

"I am Joseph of Arimathea. I bury the divine." From his pockets, he drew a handful of sunflower seeds. They were covered in lint. He offered her some.

"Don't be morbid."

"Be that way, then." Joseph was enjoying an anguish all his own. He was Joseph Henri, his father's youngest son—T-Papa's namesake in reverse. Grace could see that he was drunk. And had been for seven years. "I couldn't save him. I couldn't save nobody. Not my buddies. Or the Vietnamese. Don't touch me, girl. I'll contaminate you. I watch people die. Death rides my shoulder. Women won't have anything to do with me. The only place I feel alive is in cemeteries." He spit out shells as he spoke.

He told Grace he had walked to Holy Rosary from the coast. She didn't want to fathom how long he'd been wearing that shirt. He said he hitchhiked down the coast from Santa Cruz, where he was living off a woman who had children as old as he was. She finally gave him the boot. With the help of her children she burned all his belongings in a bonfire on the beach. He owned just enough to roast a bag of marshmallows over. It hurt him, but he kept on moving. Joseph claimed to have "squeezes" as far north as Fairbanks but, this time of year, the one in San Diego would do. He thought he ought to stop and see his mother, maybe get a bowl of gumbo before heading out again. The cemetery was the best place to hitch a ride home.

"How's Mama doing, anyway?"

"Why haven't you been in touch with her? She's been in the hospital, you know. We would have called you if anybody knew where you were."

"The hospital? For what?"

"She had a hysterectomy."

"Really?"

"Really. She was bleeding but she didn't tell anybody until she started having pains. She lost a lot of blood during surgery."

"Ooh! Do I have to hear the gory details?"

"Yes! Especially since you haven't been here to see the gory details. Look, Mama's been sick. Don't give her a hard time. And don't ask her for money!"

"What do you take me for? Some kind of bum?"

"You don't want me to answer that."

"I'm surprised to find *you* here."

"There was a funeral. I came for the burial."

"Who died?"

"Felipe Hurtado."

"Who's that?"

"Elena's brother."

"Who's Elena?"

"My lover."

"No kidding? Sounds like a girl."

"It is."

"Oh, well. She must be a very nice girl to be going out with my sister."

As they walked to Yvette's car, Grace felt a modicum of happiness. Life was unfair to be sure, devastatingly so, but perhaps it wasn't entirely unfair. Just when it all looked like death and destruction, resurrections took place. A son had died and a son had come back from the dead. A friendship had been rekindled.

She sped along Pacific Coast Highway, Joseph sleeping on her shoulder. He was different from her other brothers, for whom she felt little affinity. He smelled. "You're Joseph, the carpenter. You build things. Daddy's shed is standing empty. You should come and fill it up." Grace planted seeds while he snored.

She felt strangely free, protected. With her brother at her side—this eternally dependent child—she was large, grown, equal to any ghost. Being the youngest, Grace never had anybody to take care of. As the family aged, all that would change. She felt powerful, dangerous. She didn't need to run from T-Papa or anyone.

She would bring him his gumbo. Why not? If that was the payment he demanded of her, if gumbo was all he wanted, she'd bring it to him. Today was the Epiphany, and Joseph's homecoming would surely be an occasion for feasting. Camille would need help in the kitchen, and Grace would assist willingly. Her mother had helped her so many times, most notably on that traumatic day of her first gumbo. Grace remembered it now, more than seven years later. Those had been days and years of turmoil. And the primary reason for all the upheaval was now sound asleep on her shoulder.

Grace glanced over at her brother. She had pictured his death many times in the exploding bombs of Vietnam. When she asked him what he missed the most in the weeks and months away, his answer had been simple: "Gumbo."

What was the use in letting sleeping dogs lie? Grace would bring her father his gumbo. It's not the dead who bury the dead, she thought. Or only the young who die good.   ．

10

The First Gumbo

Saturday, September 11, 1971

Okra is a slimy food. It has the dignity of a mudslide, the integrity of an oil spill, the fidelity of liquid soap. When pressed to surrender, okra offers scant resistance; it longs to belong. Grace identified with okra. Quiet and unassuming, self-conscious and morose, okra seeks nothing more than to blend with its surroundings, to disguise itself by dressing up with onions and tomatoes. But, alas, it cannot. No matter how it presents itself, in the end it is always okra. Some people adore it; most do not. Grace managed to love okra only when she managed to love herself. It was a mess and so was she.

By the time she was twelve, Grace and okra were intimate. She knew how to pick it out in the market, how to chop it down to size, how to season, sauté, and fry it. It knew how to slip and slide beneath her knife, how to run from her groping hands, how to stick to her and soothe her. Their relationship resembled that of most married couples she knew. No matter how bad things got between them, they would not be rid of each other in this lifetime.

When she was a small child, Grace heard the pagans speak of reincarnation, which she thought was a grand idea. How marvelous to be reborn as dove or swan or eagle. If it were possible to leave the lower form of life to which she was presently confined, Grace would welcome the chance to die again and again.

She considered becoming a Hindu but rejected it on the grounds that Hindus favored arranged marriages, a practice she was trying to get away from. As presented in Catholic school, heaven had always struck Grace as a limited concept. You went there as yourself, wearing your regular clothes plus a new pair of cumbersome wings, and took up residence next to the same folks you'd known all your earthly life, give or take a few devils. By contrast, reincarnation had infinite possibilities. In the next life, a piece of okra might come back as a chili pepper. Grace held out hope for the next life.

As far as this life went, she was a hungry spirit trapped in a well-fed body. Most of the time, Grace was nervous. This was due to her wicked thoughts, which centered on all forms of gluttony and sloth. According to Yvette, she had "a sneaky little personality" and needed to be watched closely. True, Grace had been looking for a people she could run away and join from the time she was ten. It was right about then that she realized her family was all wrong for her. They worshiped false food gods, they believed in flawed concepts like heaven, they insisted on marrying each other. Grace had no place in such a clan.

These were people who professed to love okra, but their love for the seedy green vegetable was as imperfect as their love for their youngest child. They had no appreciation for its uniqueness and only approved of it when it contributed to the gumbo pot. Their love of okra as well as their love of Grace depended on the loved one's behavior. And the only acceptable behavior involved submerging oneself for the good of the stew. It was this realization, subconscious though it was, which led Grace to attempt her first gumbo.

Even though it looks like something you'd find in a swamp, Creoles revere gumbo. If you are a Creole, you get used to gumbo when you are very young, and you come to view this swamp food as the most beautiful thing you have ever seen. It tastes better than any other mortal dish, and the smell of it will drive you to distraction. It will make you drunk with pleasure. Dangerous to operate heavy machinery after eating even a spoonful.

Gumbo is the most complete of all art forms; all it needs is a little hot sauce. (If you're from Louisiana, all anything in life needs is a little hot sauce.) There is so much food in gumbo that one bowl of it can satisfy your minimum daily requirements for months on end. You could live on the streets, so long as you had gumbo. You could go without a coat in winter if you just had a little gumbo to keep you warm. One pot of gumbo could see you through famine, drought, or flood, stay the bitter tongue, rouse the sagging spirit, bring the dead to life.

Gumbo is like fine wine—its value improves with age. Three-day-old gumbo might be three times better than first-day gumbo if it were only possible to be three times better than perfection. Frozen gumbo will thaw to a tawny opulence. Indeed, if the world were a place that made any sense at all, gold would be replaced by gumbo as the monetary standard. But better to stick to gold, which has no intrinsic value, than hoard the very juice which gave life to a people.

"Gumbo" derives from the Bantu word for "okra." It is not Cajun. "Cajuns are White," Camille explained to Grace. "But there are Black Cajuns. And there are White Creoles. Don't let that confuse you. Cajuns are from France, by way of Canada. Creoles come from Louisiana. We were invented right here." This speech confused Grace terribly—she regretted asking for clarification—but it did confirm something she had long suspected. For her mother, "right here" was Louisiana, "home" was Louisiana—L.A. was Louisiana with a couple of periods. Grace had figured all along that she was being raised in Louisiana West, but this confirmation distressed her, nonetheless. Was there no leaving the homeland, no matter how far you roamed? Even if you could stop talking that Louisiana talk and walking that Louisiana walk, the gumbo in your lunch pail would give you away.

While Grace was making her first gumbo, other girls were running through sprinklers, slurping popsicles, lounging on their porches. Grace envied them. She wished she had their lives but knew this was not possible. Other girls were not Broussards. They might live their entire lives without making one pot of gumbo. For the twelve-year-old Grace Broussard, this was merely the first of several hundred pots. By her calculations, if she lived to be ninety-five she could expect to make 2,158 pots of gumbo, or 38,844 servings by the time she died. She had no reason to doubt she would live to be ninety-five—most of the women in her family did (Creoles thrive on cholesterol)—so these estimates were modest, at best. It was often said at the funeral of an ancient Creole woman, "She'd just had the whole family over for gumbo. Just the other day. That was some good gumbo, too!" The whole family could mean anywhere from eighteen to two hundred people, all of whom regularly devoured countless bowls of gumbo but each of whom responded in the same glad way upon hearing the menu—"Gumbo!"

More than her period, more than her Confirmation, the success of this venture would determine Grace's passage into Creole womanhood. She felt pressured by history. Every woman had some secret ingredient that distinguished her gumbo from all others—a little extra thyme, a heavier roux, a sweeter love. Camille's gumbo, which boasted several secret ingredients, was the rave of cousins far and wide. Even Yvette's gumbo, which only took five hours to prepare, aged well. (By Creole standards, hers was a "quickie" version akin to the five-minute rosary— just as valid but not as sacrificial. Yvette, who remained mostly a virgin, had not come to know the pleasures of prolonged duty.) The ingredients that would distinguish Grace's first gumbo were the sweat of her brow, the strength of her desire, and the depth of her guilt.

Grace had messed up, big time. She had done something no Broussard had ever thought of doing; she had talked back to a priest. A thousand times worse, she had done so at First Friday Mass in front of 286 breathless schoolchildren and seven angry nuns.

It was during Father Reilly's sermon that the spirit had moved Grace to speak. Father was talking about the War, about Abraham and Isaac and God's will. Obedience was his basic theme, as it was at the beginning of every school year. "Abraham loved God so much he was willing to sacrifice his only son." Grace looked around at her fellow lambs. Did they believe this propaganda or were they merely sporting the glazed expressions of those held captive too long? Grace had heard it all before and she was sick of it. Abraham might have loved God, but he sure didn't love Isaac, that much was clear.

Grace didn't care much for God the Father. He was too violent for her. She preferred Jesus because she could identify with him as an underdog and a fellow heretic. "Christ was obedient unto death," Father explained. He made some connection to soldiers and duty. Images of My Lai cut across Grace's mind. She considered obedience to be the least of Christ's attributes.

"I am the handmaiden of the Lord. Be it done unto me according to Thy will." Oh, here he goes bringing out Mary again. Can you imagine God coming and asking you to have His baby? Grace couldn't. She was glad He asked Mary and not her.

She was thinking all these thoughts when Father rounded a Biblical corner and landed in 1971 Watts. "Boys and girls," he said, "we must never question God's will for us. Our parents and teachers know what is best for us." Never doubt, have faith, never question. Never question? Didn't he know this was 1971 and everything was in question? How could he tell Black children in Watts not to question? The rules, the schools, the police, everything had to be questioned—everything and everybody— if they were to escape their fate. A god that could not be questioned must not be sure of what he was doing. Was he just a giant parent in the sky, who answered every inquiry with "Because I said so"? Grace questioned the direct line of descent from God to parents and teachers. She listened painfully as Father worked his way up to his rousing conclusion. "You are as nothing. God is everything!" he roared.

The intimations of this phrase were more than Grace could bear. Some brutal thing that requires children to maintain their decorum at all cost suddenly went to sleep, and something savage and honest inside of her burst its seams. "That's not true!" she bellowed from the back of the sanctuary, just as she had bellowed hundreds of times in her mind.

Father looked mortified. He fixed his steely eyes upon the eighth-grade pews from whence the trouble sprang. "Jesus wants us to obey!" he shrieked. Children huddled in holy dread, a giggle erupting here and there.

Grace tried to stuff the words back into her mouth. She sat
on her hands. And awaited her demise.

The nuns were swift. Aged claws reached for Grace's upper
arms and neck. Lay teachers watched in dumbfounded rev-
erence as she was lifted from her seat and ushered from God's
presence. Grace was stoic through it all. The last thing she remembered was the long sallow fingers heading for her hair.
After that, she descended into a towering fog, the kind that is
brought on by sudden fame. She felt like Stephen the First
Martyr being led to his curtain call. The whole thing had given
her a rush of adrenaline. She felt like Nathan Hale. "I only regret
that I have but one life to give for my conscience." When Grace
came to, she could hear the fingers dialing her mother's number.

Camille received the news with monumental embarrassment. Grace regretted being the cause of it. Everybody knew
that when Mrs. Broussard showed up at school, something serious was cooking. There was either some kind of fundraiser that
required a few hundred oyster loaves, or somebody's goose was
being cooked, usually one of the lay teachers. That day, the
goose was sitting in the principal's office, plump with fear and
ripe for the slaughter. When Camille marched by, Grace ducked
for cover. Her mother didn't stop in front of her but kept on
marching like a matador. She strode into Sister Victorine's office
and closed the door.

Grace stared at the massive door. Hadn't her mother recognized her sitting there sniffling? Was Camille storing up her
wrath for when they got home? Maybe she didn't yet know
what Grace had done and, once told, would strike the door and
cleave it in two. Grace stared after her mother, waiting.

When Camille emerged, her face was a color Grace had
never seen before. Bolts of lightning circled her brow. She was
the figurehead of a wounded ship adrift on a tortured sea.

Camille was mute except for the howling of the north wind, which was disguised as her breathing.

Grace had never seen her mother at a loss. She was more startled than if Camille had hauled off and whacked her. It's a terrible thing when parents fall silent, Grace could see this now. Parents speak at will, they don't need permission. When they run out of words, a heaviness settles over everything. Grace felt this heaviness now as she prayed for instant reincarnation.

"I don't know whose child you are." The voice was strained and narrow. Grace hung her head. She had frequently fantasized about disowning her parents, but she never expected them to disown her first. Not knowing what to do, she stood up and fell in step behind her leader. Camille made for the exit and charged down the street, her youngest child waddling behind her.

"I don't know whose child you are." The words wrung Grace's heart. She was mortally wounded, not to mention confused. Her mother disagreed with the parish priest at every turn. She condemned him as "out of touch" on every subject from civil rights to birth control. She talked relentlessly behind his back and went to confession only to accost him. Hadn't Grace just done what she'd seen her mother do every Sunday and most days in between? Granted, her dissent differed from her mother's in one crucial way: it was public. Family gossip was the stuff of life. Criticizing people, especially people in authority, was not only proper, it was duty. But public dissent was akin to treason. It could get you into big trouble. In addition, it caused embarrassment, a state to be avoided at all cost. Grace had erred, she had erred badly, but she didn't think it reason to question her lineage. *She* knew whose child she was.

The fact that Grace was a Broussard was written all over her crime. Only a Broussard would be arrogant enough to take on the clergy, self-righteous enough to question a commandment, and loud enough to be heard. It was imperative that she make amends. She worried that her family would ship her off to a hall for Catholic juvenile delinquents, where she would be made to confess her faith all day long. Worse yet, they might give her to the nuns. She would be taken into the convent, never to be heard from again. Grace fantasized about being banned from church, but she didn't think she would get off that easy.

Her crime had been the culmination of many months of subversive activity both at school and at home. Grace was waging her own private revolution. So far, she had succeeded only in destabilizing herself. She dressed like the bandits she saw on TV—surly, disheveled, hair standing on end—and her school uniform was almost unrecognizable. "I can't believe your mother lets you leave the house that way," one of her teachers had told her. In truth, she left the house looking like a proper Broussard girl, slipped into the lavatory for a quick transformation, and came out looking like a derelict, alternately flashing the Peace sign and the Black Power sign. Grace was trying to get St. Martin de Porres to offer Swahili. In the meantime, she thought she was doing pretty well to stay out of jail.

Camille was waiting at the corner. When her daughter was still half a block away, Camille shouted in a voice loud enough for passing cars to hear, "And look at you! What did you do to your hair?" Having been forcibly removed mid-stream from the day's proceedings, Grace hadn't had time to recoup her appearance. Her uniform skirt was rolled up six inches above her knees and there was a comb sticking out of her hair. "Straight to your room!" Camille enjoined. "And you'd better start saying some prayers as soon as you get there." Grace took this last comment as an indication of greater suffering to come. She decided to start praying on the spot. Up ahead, their modest wooden house had transfigured itself into the Tower of London.

When they arrived home, T-Papa was waiting in the

kitchen, reheating a cup of burnt coffee. Out back, his tools rested in the mid-morning sun. T-Papa was not known to take coffee breaks. He paused at noon for dinner and finished the day's work in time for supper. The sight of her father imitating a person at leisure sent Grace into a penitent fit. She hurried to her room, sure he would make her kneel by some statue for the rest of her life. Should she pack her bags and await her dishonorable discharge? She prayed for an airborne rescue. She could hear T-Papa thundering from the kitchen.

"I know where she got the notion," he was saying. "Where do you think she got the notion? Who did I have to come pick up out the street, running around in circles and talking crazy?"

The incident to which he referred was one that he and his wife had agreed not to mention in front of their seven children. Grace had no knowledge of the scene her father was describing. The only thing she could glean from the words coming from the kitchen was that, somehow, her father was blaming her mother for what she had done.

Camille's answer came in a gust. It stunned T-Papa. "You could have left me there," she spat. "I was doing just fine."

"Foot, woman!" T-Papa scowled. "You don't know what you talkin'!" With a sweep of his hand, he cleared the counter, sending the gravy boat crashing to the floor.

"Look what you done!" Camille cried. "My good gravy boat. You settle down. Before you go and break something you can *never* fix." Her words were followed by a furious sweeping.

T-Papa was not done. "I'd like to wear out the both of you!" he snapped.

The sweeping stopped. "When you want me this weekend, I'll be in church," Camille replied. "Praying for your soul."

She dropped the broom and retreated to the other side of the house. T-Papa did not follow.

Camille had vowed to obey, but she hadn't meant it. It was

the one major lie she had told in her lifetime and she felt guilty
about it still, thirty-six years later. She loved her husband
ardently, honored him daily, but she was not his to order
around. They each performed their separate duties with few
complaints, and they cooperated in every task that required co-
operation. If it hadn't been for the War, she would have stood
by him in everything.

The Broussards were a steadfast people. They were loyal
down to their teeth, often to their cavities and fillings. If they
loved you, they would stand by you like a reflex. But as with
many people who love, they confused unanimity for unity.
While they lived to scourge and scour one another, it hurt them
to truly disagree. The Vietnam War had torn them to pieces.

On one side of the family was T-Papa. Patriotic, patriarchal,
patronizing, he was devoted to the idea of defending women and
children, even if you accidentally killed them in the process. On
the other side of the fence was Camille. Sanctified and sanctimo-
nious, she was convinced the War was morally wrong. The Vietnamese could solve their own problems, they didn't need our
interference. Camille was an isolationist. To T-Papa's assertion,
"You can't just stand by idle while your friends are being
slaughtered," she countered, "Why go running all over creation
looking for trouble when there's enough things need fixing right
here?" Camille liked to control things as much as anybody, but
she was sure that Southeast Asia was beyond her jurisdiction.
T-Papa defended his position. Like family, war was duty. Family
was duty, maintained Camille. War was only duty if it meant
protecting family. Since neither would ever admit defeat, they
would argue until they stopped making sense. And then they'd
go to bed.

In a sad attempt to remain loyal to both parents, the
Broussard children vacillated wildly between poles. The boys

hovered around their father's camp—they didn't really believe in the War, but it was like Catholicism to them, something you were born to do. That you might die doing it was a crying shame. That you might kill doing it was never discussed. Yvette gravitated toward her mother's stance, but she could not be sure what God wanted. Suppose He wanted to save the world from Communism? Would they not be wise to do His bidding?

Only Grace held her own during these days and years of disagreement. Of her treason she was sure. All war was wrong, not just this one. God had no part in any of them. Duty was not a reason to act. Love was. Duty without love was meaningless. She had read *The Prophet*. She knew.

When Joseph's number came up, the family gathered in shock. No Broussard child had ever gone away from home, not for college or marriage or work. To the Broussards, leaving home meant eating at a restaurant; it did not mean being away from family. When T-Papa and Camille left Louisiana in 1936, extended family had followed them. If Vietnam had only been closer, they could have all gone.

T-Papa told his youngest son, "We'll be there with you. You won't be alone." Yvette promised to write every week. The older boys offered their prayers. Grace suggested Canada, but no one paid any attention to her. Joseph tried to comfort everyone by saying, "I'll be home before you know it," but his voice was shaking.

During the presidential campaign of 1968, Joseph had teased his little sister mercilessly by pretending he was for Nixon. Not even the Burbank Broussards were for Nixon, but Grace had taken him seriously, and they had argued so bitterly that T-Papa had made them turn off the television. Grace remembered that argument when Joseph got his draft notice. How could he go and fight for Nixon? She was thoroughly depressed

by her brother's departure, sure he was going to die. She refused
to say any prayers to a God who was careless enough to permit
the use of napalm.

Camille, for her part, joined a group called Mothers Against
the War, which held a prayer vigil every weekend at Our Lady of
Perpetual Light Church. It lasted from Friday evening to Saturday morning, when it culminated in eight o'clock Mass. In
addition to the vigil at the church, they also kept a Tuesday
afternoon table outside the local supermarket. There they
harangued innocent shoppers with intimations of Apocalypse.
MAW was a scraggly group of women, worn thin by attempts to
be ecumenical. Their ranks included a couple of Methodists and
Lutherans, a bevy of Catholics, and an occasional Jew. They
were linked by an unjustified belief in the power of prayer.
Camille was the best thing that had happened to them. Under
her influence, MAW sharpened its focus. Instead of just praying
for peace to fall from the sky, they prayed for the strength to
bring it about.

The War was now off-limits as a topic of conversation in the
Broussard home. As the occasional letters from Vietnam became
more and more occasional, family members managed to talk
about Joseph without mentioning the War. "When Joseph
comes home, we're going to build that fence and put a big dog
behind it. Joseph always liked a dog," T-Papa would say. Yvette
would talk about a girl she met who would be just right for
Joseph. And Camille would speculate about how sorry Joseph
would be to have missed the crawfish bisque carried all the way
from Baton Rouge. Once, when his name came up, she left the
table in tears.

A horrible silence descended upon the family. In the absence
of open conflict, Grace decided to become the problem. Camille
soon found her daughter uncontrollable. Her grades plummeted

as her hair peaked. The nuns expressed concern. The family was falling apart, with Grace in the lead.

"I ought to drag you to church and make you apologize to Father." T-Papa was now standing in her doorway, trembling with rage.

Grace waited to be hit. She had been waiting since Camille came to get her from school, and she couldn't account for the delay. She had only been struck three times in her life, but, as those three offenses taken together didn't add up to this one, she was sure she would be whacked long and hard. Her siblings always told her she was lucky to be the last child; by their accounts, they had all been struck more times than they could count, with the exception of Yvette, who swore she'd never been hit at all. Grace waited for her father's hand, but T-Papa didn't move from the doorway.

"Embarrassing me in front of the whole neighborhood... I ought to make you kneel in front of the Sacred Heart. What's the matter? Can't you talk now? You could talk plenty good in church!" He waited for a reply. From the way he was shaking, Grace could see the reason for his leniency. He was too angry to smack her.

Grace said nothing. Her parents were losing it, right before her eyes. She was astonished. T-Papa turned and made for the yard. Grace heard the screen door slam, and she knew he had taken to his shed, as he always did after a tiff. Usually, he and Camille fought about who was right. They never fought about who was to blame. Camille remained in her bedroom with the door closed. Grace listened in wonder.

She rose and looked around her. The wallpaper strawberries of her room seemed like tiny grenades waiting to explode. Things had taken a definite turn for the worse. Nothing she had done before had caused her parents to turn on each other. The gravy boat had been the first casualty. Would their marriage be the next? Grace prayed for reconciliation. An hour passed and nobody moved. Grace feared that the chasm between her parents had grown to unbreachable dimensions. Her fears were confirmed when she saw her mother standing in the doorway with a suitcase.

"I'm going to pray," she said. "You're not to go anywhere."

"When will you be back?"

"I don't know. Give this note to Yvette. I'm putting her in charge. I want this house cleaned. I want the statues dusted and the furniture polished. I want the refrigerator emptied and wiped down. Underneath and on top of it too. Make sure to wash the kitchen floor. And don't forget the blinds. If I come home to a speck of dirt, you've had it."

On top of that, Grace was to labor in silence. "And no talking. I mean not a sound all weekend. If there's a fire, I want you to point and gesture. If there's a riot, I want you to run and hide. There's a time to talk and a time to listen. This weekend, you listen. If you make a noise, I'll know about it."

With that, she vanished. Grace was frightened. She had frequently contemplated running away, but she never expected her mother to fly the coop. A car pulled up in the driveway. She recognized it as one of her mother's prayer companions. Would Camille take refuge with a non-relative? It was too much to think about. Grace watched her mother open the car door, step inside, and disappear. Camille never looked back.

Grace didn't bother to read her mother's note to Yvette. She knew it comprised her sentence, which could be summed up in a single phrase: house arrest. The instructions to the guard were insignificant. Regardless of her good behavior, she would not be paroled until Sunday, at the very earliest. Yvette would obey the spirit of the law no matter what the letter said. Grace put on her pajamas, which were striped and droopy, and settled into her solitary confinement.

She prayed herself into a coma. She didn't hear Yvette enter the house hours later, humming a lala song. Yvette had plans to go dancing and she wasn't going to have them interfered with. She lived for lala dances, for circles of bustling Creoles jiggling to zydeco. Somewhere amongst them might be a husband— transplants were arriving from Louisiana daily. There were bound to be a few handsome visitors, at least one of them looking for a proper Creole wife. Yvette was a little old at thirty-five, but she could pass for twenty-six, and being able to pass was a vaunted talent in some Creole circles. She would spend Friday evening deciding what to wear and all day Saturday doing her hair. On Saturday night, she would dance until her feet ached. That was her plan.

"Hey, Mama, it's your favorite," Yvette announced upon opening the door. No response. "Your oldest favorite daughter," she sang again, but she didn't hear her mother anywhere, not on the phone, not at the stove, not in the bath. In fact, there was no noise at all. No TV laughing, no sewing machine humming, no washing machine clanking and convulsing. No filing or sawing coming from the shed. Yvette, who was always complaining about the lack of peace and quiet on the premises, a lack to which she was a chief contributor, found the unsolicited silence to be most disquieting.

She bobbed her head in Grace's doorway. "Where's Mama?" Grace, flopped on her knees with her head resting on the bed, failed to respond. Her eyes had a torpid look and her hair was arranged as a sort of leaning tower. Yvette flapped her hands in front of Grace's face. The eyes did blink, but the face remained frozen. There was a pulse in the wrist, the body was warm, but clearly something was amiss.

"You look like a prisoner in the land of the doomed. Where's Mama?"

Yvette waited for a reply. When none was forthcoming, she decided to employ irritation as the tactic most likely to produce results. "What's your story, little one? Does my beauty render you speechless? Don't let my glamor intimidate you. Speak!"

Grace rolled her eyes.

"So, there is life, I see. Critical, judgmental life. Good enough. Nod your head if you can hear me. Where is Mama?"

Grace covered her ears. Yvette was undaunted. "Are we engaged in some kind of scientific experiment, the object of which is to torture your elders?"

Grace handed her the note.

"My, but aren't we becoming formal around here? Am I to conclude that the lines of communication are a bit strained?"

Grace had no thoughts on the subject, or none she wished to share, so Yvette proceeded without her. Reading the note out loud, like the schoolteacher in training she was, Yvette paused every now and then to add illumination. "'Grace is not to leave the house this weekend.' Well, my goodness, you *are* a prisoner! No wonder you look so pathetic. 'She is not to talk on the phone.' Underlined. No communication with the outside world. 'No radio. No television. She may leave her room to eat and clean. She may not tie up the bathroom.' Oh, dear. Whatever did you do?"

The prisoner did not reply. "Come on, you can talk to me," Yvette coaxed, "Mama'll never know." When the soft approach did nothing to loose the youthful jaw, Yvette added more muscle. "Tell me what you did or I'll tickle you to death." Grace looked annoyed and Yvette knew not to touch her. When repeated rounds of interrogation did not produce an answer, Yvette got tough. "Where's Daddy?" she said. "Is he hiding out in that shed? I think I'll just have a little talk with Daddy and get to the bottom of this."

At the sound of this suggestion, Grace dove into a panic. She might have been forbidden to talk but she wasn't forbidden to cry. Treacherous sobs wracked the small house. They flew off the walls, rebounded against the windows, and flung themselves under the doors. Yvette had never seen anything like it. Her first impulse was to stoop down and cradle Grace in her arms, but she found her little sister's behavior so disturbing that she could do nothing but stare. "Whatever is the matter?" she waited to no avail for Grace to collect herself. When Yvette moved toward the bedroom door, Grace lunged at her sister's feet, shaking violently from side to side.

Yvette felt as if she were talking to the criminally insane. "Don't stand in my way," she whispered slowly. "I know you've done something really awful and I feel sorry for you, I truly do. But that's what growing up is all about—suffering the consequences. There's nothing anybody can do for a sinner unless she herself repents and begs God or her big sister for forgiveness."

Yvette rummaged through Grace's desk for a scrap of paper and a pen. Tissue was too much to ask for in the heap of refuse that constituted Grace's effects. The desk had once been Yvette's—so had the room—and looking at them now caused Yvette to contemplate the mystery of genes. While Grace was occupied with paper and pen, she straightened up a bit, careful to avoid the ancient scrolls of homework which might someday provide important evidence that Grace had indeed done something worthwhile during her eighth-grade year at St. Martin de Porres.

Grace handed over the note. "Suspended from school?" railed Yvette. "What could you have possibly done to get kicked out of school? A Broussard behavior problem! I see why Mama went to a prayer vigil. I suppose things got a little out of hand," Yvette concluded. "Did Mama and Daddy fight?"

Grace nodded mournfully.

"Was it bad?"

Grace nodded and shook. Yvette threw her arms around her little sister, remembering in the gesture all of the baby siblings it had been her job to comfort.

"Oh, they growl a bit," Yvette soothed, "but they'd never quit each other. Not in this lifetime. Sparring keeps them young. Since you're so pitiful, I'm going to tell you a story. Once upon a time, before you were born, Mama Bear and Papa Bear got into a huge fight that rocked this house to its very foundations. It seems that one of the baby bears, who shall remain nameless, got himself arrested for loitering in front of the liquor store. A friend of Anthony's, I mean, Baby's (oh, well) had watched the whole thing from across the street, and as soon as the police left he beat it over here and told Daddy the entire story. Daddy thanked him and walked him to the door. That's when the showdown began. Mama wanted to go get her baby right away, but Daddy thought a night in jail would teach him a valuable lesson. 'Now is not the time to teach lessons," Mama said. They went back and forth for hours, getting louder and louder until, finally, Daddy left and barricaded himself inside his shed. Mama put on her coat and hat, took the money Daddy kept in his top drawer, and disappeared for a few hours. Late that night she returned home with Anthony in tow. Nobody said a word. I tried to get the convict to talk about it the next day, but I didn't have any luck. Mama had forbidden him to speak. Shortly after this incident, Anthony started working with Daddy. Years later, during the Riots, the liquor store burned to the ground, erasing all memory of his sin. As far as I know, he never did another bad thing in his life. He was cured forever. Maybe you will be too. What did you do, anyway?"

Grace opened her mouth to speak, but Yvette used her hand to block the words. "Don't talk," advised the older sister. "You have to erase your sin."

Grace had never really thought much about Anthony. There was no reason to. He wasn't Joseph, who had tormented her on a daily basis until he had left for Vietnam and tormented her with his leaving. Nor was he Marc, who thought so much of himself it was impossible not to think about him, one way or another. He was only Anthony—Antoine, actually, but he hadn't liked the foreign sound of his name and had changed it to be more common—who did nothing to make her life easy or difficult, who was distant and benign. It was hard for Grace to imagine him as a young man hanging out on the corner. At thirty, he was the picture of Broussard acquiescence. Grace wondered if she would end up like him but quickly decided against it. His misfit nature must not have run as deep as hers.

Yvette fried some oysters for supper. The sounds from the shed rose and fell like a rusty swing. Sooner or later, T-Papa would come in. Grace washed the dishes, as she did every evening, but this time she was extra careful to wipe the backs of the plates, following Yvette's detailed instructions. While Grace labored to "make the dishes sparkle the way they do on TV," Yvette entertained her with talk of the dance, which she would attend with her cousin Lisette who was "recently annulled." The two of them would gossip and devour lemon pie before going to meet men. Even if they only met the same men they had met before, one or two might be single again since the last dance. By the time Yvette launched into her fashion show—"You can help me decide what to wear tomorrow"—Grace was nodding off at the sink.

The sun had set, the moon had risen, Yvette had gone through five and a half outfits, and T-Papa was still filing away in his shed. A brave figure slunk down the driveway and called

softly through a crack in the shed door. T-Papa heard the call
and stuck his head out to see who it was.

"Broussard. It's Pep. I came to see how you was doing."

"Hello, sir. Long time no see." T-Papa stepped out into the
balmy night, file in hand. "How you been?"

"Very fine, thank you. What about the Broussards?"

"Oh, just fine," T-Papa nodded.

"I see that pretty miss sometimes, the little one."

"Yeah, she's not too little anymore."

"Lots of hair. I hardly recognize her."

"Yeah, she's a little hard to recognize. How's Miss Alma?"

"Very busy. Gets me up early. We got a paper route now,
you know. Got to make a livin' some kinda way."

"Very good."

They stood side by side, staring off into the night sky.

"Yeah. Wakes me up in the middle of the night to get
started," Pep chuckled.

"You must be tired." T-Papa wrinkled his nose, suddenly
ashamed of all the noise he'd been making. The two said good
night. T-Papa watched his neighbor lumber back up the driveway. There was something to be said for a gentleman.

Yvette was in the living room giving Grace the last of her
best pivots. They scattered when they heard the screen door
close. It was the first time either one of them could remember
their father skipping a meal. He was bound to be grouchy.
Yvette retired to her room to admire herself in front of the mirror. Grace retired to her bed to pray. Both were soon dreaming.

The house was homely without Camille. T-Papa had never
noticed how old everything was getting. He had built that house
in 1937, when Yvette was just a toddler and Grace wasn't even a
notion. The wooden floors needed a new finish, a few tiles on
the service porch had broken, and the faucets always seemed to

be leaking. These signs of aging didn't bother T-Papa as long as Camille was concocting in the kitchen or laughing round the table. Amidst the smells and tastes and colors, he barely noticed that anything was wrong. But tonight, without her voice and flesh and spirit, the house looked dingy, out of sorts. He fitted himself into Camille's favorite chair and waited for sleep to comfort him. The conch shell that lay by the front door needed dusting. He would instruct Grace to get to it in the morning.

When Grace arose at eight, the house was quiet except for her sister's whistling and her father's snoring. The events of the day before seemed surreal and far away. She couldn't remember exactly what had happened, only that there had been bold adventure followed by endless, deafening silence. When she spotted her father still asleep in the living room chair, it came back to her how the universe had caved in on itself, and how she had been the impetus. T-Papa stirred and mumbled in his sleep. Grace dusted around him.

Two hours later, when T-Papa had risen to take a bath and Yvette was in the kitchen finishing her grits, a truck roared up the driveway and Anthony hopped out. Now that he was a father, he moved with much more purpose. He had his own furniture shop in Long Beach where he lived, but he still came around to help T-Papa with large orders. Most of T-Papa's orders consisted of china closets for newlyweds or cribs for newborns. Occasionally, bedroom sets cropped up for silver anniversaries. In the old days, he had built everything from cabinets to coffins, chairs to choir lofts. Today, Anthony had come to ferry his father to his new home, which his cousins the bricklayers had built for him. There, he and T-Papa and those same cousins would labor all day to erect a shrine to the Blessed Mother. Part crèche, part birdbath, part barbecue pit, the shrine would be the finishing touch on Anthony's house. He would

take great pride in showing it off to his neighbors and friends —
not everybody had a shrine in his back yard. He entered the
kitchen with spirit.

"Great day out. Why don't you come with us and see the
new place?"

"Well, I've got to do my hair for the lala dance," Yvette
began, "and Grace here is dusting the statues."

"Dusting the statues! Whatever for? She should be outside
enjoying her youth. You could at least open the blinds." He
reached behind the sofa and let in the light.

"A glimpse of the outside world only makes the prisoner
yearn for her freedom," Yvette confided.

"Prisoner? Who? Our little Gracie? I see. I didn't think she
was dusting statues of her own free will. What'd she do?"

"She can't speak. But it must have been something awful
because Mama's spending the entire weekend praying for her."

"No kidding. The whole weekend, huh? Must have been
something spectacular! In my wildest days, I only got a couple of
rosaries. Inflation."

"She's a whole different generation. She gets her ideas from
television. Be careful, or she might take you hostage."

They laughed. Grace resented being discussed as though she
wasn't there. Yvette and Anthony were like all adults in this
way; they had purposely forgotten the trauma Grace was living.
She disliked them for belittling her passion, which had led to the
outburst for which she was imprisoned. It was better than being
arrested for loitering.

"Where's Daddy?" Anthony moved on to weightier topics.

"Taking a bath."

"At this time of day? Is he sick?"

"Lovesick. He slept in the chair."

"Those two!" he exclaimed. Grace could hear the smile in

her brother's voice. "She left for the whole weekend, huh? Who's going to make the gumbo?"

"Campbell's can make it, for all I care," Yvette offered, and the two of them squealed with pleasure at their own irreverence.

Grace couldn't comprehend their cavalier manner with respect to the family. "Those two!" Anthony had said of his parents, as though they were exasperating children only playing at being hurt and not the aging monarchs that Grace knew.

T-Papa emerged in his work clothes, looking sullen. Anthony waved goodbye to Grace after sitting down to a second breakfast and leaving more dishes for her to wash. "You do what Yvette tells you," he advised, laughing. T-Papa left without a word.

By noon, Grace was feeling somewhat morose. She finished dusting and settled in for a few hours of polishing furniture and sweeping floors. At three o'clock, with her father and Anthony out of the house and Yvette under the hair dryer clipping her toenails, Grace figured she could safely take a break. She lay on her bed and stared at the ceiling. There were spiderwebs on the sconce. She could stand on the mattress and use a broom to try to get to them. The thought made Grace dizzy. Depression lulled her to sleep. She didn't wake up until Yvette roused her to button the back of the winning dress.

Yvette left around eight. "Daddy should be home soon," her voice trailed off unconvincingly. As soon as she closed the door, Grace knew what loneliness was.

She was almost thirteen, but she had rarely been left alone. In the Broussard house, company was never far away. T-Papa was the only one who was often alone, at work in his shed, but he was never really alone. He had the ancestors. He had the saints. He had his chickens until the city made him get rid of them. Now he had the memory of his chickens.

Grace did not like the sound of alone. The house was always full of voices, complaining, gossiping, teasing voices. Now the only voices came from the street, where happy, drunken talk lit the night with promise. The sound of gunshots in the distance reminded Grace of firecrackers. The silence they left behind scared her. The sound of her own voice would have been a comfort.

Still, she was unable to speak. Camille had put a hex on her, which could only be lifted by a special dispensation from the Holy Mother herself. Just as a mother knows when her son is killed in battle, she knows too when her daughter betrays her. Grace was afraid to utter a word.

She was lacking in things to do. She couldn't call anyone. She was forbidden even to answer the phone, which was cooperating by refusing to ring. She speculated as to how many rosaries she could stomach before someone returned home to find her prostrate on the floor wearing the stigmata. In all the stories she had heard about the stigmata, it was unclear whether the hallowed wounds came on like a bad cold and faded with a proper rest or whether they were more like tattoos that hung around indefinitely. Grace decided not to risk it.

She felt herself growing faint with fear and hunger. To her sentence of silent penance she had added a purifying fast. It was all the snack food she consumed that caused her to yell out in church. If she seemed sufficiently wan and wasted when her mother returned, Camille might look down on her wretched little form with something resembling compassion. But fasting was not, in and of itself, an activity. Eating could take up lots of time and energy, but fasting really didn't take up any. Grace opened the refrigerator and regarded its luscious contents. If she was going to indulge, the food she chose should be more punishment than reward, a sinner's repast.

It was a buxom summer's eve, 90-some degrees outside, 110 in the kitchen. Double-dutch-jumping girls were playing raucously under the one working streetlamp, which happened to be in front of the Broussard home. (All the city complaint lines knew Camille by name.) Grace grabbed a pickled okra and watched them out the window. All of them were younger than she was, and freer too. They didn't have to go home when the lights came on. Their mothers didn't stand on their front porches shouting their names. They could eat dinner whenever they wanted to, whenever they made it for themselves. Grace envied them as they slapped the sidewalk with furious precision.

"Gotta pain in my stomach 'cause the baby's comin'. Gotta pain in my spine 'cause the baby's cryin'. Gotta pain in my back 'cause the baby's black!" One, two, three, four, Grace counted along.

She wondered what her mother must have looked like pregnant. Big, no doubt. Indulgent, maybe. Tired, perhaps. Yvette would have been no trouble at all, Grace was sure of it. The boys would have fallen out, one after another like a battered platoon. She must have clung. That was her job as the youngest child, to cling until the hospitality ran out, until she was shoved, head first, into the abyss.

The girls outside were laughing, taunting a passing boy. They were tarts, those girls. Everybody said so. They were tarts and Grace was pound cake. They were candied yams and she was mashed potatoes. No one in their right mind would prefer Grace to one of those girls. But today she was their equal. She had spoken out. She had risked her soul. Today, her breasts were as big as the next girl's, her lips as moist and succulent.

Her action had not been one of youthful defiance but a costly show of heroism. She had become an adult in the eyes of the Church, the 572 round eyes that followed her down the aisle

to Armageddon. Vietnam had brought it home to her. Grace
was a conscientious objector. While her family languished in a
moral fog, she had transfigured herself atop a mountain of
angst. The ancestors had appeared to her there and bathed her
in a terrible light: to be true to oneself, one must stand alone.

Having staged her own rite of passage, Grace could not expect her family to recognize her, to see her in her glory. When
they looked around, they had not found the child amongst them.
She had gone to the temple and preached to the elders. She had
left them days before, years even, but they had not noticed, so
trusting were they, so fixed in their powerful customs.

"Why hast thou thus dealt with us?" Camille had wanted to
know. "Behold, thy father and I have sought thee sorrowing."

"How is it that you sought me?" Grace glared in wordless
contempt. "Wist ye not that I must be about my business?"

But they had not understood her look.

So she had returned to them and was again subject unto
them. And she would increase in wisdom and stature until, one
day, she would leave them.

And all these things her mother kept in her heart.

Growing up Black Creole Catholic in Vietnam America
Watts was a heady experience. Grace frequently got carried
away with the drama of it all.

She fondled the pickled okra. She took little bites from the
tip, rubbed her thumb along the grooves and ridges, licked the
stem, and swallowed the crown. With increasing antipathy, she
bit into her savior, unaware that at this very moment the future
was entering her. The body was broken and the juice ran across
her tongue. In the release of the fragile seeds, Grace felt an
epiphany. With the first sour breath, a monstrous vision. Her
quest was over. She knew what she had to do.

She would go back to the church and sleep with God, beg

His forgiveness. Grace grabbed another piece of okra, raced to the hall closet, took out her mother's shawl, and threw it over her pajamas. She strode past the sofa and unlocked the door. It was dark outside. It was late. To get to the church, she would have to pass a row of burnt-out enterprises, somber memorials left over from the '65 Riots. At the end of the row was the newly reconstructed liquor store, resuscitated due to popular demand, some of whom were sure to be testifying out front on a Friday night. Add to this scene a bunch of fast girls jumping double-dutch on the Broussard sidewalk, and Grace began to reconsider her plan for redemption. She was unclean, she was scared, she was nothing. She took off the shawl. The okra, which she had been clutching like a bent crucifix, fell onto the floor and landed under the sofa. It lay in limp indolence, mocking her. Grace wept loudly at the idea of the afterlife.

After a few moments of this, Grace grew bored. Instead of returning to the church, which was bound to be locked, she returned to the refrigerator, determined to add gluttony to her list of sins. She searched the shelves for something dangerous, but nothing appeared. One by one, she filled the countertop with items rejected as entirely too wholesome. Grace was hungry. She surveyed the counter for a quick fix. Crab, shrimp, green peppers, onions—nothing spoke to her immediate desires. Her eyes fell upon the Louisiana sausage. A few slices of sausage on a piece of French bread might go a long way. She found a knife and sliced her way to satiety. Several small sandwiches later, it occurred to her that the sausage was being saved for gumbo. So was the bread, for that matter. Panic seized Grace mid-chew.

"Who's going to make the gumbo?" Anthony's question beckoned. Grace had prayed for a sign and here it was. She would make a gumbo to bring her mother home. Alone with her ingredients, terrified by the magnitude of her mission, she began chopping. Angels, sounding very much like the Boys' Choir of Harlem, harmonized to "Ezekiel Saw De Wheel." The ceiling parted and a light shone through. "Behold, my beloved child, in whom I find great favor." Grace couldn't tell if the voice was coming from inside her brain or from the police helicopter overhead. At any rate, her task was clear.

Onions, green peppers, scallions, garlic flew in every direction. Grace was cheerful with the work of generations. Like her Haitian foremothers, she gathered and plucked with an eye to vexation. In fact, the only difference between Grace and a *voudou* priestess was that she didn't know what she was doing. Her gumbo was more the work of Macbeth's witches—eye of newt, toe of frog, did anybody know the exact proportions? It didn't occur to her to look for a recipe.

Camille never so much as looked at a cookbook; one year for Christmas, a distant cousin had paid her the highest insult by giving her one as a present. It was all about cooking like a French chef, and Camille had dismissed it with one comment, "If I wanted to cook like a balding Frenchman, I would have been born on another continent with a soup tureen for a nose." As far as Grace knew, that book had ended up at the parish rummage sale, and the only recipes to be found in her mother's kitchen were the ones on the back of the Bisquick box. Grace felt her way around the ingredients. Her vision was blurry as she approached the cauldron. A chunk of butter was soon sizzling at the bottom. It was time to sauté.

Sauté was Grace's favorite word. While others burned in hell's fury or froze in heaven's sterile clouds, Grace would be content to sauté her time away. With wooden spoon in hand, she set about her business. She had a feeling she was adding too much salt, and maybe she was overdoing it on the cayenne as well. She couldn't remember all the right seasonings, so she settled on parsley, sage, rosemary, and thyme because she knew of a song that advocated this mixture. She didn't think the song had anything to do with gumbo, but that was the beauty of gumbo: you could put anything in it. Bay leaves, she remembered bay leaves. Camille put bay leaves in everything—gumbo, jambalaya, red beans—the Broussards were always fishing bay leaves out of their food. Grace found the bag of bay leaves and dumped them into the pot. Satisfied with her creation, she added a few handfuls of flour and watched everything sauté.

All was going incredibly well. Grace lined up the cans of stewed tomato and located the can opener. After several attempts, she succeeded in opening each can. She was all set to pitch them in when she realized that something was missing from this dish. Something slimy and base and essential.

Grace searched the freezer for okra. She didn't see it anywhere. Just as she was poised to panic, a little brown bag appeared on the counter in front of her. It was filled with fresh okra from the Caribbean store. Grace regarded the curious green cones. She took one out and washed it.

It was a fuzzy little thing. Much rougher than she remembered. She felt around in the bag for a better specimen, but they all felt coarse and hairy. Grace didn't recognize it as the same okra that ended up in gumbo. She washed and washed but the disappointment wouldn't go away. Maybe this wasn't the right kind of okra. She had better chop it up and see.

Grace chopped herself into a frenzy, but the okra didn't behave any better. In fact, it acted worse. In response to her jabs, it was bleeding, oozing, salivating. She was chasing okra across the cutting board. Okra was escaping onto the floor. It slithered and writhed against her knife.

Grace had never met such an expressive batch of okra. It simply would not obey. The problem was with the skin.

It smashed together when she chopped it. She would have to skin the okra before chopping it. A carrot peeler would do nicely. It wasn't necessary to take off all the skin, just enough so that the okra in her hand would look like the okra in gumbo. She peeled a piece and tried to cut it. The result was an okra pond with lily pads of seeds.

The pot was crackling, asking for more food. Grace threw in the few chunks that were clinging to her knife. She watched them sizzle and bubble over. Grabbing the pond with her hands, she shook it into the stew. Grace stared at her first gumbo. There was only one thing to do with it: bury it. Lava was rising inside the pot. The smell of burning flour permeated the air. As Grace threw water into the muck, acid tears flowed down her cheeks. She had created a perfect disaster. She was of no use to her family. Federal troops would have to be called in for the cleanup.

She didn't hear the car pull into the driveway or the passenger door closing or the key turning in the lock. Grace was stirring a large vat of what looked to be mud when Camille stepped into the kitchen.

"What are you doing?" Camille turned off the pot.

Grace sniffled and sobbed. She couldn't talk. Tears like words flowed out of her eyes, her ears, her throat.

"It's a good thing I came home early. Look at the mess you've made. Where is everybody? Are you here alone?"

Camille unloaded her things—suitcase, purse, rosary, church bulletin, pillow, MAW newsletter, handkerchief, fan, and scarf. She scooped Grace up in her hands.

"Where's Daddy? Where's Yvette? Why did they leave you alone?" Camille was crying now too. "It's okay. You can talk now," she patted Grace. But Grace still couldn't talk.

"Did you season the pot? Here, you stir. Mmmm, smells good. Whatever gave you the idea? Tastes good too. It's just a little hot. Here, chop up some more green peppers and onions.

I'll just put this over here and we'll get started fresh. You can stop stirring now. Why don't you add a little water to that? And open the window a little. I'm just going to take off my girdle. I'll be right back. You can wipe up the floor in the meantime. Fish some of those bay leaves out of the pot. We can use them again. Do you want to make another roux? This is your gumbo, you know, so you tell me what you want in it."

They labored into the night. It was one thirty in the morning when the first guest arrived. Yvette came home sweaty but invigorated. The sight of Camille made her wilt. "Why did you leave your sister alone? I asked you to watch her, didn't I?" Yvette stammered out a "yes, ma'am." Grace was busy stirring and didn't look up. "We'll be eating about three. You go take a bath. And then come on back here and make a salad and get the table ready. I'm surprised at you!"

"Yes, ma'am." Yvette hurried off.

When T-Papa and Anthony rolled in, it was 2:39 by the kitchen clock. They had been drinking, not enough to make them drunk but enough to make them happy. Camille squinted at her husband. "Why did you go off and leave my baby? Didn't you know she'd be scared by herself?"

"Where was Yvette?"

"Out dancing."

"Well, I didn't know Grace would be by herself. She could have come with us."

"Yvette's setting the table. Why don't you bring in some cold drinks and see about some ice? Anthony, you can butter the French bread."

"Oh, I can't stay, Mama. I got to get back to Long Beach. We ate us a big barbecue tonight and I can't say I'm hungry."

"Well, you're going to eat some more. This is your sister's first gumbo. She wants you all to taste it."

At that late-night dinner, there was much exclaiming. People

looked at Grace as if they were seeing her for the first time.
Yvette toasted the chef. Camille led the benediction. She asked
for a blessing on Grace's first gumbo and for a special blessing
on Grace. When Anthony asked for some salt, she silenced him
with a glance. In a complete break with tradition, Grace was
served first. T-Papa saved her the largest piece of garlic bread.
Grace savored these gestures. She was very hungry.

The dinner conversation centered on Attica. T-Papa said the
prisoners were foolish. The State of New York would surely use
force to "retake their property" and no one would sympathize
with "a bunch of colored criminals." Anthony said the governor
wouldn't have to use force. "All he has to do is wait a few days
and they'll destroy each other." Yvette predicted they would
negotiate "at least until the Super Bowl is over." Camille said
they should keep negotiating until they found a real solution.
"The prisoners are scared, too. They'll back down eventually."

Grace listened but said nothing. She was aware of what was
going on at Attica. Before her news blackout on Friday, she had
heard the word spoken. Since then, she had heard snippets of the
news—thirty-three hostages, cell block D, bats, billy clubs,
lengths of pipe—which Yvette had listened to on full volume
while under the hair dryer. Prisoners were scary people, and the
prisoners at Attica were scariest of all. Here in the clutches of the
dungeon, stripped of their freedom and surrounded by gallows,
they were full of power and strength. They would be caught and
punished. Grace felt sorry for them. Anthony had been in jail.
And she herself knew what it was like to be deprived of rights
for committing a mortal sin. Even if the prisoners at Attica were
evil people, Grace felt they must have reasons to stage a rebellion. She wondered if anyone had asked them why they had
taken those guards hostage and if anyone dared to listen to their
answer.

Why? It was the one question Grace had longed to hear all weekend, but no one asked her why she did the things she did. It was the one topic she yearned to talk about. Things had swelled up inside of her that she could no longer contain.

Camille asked if anybody wanted seconds. Anthony ate a surplus spoonful before begging off for the night. Camille dispatched T-Papa to bed when she was satisfied that he had eaten enough. Yvette was left to do the dishes. Camille went to draw a bath for Grace, who had fallen asleep at the dining room table.

"Come on, baby. You can't go to sleep like that. You have okra in your hair." Grace let her mother lead her to the river, part the waters, and wash her down.

"I don't know whose child you are. Sometimes I think you're your father's child, strong-willed and self-righteous like him. But he thinks with his head. In truth, you're Yvette's child. She's the one who raised you. But you and Yvette don't have much in common, do you? You're really the child of my desire. Everything I ever wanted to do, I do through you. Things I didn't know I wanted to do, like shouting out in church and rolling up my skirt. Who would have ever thought these days would come? You're not mine or your father's or anyone else's. You're somebody all to yourself. Not like your sister or any of your brothers. You really think about things. With your whole body. You really know things with your soul. Sometimes I don't know whose child you are. Then I realize you're God's child." Grace looked like she was sleeping but she was wide awake.

That night, the Broussards tossed and turned on too much food and too much feeling. It would be four o'clock before the last of the family drifted off. Grace lay in bed, waiting for the others to go to sleep. When she could no longer hear them wrestling, she rose in the night to recover the okra she had carelessly left on the living room floor.

11

The Announcement

The Epiphany, January 6, 1979

Resentment makes the world go round, but within a family it can be quite debilitating. Smoldering for years under flaccid smiles, it can savage a household in one afternoon. If nobody steps in to smother the flames, or if the cynics fan them, resentment will burn out of control, scorching everything in its path. It won't stop until it has drunk its fill, until it has eaten somebody's heart out.

For the Broussards, the Epiphany was a chance to capture the lost glory of Christmas, specifically the glory of all the gumbo they missed with Camille in the hospital. It was no mystery why Camille's brood generally preferred the Feast of the Magi to the Birth of Jesus. While the latter involved clamoring children, copious gifts, and severe financial stress, the former only involved work for their mother. To them, Camille's gumbo was mother's milk over rice. They looked forward to plopping down at her table and consuming vast quantities of it.

As far as Grace was concerned, Christ was just another baby lying in a manger until a multitude of heavenly host appeared to some shepherds who were watching a star that would guide three wise men to their new king. This was the kind of recognition Jesus needed for his career to take off. Grace didn't need anything quite so elaborate. A kind word, a sympathetic glance would be enough to launch her on her way. She doubted they would be forthcoming.

The Broussards were having a dinner, and Grace was to be the main course. Over gumbo, she would make her Announcement. "I'm running away." She practiced the words while sweeping the dusty floor.

By Grace's own reckoning, dinner would be the most appropriate time to throw herself to the wolves. Picking at the bones was the Broussards' favorite family sport. As the family's black sheep, Grace knew she'd be eaten alive. It was all part of her Plan. Scoff and sneer all they want, but she was moving out. Salvation requires sacrifice, and one ruined dinner is a small price to pay for the redemption of a soul. Grace could hear the jolly voices of ridicule, and she was prepared to meet them head on. For every taunt, she had a scowl, for every doubt, a grimace. In front of her bedroom mirror, she practiced flinging dirty looks.

The wolves would begin arriving at noon. It would take a miracle for them to show restraint. In the absence of a miracle, Grace hoped her entire extended family would choke on their collective scorn. She'd give them something to chew on, all right, something so fat and succulent it would dull their resistance and lay waste their resolve. Then, when they were too bloated with self-satisfaction to move—as they cradled their stomachs from the joys of bellyaching—she would step right over their corpulent bodies and head on out the door.

"I'm moving out. No matter what you say." This she would announce as all heads were cocked to meet their spoons.

"With what?" From one of the heads slurping okra.

"I've been saving my paycheck."

Slurp. "Thirty-five dollars won't go very far." All heads chuckling.

"Just watch me." Eyes squinting, nose twitching.

Head gnawing on a crab leg. "Where you moving to?"

"Inglewood."

"Inglewatts? Why pay to move to the imitation, when you're already living in the real thing? For free?"

More laughter from the slurping, sucking heads.

"Why not move to Beverly Hills? We can come swim in your pool." A mouth full of shrimp and sausage.

"I don't want you swimming in my pool."

Laughter all around.

"You're not moving in with that Mexican girl, are you? Aren't you two tired of each other? Pass me the rice."

"Why don't you wait till you get married? Like the rest of us did. What can you do in an apartment that you can't do here? Sin, that's what. Who's got the hot sauce?"

Grace was prepared for their ridicule. She had been praying for strength ever since leaving the cemetery. She had waited for this day to make her Announcement because intentions raised on a holy day carry the most weight. Creoles pray every day of the week, every hour of the day, and on holy days they pray double. With all those Creole prayers making their way to Heaven at the same time, God would have trouble keeping straight which prayers went with which intentions. The resulting confusion might work in a girl's favor. If she could only hurl her little prayer at the proper angle and force a collision with other nearby supplications, thereby throwing them off course and converting them to her cause, her prayer would gather strength in the ascent. To face the Broussards with her news, Grace needed all the strength she could pirate.

It wasn't as if none of the Broussards ever moved out. There were at least two legitimate ways to escape the family den. You could marry yourself out or drop dead. Sin was no excuse, school was no excuse, work was no excuse. War was a flimsy excuse. Duty to family came before duty to church, state, or employer. Only the family had eminent domain over its members' hearts.

"Sure, it's closer to work. Everybody knows there aren't any jobs in Watts. But this is where your family lives. Shouldn't that count for something? Who wants some more wine?"

"A young girl living alone. I don't like it. Are you going to eat that shrimp?"

"What's the rush to move? You're barely twenty years old. Look at Yvette. She's pushing fifty and she's still here. Are we all out of garlic bread?"

"You sure you want to leave your mother's gumbo?" Grace anticipated every possible reaction to her news. Acceptance wasn't one of them.

Camille called from the kitchen. "What did Joseph look like?"

"A prisoner of war. He hadn't bathed in a while."

Joseph had had Grace drop him at a buddy's house, saying he needed "to get cleaned up" before presenting himself to Camille. "Tell Mama to set an extra place at the table," he hollered as she drove away.

"Oh, Lord," said Camille. "I don't have any more fatted calves to slaughter for that boy."

"He's not a boy anymore. He can buy his own hamburgers."

"Don't talk about your brother that way. Company's

almost here and you ain't set the table yet? That's enough
sweeping for now. Get on in here and help me out." Grace resented her mother's tone. All the same, she found it useful. It's
easier to separate when you're angry, and Grace was a veritable
cauldron of irritability. She pushed the porch dirt into the yard
and let the screen door slam behind her.

In less than an hour, the "company" would begin arriving. It
was hard for Grace to think of Joseph or any of her brothers as
"company." Raymond, Anthony, and Louis would make the
journey with their respective broods. None of their wives
cooked very well, and their households were so fractious as to
make digestion difficult. Uncle Claude and Aunt Julie did their
best never to miss a gumbo. Marc and Vanessa would "drop in
for a bite" and stay until closing. And no meal was complete
without Rouby, who could lick the pot with his last piece of
bread on his way to the dessert line.

The Broussard descendants numbered as the stars. The
nieces and nephews born in the three short years since T-Papa's
death could have stocked a small orchestra. The kitchen table,
the dining room table with two leaves added, two card tables,
and four TV trays were needed just to accommodate the immediate family, their ever-expanding progeny, and the handful of
freeloaders who showed up for every feast. For occasions that
featured the extended family (all the relatives with plots at Holy
Rosary) Camille had to get down the pot you could stand in. By
the way they lined up with their bowls, the house on Compton
Avenue might have been the Union Gospel Mission. Camille
dished it out like the Messiah Himself, multiplying as they came.
Today the Broussards would be joined by a visiting cousin from
Louisiana. He was the only real company as far as Grace was
concerned.

It fell to Grace to arrange the tables. The card tables were for the younger children, who had to be seated in certain configurations for the benefit of the adults. Two of the TV trays were for Rouby and Cousin Paul. The other two were for Camille's no-count brother Claude and his no-cooking wife Julie. The kitchen table was for the older children, led by Raymond's son Gregory, who was almost as old as Grace and half again as tall. The oak dining room table, made by T-Papa himself to last an eternity, was the exclusive domain of Camille, her children, and their respective spouses. Joseph would get the place of honor, his father's chair. Grace and Yvette would crowd next to each other in the spinsters' corner closest to the kitchen.

Setting the tables had always been Grace's job, but now that she worked in the China Department she was expected to add a flourish to the napkins and a polish to the silverware. For Christmas, Grace had presented Camille with twelve porcelain napkin rings. Because she was saving her money for the move, she hadn't yet delivered on the cloth napkins. She was reminded of this failure as she commenced setting the tables.

The news of Camille's First Post-Hysterectomy Gumbo excited all the Broussards immensely. For almost three weeks, they had suffered through Yvette's quickie versions. The Broussard siblings had each dreamed of Camille's fleshy concoction while sipping Yvette's watery stew. Camille had barely had time to whip up one good pot before going to the hospital for surgery; with help from their suckling brothers, Yvette and Grace had finished it off by Christmas Day. By now the clan was languishing in a state of withdrawal. Grace had risen at dawn to chop, season, and stir, but once the gumbo was served, Camille would get all the raves. While daughter adorned the tables, mother added the last batch of shrimp.

In those final moments of solitude before Yvette came home from ten o'clock Mass, a cleaned-up Joseph made his grand entrance, and the grandchildren razed the back door, Grace considered approaching her mother privately and dropping the Announcement in her lap. Because her news was really meant for Camille, this would have been the honorable thing to do. But how could she tell her mother, fresh from a hysterectomy, that her last child would be leaving her? And leaving not as the others had left, to go off to war or marriage, but leaving to go off to herself, that sequestered place where no parent can follow?

Designed to soften the blow, Grace's Ten Point Plan had been a dismal failure. Three of the points had been executed, but not one of them had been executed well. She had skipped Mass (Point One) on Christmas Day, a transgression that met with praise instead of condemnation. She had ruined her hair (Point Two), but this hadn't garnered the desired shock, only the usual disparaging remarks. Elena had worn the red dress (Point Four), but not to a family dinner (Point Three), and Grace's faint determination to stay out all night (Point Five) had fallen prey to her own jealousy. Points Six, Seven, and Eight all had to do with moving, and Grace was still in her mother's house bearing the last name she couldn't bring herself to change (Point Ten). She had yet to attempt Point Nine (refusing her mother's gumbo), and she very much doubted that today would be the day.

"Mama, I have something to tell you."

"Do you think this needs more cayenne?"

"Mama, I'm moving out."

"Seventeen days in bed and I've lost my touch."

"Mama, I'm going to live in Inglewood."

"Now, don't forget to set a place for your cousin Paul."

"Mama, I really love you, but I can't live with you anymore. I want a divorce. A friendly divorce. You can come visit me every once in a while. Just don't bring any gumbo."

"These shrimp don't look as big as before."

"Mama, did you hear me? I said I don't want your gumbo."

"No gumbo? You aren't sick, are you?"

Grace couldn't do it. She listened to the sounds coming from the kitchen. Her mother was getting old. Sixty-one wasn't old for a grandmother, but the future of a sixty-one-year-old mother who was already widowed and recently downed could not be taken for granted. Camille moved haltingly about the kitchen, forgetting to bang things around with her usual élan. Grace was afraid her Announcement would meet with the worst kind of opposition possible: tears. She said nothing.

Yvette danced through the back door singing the "Lamb of God." She was in rare form, even for Yvette, and Grace guessed it was due to one too many brownies at the social following Mass. The killer of San Francisco's Mayor Moscone and Supervisor Harvey Milk was citing "too much junk food" as part of his defense. Grace didn't believe the murderer, but she was ingesting with caution, nonetheless. Yvette, who hadn't gained a pound in thirty years, had no such prohibitions against sugar or any other food. The more she ate, the more energy she discharged. Today, she had the vigor of a serial killer. The "Twinkie Defense" was not likely to wash with Camille.

"Mama, you'll never believe what happened! Grace, how was the funeral? It's just awful what happened to that talented young man. I feel embarrassed to tell you my news on such a tragic day, but I'm just about to burst. Mama, Sister, you'll never believe it, but Mr. Juge proposed to me!" Yvette announced through tears of joy.

"Well, of course, I didn't take him seriously. I mean, what would I do with an old man like that? Anyway, I told him I would think about it, so as not to hurt his feelings, but I wasn't going to give it another thought. It just gave me a good laugh, that's all. Well, don't you know, after Mass, the Blessed Virgin

called me to her altar. It was her, all right. Irresistible. Before I
know what I'm doing, I'm on my knees praying for a sign. You'll
never believe what happened! Just as I was getting up to go, she
nodded toward the back of the church, and here comes Mr.
Juge, carrying a red candle and looking twenty years younger.

"My heart just about fell out of my chest! He grabbed my
hand and kissed it, right there in front of the Altar Society ladies.
It was the most exciting thing that's ever happened to me. We
knelt together for a moment, our hearts pounding like scared
little sparrows, and you'll never guess what happened. She
smiled at us, Mama. The Blessed Virgin Mary smiled upon our
union. I'm going to marry Urbain Juge!"

Grace dropped the bowl she was holding. It clattered onto
the plate below. The news was astonishing. She had never considered that Yvette would get married. No one had ever considered that *Yvette* would leave. This was not within the realm of
possibility. Urbain Juge? The old man who haunted the cemetery? The man from whom all sensible women ran and with
whom all sensible men took issue? How could Yvette leave her
mother for Urbain Juge? Grace could never leave now. Her skin
bristled with outrage.

"Sit down," was all Camille said. "Sit down and quit this
foolishness. You're not marrying anybody, least of all some
crazy old man who's already had two wives die on him. If he was
insulting enough to propose, you don't have to be foolish
enough to accept. Your father has to approve. He's not here,
and if he was, he wouldn't even consider it."

"It's my choice. It's not Daddy's choice or your choice. It's
my choice. Urbain is my choice!"

"You have to choose wisely. For our sake. We have to live
with this person!"

"What about me? What about my life?"

"What about it? All this time, I've been thinking you were going to the lala to dance and, truth is, you've been running out to meet some old simpleton! Well, don't think I'm going to stand by while you make plans to ruin your life. Go help Grace straighten the living room. And act like you got some sense!"

"Mama, I'm trying to tell you something. Something about my life!"

"I don't want to hear nothing more about it. I don't care if Jesus Himself came down and whispered in your ear. You are not going to marry Urbain Juge!"

What came after that was hard for Grace to decipher. Camille let fly a string of invectives that ended in Yvette crying, "You would go against the Blessed Virgin?"

Camille replied with the pointed Gospel passage, "Forgive them, Father, for they know not what they do." And she added for effect, "There's things about that old man you don't know."

"What things, Mama? What things?"

"Like about his wives. You don't know how they died."

"They died of cancer. Everybody knows that. What are you saying, Mama? Are you saying they didn't die of natural causes? Are you saying Urbain is a murderer?"

"I'm not saying nothing. He's from New Orleans, you know. His mother practiced the *voudou*. So, you just stay away from that old man. Cause you don't know what you getting."

"Are you saying Urbain is a *voudou* priest?"

"I don't know what he is. I just know you saw him carrying a red candle and looking like a suitor. And you saw a statue smile. So, you either gone and lost your mind, or Urbain gone and taken it from you!"

"Are you claiming he has special powers over me?"

"I don't know what he has. I just know that now is not the time to talk about it. We got company coming over. Your brother just got back from God knows where. We'll take this up tonight when we have some privacy. In the meantime, don't you breathe a syllable to anybody. Do you hear me? If you truly want to marry Urbain Juge, there ain't a thing I can do about it. But I've got plenty to say till then, and I'm not going to bite my tongue!"

"Mama, you are confusing me!" Grace caught a glimpse of her frazzled sister as she tore through the dining room on her way to seclusion. The wind from Yvette's retreat knocked over one of the TV trays.

The scattered tray, the naked card table, the glasses waiting for ice—all were insignificant in the wake of Yvette's revelation. Grace's first reaction was shock, followed by raging disbelief, rapidly followed by the louder voice of disgust. How could Yvette lie down with a snake like Mr. Juge? Grace smoldered with resentment. Today was to have been her day to bring the house down. First, Joseph's reappearance had stolen her thunder. Now, in one torrential broadcast, Yvette had managed to grab center stage.

The news put a kink in Grace's plans. If used properly, this kink might work to her advantage. The more she thought about it, the more she was taken by a feeling of restrained joy. The spotlight had been diverted; she could now relax outside of its merciless gaze. With Yvette set to marry Urbain Juge, Grace's departure would become of secondary importance, hardly worth noting at all. Oh, the opportunity in obscurity! Now was the time to strike.

"Mama, I..."

"Hand me that spoon."

"I just want you to know..."

"Not that one. The one over there."

"I just want to tell you..."

"Don't you start with me too."

"I'm not starting anything... I'm just thinking about..."

"And don't you mutter a word about Yvette. She's getting older, that's all. She must be coming upon her change."

Camille threw Grace one of those threadbare looks, and Grace backed off. Camille never talked about personal things like "changes," and Grace took this as a signal that her mother was coming loose at the seams. Her announcement would have to wait. She went back to setting the tables.

The company began arriving at 11:56 in the morning. Since their usual cheery greeter was perishing in self-exile, Grace met them at the door with a warning look. Anthony figured the look pertained to Joseph and decided to make a joke out of it.

"Was that the guest of honor I passed by the liquor store?" Anthony called out on his way to the kitchen. Grace rebuked him with a flash of her eyes. He straightened up.

Her other brothers smelled the tension long before they hit the kitchen, where Camille was steadily watching that pot. So did all their wives and all their kids. So did Rouby, Uncle Claude, and Aunt Julie, who had just come from seeing Zippy's baby, which had put them all in a thoughtful mood. The only one who didn't seem to realize he had landed in a smokehouse was cousin Paul. He kept telling Grace how pretty she was look-ing these days—and wasn't it something that no California boy had scooped her up and married her?

Grace remembered Paul from her girlhood visits to Grimelle. She had seen him last when they were both twelve. After that, Paul's family had discovered oil on their land, migrated to Metairie, and lost themselves among the Whites. Paul was here in Los Angeles searching for his "roots." Alex Haley's book had sent lots of people scampering about their family trees, and Paul looked to be no exception. His wavy hair

was picked out in a "natural" so prodigious that he appeared to
have been hit by lightning at some point in his journey. Grace
figured he had been hopelessly addled by that schizophrenia
known as "passing." But she remembered that he had once been
kind to her, so she tried to temper her disdain.

With T-Papa dead, Camille in the kitchen, and Yvette deep
in hiding, there was no one capable of leading a conversation.
No one outside of the central Broussard clan was comfortable
taking the lead, not even Camille's brother Claude, who had
gotten as far as he had by taking orders. Grace was much too
self-absorbed to offer her services, which had never been more
than minimal at best. Rouby, a prolific talker who whispered
secrets in his sleep, had learned years before that he should never
be the first to dive in where others feared to wade. The "boys'
wives" were all in competition with one another—each of them
being miserably aware of her status as a near-Broussard—and if
one tried to start something, the others jumped in and cut her
off. The older grandchildren, who were quite adept when it
came to adding comic relief, had been sent to the back yard to
play. The youngest two had the good sense to fall asleep the
minute they hit the couch.

As for the Broussard brothers, family gatherings rendered
them practically comatose, all but Marc, who relished the authority conferred by his architectural degree. He was no longer
simply a Broussard; he was Marc Gilbert Broussard, M.A. And
as proof of his superior verbal marksmanship, he now zeroed in
on poor cousin Paul.

"That's some hair you got there. How long you been
growin' it?"

"Oh, it just grows itself. I ain't got to do nothin'." Paul
knew how to play. Wives clucked their appreciation.

"It matches Grace's. Y'all should get together."

"What would Grace want with a country boy like me?"

"Hear that, Grace? Paul says he's available."

"Did I say that?"

"*He* might be. But *I'm* not." No one wanted to touch that one.

"So, Paul... what about your little girlfriend back home?"

"What girlfriend?"

"You must have more than one. Can't even remember all their names. Plenty of little country girls... sitting on they po'ches just waiting for you to wander by."

"Who told you that lie?"

"Don't you bring them flowers and candy? Like a good Lou'siana beau's s'posed to do?"

"You only brought me candy. You didn't bring me flowers." Vanessa flipped her hair at Marc.

"And this ain't Lou'siana, is it?" The tension was traveling.

"Lou'siana ain't even Lou'siana anymore. Nowadays the girls bring the boys candy." This enlightening piece of information was courtesy of Uncle Claude.

"Oh, I see. That must be why Paul's grown to be such a nice size. He must have a girlfriend or two bringing him candy."

"I buy my own candy. It's cheaper."

"That's right! You got to have lots of money to keep a girl-friend." Everyone suspected Marc knew what he was talking about. Vanessa would have silenced him if it weren't for the fact that she encouraged his candy-buying. She liked having a hus-band whom other women found attractive.

"Maybe Paul come to L.A. looking for one," said Raymond, waking up.

"Did you hear that, Grace? Paul says he's looking for a girl-friend." Louis joined in the fun. Deborah shot him a warning look.

"Did I say that?"

"What's wrong with Grace?" asked Raymond.

"Oh, nothing a good man can't cure," said Marc, sucking up to the challenge. "She's a little snarly, but she makes a mean gumbo."

"You better be careful I don't poison your bowl." Grace hated to resort to threats, but growing up in the Broussards was like growing up in the balcony of the Apollo Theater. Grace was used to the heckling, but it still hurt to be booed off the stage.

She wished suddenly for her father. She fancied that he would protect her from all the fiendish suggestions and inquiries. For a moment, she remembered him not as her tormentor but as her stalwart defender. Though this memory was entirely false, it calmed her now to dwell on it.

"Hey, Grace?" Louis offered. "Why don't you take Paul for a ride after dinner? Show him the town?"

"Yeah! You could show him Watts," suggested Marc. "Grace knows all the happ'nin' spots."

"Leave Grace alone," said Anthony, finally speaking up. Lord knows, he had been picked on in his day.

"I don't think Grace is talking to us anymore anyway," observed Vanessa.

"I think you're right," agreed Marc, leaving off Grace to begin a new round of speculation about Joseph. Grace felt like introducing conversation that would really shake them all up ("I saw Daddy. He said to tell y'all hey.") but she knew they would just ignore her. The Broussards ignored any comment that broke with convention. So Grace turned her attention to the smell of garlic bread as her brothers and their wives engaged in stream of consciousness gossip about those absent and those sitting right there in the living room. That was one thing about the Broussards—they didn't play favorites. They talked about people behind their backs, in front of their backs, and back to back. Grace knew they would go to their graves with the drool of unspent criticism on their lips. She didn't really believe the dead would intercede on her behalf. People did not change in death; they merely hid.

Yvette emerged from her tight chamber, shrouded in a black lace veil. She greeted no one. Even Marc knew not to tease her as she made her way to the table. The house drooped under a cloud of silence. Paul alone did not seem to notice the change in weather. He hurried over to Yvette, kissed her cold cheek, and told her how pretty she looked. Yvette smiled morosely, batting Paul's hair out of her eyes.

Camille gusted in from the kitchen. "Gumbo's ready. Line up." The Broussards sprang into action, rounding up children from the yard, stopping in the bathroom to wash their hands. Paul was pushed to the front. Grace brought up the rear. As they dished up their bowls, Grace looked around at her siblings and their lives. She didn't want any of them.

Yvette's life? How it haunted Grace! Yvette had had a young love. He had been killed in a construction accident. She had been in mourning half of her life and all of Grace's. Yvette had tried once to leave her parents' house and move back to Louisiana to be with him. But somewhere along the path, while home was still in sight, she turned and looked back longingly. And the Creole God, in his infinite wisdom, had reduced her to a pillar of salt, fit only for seasoning her mother's gumbo pot.

Raymond was not salt but stone. Petrified inside his marriage for as long as Grace had known him, you could not strike him and draw water. Grace had never seen him cry and rarely seen him laugh. His children seemed remarkably immune to him, which Grace judged to be a good thing.

Grace looked to Louis for inspiration and found none. He

seemed to be happily married enough, but his wife clearly wasn't, and that fact was starting to take its toll.

Then there was Anthony, who had been hoodwinked into marriage just as he had been cowed into respectability. The titles Husband, Father, and Devoted Son suited him well. Therein lay Grace's disappointment. What had happened to Anthony's nerve? She had only heard tell of it, never actually seen it. In her mind, he was the worst kind of diplomat, one who never contradicted his bosses no matter how much they lied.

And what was there to say about Marc? Love, for him, was an acquisition. Career, money, admirers—he and Vanessa had plenty of all three. They had the carefree air of people with no children, and they were roundly resented for it. Family gossip suggested that infertility was involved, brought about by excessive birth control.

Vanessa worked at the Automobile Club. She had taken over Yvette's job when Yvette decided to go back to school and become a teacher. While Yvette had remained a clerk typist for her entire tenure with Triple A, Vanessa had advanced all the way from clerk to supervisor. Yvette, who had practically arranged their marriage for them, was repaid for her kindness with a disinvitation to ride in their car.

Marc was the most American of all the Broussard children, but Grace did not take him as a role model. Her parents' generation had only recently won the right to vote. Where did he and Vanessa get their sense of entitlement? Hadn't they taken this pursuit of happiness thing too far?

And where was Joseph, defender of life and liberty? Grace felt sure that Joseph had tasted love long before he tasted war. Women seemed to be his only cause for motivation. Grace couldn't see what he had to offer them, but it must have been good. The Joseph she knew was a lost soul. His hero was Superfly.

It was impossible for Grace to think of any of her siblings as people to emulate. That role went to her parents. Camille had married her love. T-Papa had married his love. They had worked hard and lived simply. Both of them had maintained their strength of mind and independent spirits. Grace wanted the love life her parents had had.

If Grace was having a hard time of it, Yvette was having the hardest time of all. She showed no interest in the feast. "Aren't you eating, Yvette?" Camille brought a bowl and placed it before her eldest daughter. Yvette turned away. Camille went on to other things.

"Who wants to say the blessing?"

Marc jumped up. "I think it's my turn."

"You sure you remember the words?" Raymond looked smugly at his brother, the infidel. "When's the last time you were in church, boy?"

"I don't need to go to church to get practice blessing the table," Marc countered.

"All you have to do is eat. And Marc does plenty of that." Vanessa patted his stomach. He smiled down at her.

"Heavenly Father, we thank Thee for our mother's health, for the loving hands that cooked this food. For our holy mother who gave birth to this great family. Of which I am the brightest part. And to our holy father, whom we miss with all our hearts. And for our brother Joseph who, rumor has it, has blown into town to grace us with his presence. May his visit be sunny and dry. We thank Thee also for bringing our cousin Paul to us and for gathering us safely together for another delicious gumbo. Lord, we thank Thee for gumbo, the food of the gods…"

"That's enough," Camille interjected. "Amen."

"Amen." The spoons were clicking.

"Hold on, everybody." Marc held up his glass. "This is truly an occasion for celebrating. Vanessa and I have an announcement." He patted Vanessa's belly. "To family," he said. "More and more of it." Yvette began to cry.

The wives exclaimed unhappily. One by one, they examined the imperceptible roundness under Vanessa's silk blouse. They had all assumed that she and Marc were either infertile or uninterested. Now they were quite unsettled by the thought of a princely little replica sitting in the back seat of their convertible, a little silk scarf blowing round its thick Broussard neck. Grace eyed Vanessa's stomach and sank lower in her chair. Camille waddled over and hugged Vanessa, whom she had considered worthless until that very moment. The husbands teased Marc about his prowess. The wives sang Vanessa's praises, not because they thought she would make a good mother, but because she would look so lovely pregnant. Paul nodded his natural approvingly. Yvette blew her nose and kissed Vanessa on both cheeks. Grace seethed in garlic acrimony.

"To my lovely wife, who I showered with candy over the years and who now presents me with the greatest happiness the world has ever known, a perfect image of myself." Marc wound to an end amid snickers and the sound of the doorbell ringing.

"Well, that might be the stork now," quipped Paul, but nobody noticed.

Grace got up to answer the door. Standing there in lively disarray was the guest of honor himself. "Where have you been?" Grace snarled. The answer to that question was painfully obvious.

"This the Bruzzard fambly rez'dence?"

Camille was rising from her seat. Raymond and Anthony

held her down. "How dare a son of mine disgrace me in front of my neighbors!" she began.

"Whass e'rybody eatin'? Sho do smell good. Ah'll take a bowl a' dat!"

"Come on, Joe. Let's go clean you up." Anthony had him by the arm. Joseph pulled away.

"Ah needs me some grub!" He fell on the couch. "Where the wine at?" Within seconds he was fast asleep.

"Paul, may I serve you some garlic bread?" Yvette was the first to recover. "How about a little wine?"

While Camille was being comforted by her daughters-in-law, Raymond went to calm the children, who found the whole scene with "Uncle Joe" worthy of uncontrollable giggles. Aunt Julie went to censure Uncle Claude, who was out on the porch fanning himself after leaving the table in a coughing fit, which everyone suspected was a laughing fit. Yvette repaired to the kitchen to make good on her offer of wine. Louis retreated to the bathroom. Marc began eating. Grace headed for the door.

"Come on, Paul. Let's go."

"Hey, Gracie, take it easy," Anthony protested. "Give the man a minute to eat his dinner."

"You take it easy. My name's not Gracie."

"For goodness sakes, Grace! Demonstrate some manners, would you?" Raymond was still trying to stifle his children.

"You're the ones who said I should show Paul around."

"Whose car you taking, Missy?" Marc wanted to know.

"Can't I take yours?"

"Take my car where? I just waxed it." Marc looked up from his food. "Why don't you take the Buick? I heard you got it started and took it for a little spin. How much did you have to pay to get it towed back here?"

"Marc, don't tease your sister."

"We could take my car. I mean, I could show Paul around. I wouldn't mind. Grace could come too," said Rouby.

"Yeah, go in Rouby's car."

"I'll wait for you outside, then," said Grace, who hadn't eaten a bite and didn't want to be tempted.

"You can't go outside looking like that. You're liable to get arrested," said Camille. "Go comb your hair."

"Oh, Mama, nobody cares about my hair but you." Grace escaped before Camille could say anything.

Yvette came back carrying a bottle of wine. "Doesn't Paul get a say in what he wants to do? Poor thing, he doesn't know which way to turn."

"He doesn't need to know which way to turn. He just needs to know which way is out."

"Thank you, Anthony, for that insight."

"Look, Paul, this here's the center. Watts. It's where everybody's trying to get away from."

"What a terrible thing to say! I like living here," protested Yvette.

"Sure you do. It keeps you from being bored. Mother Teresa likes living in Calcutta. The Devil likes living in Hell. Don't pay any attention to Yvette. She's lacking a sense of direction in life." Anthony was feeling reckless and mean.

"I've got more sense than you'll ever have." Yvette was on fire. "And let me tell you one thing, Mister Antoine Anthony Broussard. I'm getting out of here. And I'm going somewhere you've never been. I'm going to be happy!"

"I'll believe it when I see it. Anyway, Paul... to your right, there's nothing but Disneyland, which you're too old for."

"You're never too old for Disneyland."

"Not if you live there all the time."

"Wait a minute, that's not far from where *we* live."

"Another baby born in Disneyland. And they wonder what's wrong with kids these days."

"Paul, it's quite nice to the east of here. You just have to go far enough. Marc and I have a wonderful little ranch-style in Fullerton. You should come for some barbecue."

"Nobody barbecues in January."

"In Fullerton we barbecue year round. We just don't invite you."

"Thank you, Vanessa. Like I said… If you go south, you're in the harbor. There's nothing but an old boat named after some queen who's about as relevant to your life as a powdered wig. That's where I live, but I wouldn't recommend it."

"Speak for yourself."

"I'm sorry, darling. Your mother still powder her wig?"

"You'll pay for that, Anthony Broussard."

"Never get married, Paul. It's like barbecuing in hell."

"I like to barbecue."

"Did you hear that, honey? Paul likes to barbecue."

"He'll make some woman a good wife."

"A good wife!"

"A good husband! I'm sorry, Paul. You know what I mean."

"That's just what she means, son. Women don't want husbands," said Anthony. "They want wives. So they can sit around all day and do nothing but complain while somebody waits on them."

"Hah! I'm raising your children, ain't I? You don't hear me complaining. You complain more than anybody I know."

"Now stop all this crazy talk! You all have company." Camille was tired.

Silence. Lots of spoons scraping the bottoms of bowls. Everybody searching for a way out. Grace came in from the porch.

"Hey, Gracie's back. Where'd you go?" yelled Marc.

"For a walk!" Grace looked at Paul and Rouby. "Are you coming?" She made for the kitchen.

"You can't go for a walk in Watts." Laughter all around, followed by tales about the last time anybody could remember going on a neighborhood walk and the evils that had almost befallen him. Their smugness infuriated Grace. Their arrogance, their superstition, their prejudice. In truth, she had not gone for a walk. She was a Broussard and well-trained. She was afraid to go for a walk by herself. Disgusted, Grace returned to the porch, a tiny bottle stashed in her pocket.

Mr. Pep was on his porch now. "Pretty Miss Grace," he called to her, "have you seen my Pretty Miss Alma?"

"No, Mr. Pep, I haven't."

"She's flown the coop again."

"Oh, Mr. Pep, I'm sorry."

"Don't worry yourself, Miss Grace. You got worries enough of your own," he chuckled. "Is that Casper still giving you a hard time?"

"No, not so bad."

"That's good. I wish I could get somebody to haunt me. Then maybe Mr. Pep wouldn't be so lonely."

"I'm sure Miss Alma will be back."

"Don't you know she will. She always comes back to her Mr. Pep."

Rouby called to Grace from his car. She said goodbye to Mr. Pep and climbed in. Paul sat in the front with Rouby while Grace brooded in the back. They turned on some raucous radio station that suited her just fine.

"This whole car smells like gumbo!" Paul said. They laughed and fell silent. There was no need for talking on this trip. Paul shook his hair to the music. Rouby tapped the steering wheel of his new Toyota. With no trinkets to distract her, Grace settled into her thoughts. After two hours of detours, they landed at Playa del Rey.

Paul and Rouby stripped down to their jeans. Paul was a lion, Rouby a stallion. They chased each other out to sea, kicking up seaweed, sand, and both of their sabers. Ah, lust! Grace hated how easy it was for them to be together. Would they dream all night of sleeping in each other's arms? Would they pine for each other in the morning? Would they make plans to move in together? Would they remember this day when they were old men, old married men with grandchildren? Paul's hair was rather nice, once it hit the water. Rouby's breasts were a bit more taut than Grace remembered them. The two young men shivered beneath broad smiles. She watched them disappear inside a wave.

Suddenly, Grace saw. All the things she had been trying not to see—here they were, spread before her in the sand.

"What you go so far out for?"

"I wanted to see what was out there."

"Ain't nothing but water out there."

"I wanted to see the shore."

"You'll drown if you go out too far."

"It wasn't that far."

"It was far away from the rest of us."

"You don't understand. I'm different from you."

"Different how?"

"I'm not your little girl! You don't own me!"

Grace's words had been a slap to her father's honor. She remembered his look of horror, his glazed eyes, his trouble breathing. The hand at his throat. She could see it now as clear as day. T-Papa was having a heart attack. She hadn't known it then, but he had known. From that day forward, he had known

he was sick. Without their knowledge, he'd grown sicker and
sicker until one day he had died. Why hadn't she seen it? Why
hadn't anyone? He hadn't wanted them to see; he had wanted to
protect them.

"Look at this white Negro with his colored family."

"We was just passing through."

*"I'll have to take these boys down to the station. You take
the gals with you."*

"Hail Mary, full of grace, the Lord is with Thee."

"Coming in with a carload of coloreds."

The pain in her stomach. Her touching herself. Her first experience with sex of any kind. Her needing to use the bathroom.
The blood. Her father's tears. He had imagined the worst. So
had she. She thought they were going to kill him.

*"I ought to make you kneel in front of the Sacred Heart.
What's the matter? Can't you talk now? You could talk plenty
good in church!"*

Grace could still see her father shaking with rage. She no
longer feared him. She no longer wished he would leave her
alone. She wasn't the one who had killed him. It was simply his
time to go.

Grace pushed herself up from the sand. A lone surfer rode
the tide in his wetsuit. A couple huddled in front of a fire. A
toddler scouted for shells. Rouby's keys were in his boots. Grace
waved to her cousins. They were swimming side by side, trans-
fixed by the power of the sea and by their own virility. Grace
turned away without waiting for them to signal back. She knew
they wouldn't miss her. She walked to the car and climbed in on
the driver's side.

Grace sat in the quiet and watched the waves. *How come
the water never gets tired?* T-Papa had laughed at his little girl's
query, but he hadn't known the reason. All these years later,

Grace had discovered why, but it was too late to tell him. The water was mad with desire. It craved the shore, lapped at it, swallowed it in a rush. At times it shouted. At times it whispered. But it never stopped speaking of its desire. Life was hunger, life was feast.

By now, dinner was a distant memory. The dirty dishes, the bones from the chicken, the crab shells would be heaped on the kitchen counter waiting for Grace to dispose of them. She had not eaten and she was hungry. She was tempted to drink the spice jar of gumbo in her pocket, but it was not that kind of hunger. Grace missed Elena. Every part of her body longed to be held. She leaned on the horn and announced her desire. She kept on announcing it until the last waves of hunger had disappeared.

12

The Resting Place

Afternoon, January 6, 1979

It is hard for a Broussard to rest. T-Papa had lost a lot of weight in death, and this worried him. He worried that his opinions no longer carried much weight with his daughters and sons. Many a night, he stayed awake worrying. Many a day, he roamed from pond to grotto to hills, looking. Finally, he saw. By the way they gathered at his grave and kept gathering until the last one came—the one who never came, the young one who didn't understand the importance of coming—he knew he was not forgotten. Like salmon, like pigeons, the Broussards were a homing people. T-Papa would never be abandoned. He rested in this knowledge.

S he came carrying gumbo, a little vial of it. In an old cayenne jar, it had stewed until its colors were wet sand and seaweed. Gumbo—the original food. *You a Broussard. You gots to want gumbo.* She could hear him taunting her and her own shrill voice answering back. *I'm tired of being a Broussard. I'm tired of gumbo.* And now here she was, a scientist trading secrets, guarding the recipe that would bring the world to its knees, make him captive, the way she was. His one final taste, the one for which he had been staying awake. One drop of this stuff had the power to wake the dead... or put them to sleep forever. The coup de grâce.

Grace had been so sure of herself only twelve days before, so sweetly defiant. Now, she didn't know who she was. She could have just left the gumbo, turned around without so much as a parting glance, headed back to the beach to collect the boys, never come to this place again. But she wanted to be there to greet him. She wanted to see him off. She wanted to apologize.

Every day for three years, his memory had dogged her. Her father was a big, strong man, but Grace remembered him in times of weakness. Those were the times when she felt closest to him, when he was vulnerable and human, a mere mortal like herself who would one day die and turn to dust. She could still hear his awful "yes sir, yes sir" to the sheriff in Texas, his crying by the roadside, his massive nose honking into his linen hand-kerchief. For three years Grace had felt his unrelenting absence. For three years she had blamed herself. Not a heart attack, but a broken heart in need of stitching. Nobody had noticed, nobody but Grace, who couldn't sew if her life depended on it. She had made things worse by yanking on the threads. Grace's regrets weren't many, but they ran as deep as the hurt and bewilder-ment on a father's face. Children are supposed to protect their parents. Grace hadn't been able to do that.

It was getting late. In an hour it would be dusk and the cemetery would be closing. And even though Yvette claimed there were very nice men who came around and gave you a fifteen-minute warning so you wouldn't get locked inside the gates, Grace didn't want to chance it. She hurried along.

She had Yvette's sweater draped around her shoulders, a

creamy peach cardigan with fake pearl buttons. It was too small
for her. She pulled it tight against the January wind. The evening
chill made the cemetery seem oppressive. Grace pictured herself
old. Yvette would be gone. All of their brothers would be old,
gone. She would be the one to bring the flowers, wipe the stones,
pull the weeds for all of them. And who would do it for her, once
she was too frail to make the trip, once she herself was lying with
the rest of them? Raymond's son Gregory? He was only a few
years behind her. One of Louis's kids? She barely knew them.
Some unborn niece or nephew? Where would they bury her?
Would she be in a plot by herself? Would she and Yvette share
the Tomb of the Unmarried Sisters? Grace no longer wanted her
ashes scattered on the beach, but she didn't want to be buried
alone in the cold damp ground. She wanted to lie for eternity
next to her beloved. She hoped it would be possible.

Grace hesitated as she walked up the hill to T-Papa's grave
clutching her little offering. One strand of crab, a curl of shrimp,
a taste of sausage, a few okra seeds—such a small thing. T-Papa
had been the biggest thing she knew. When he laughed, the seas
howled their pleasure. When he raged, the wind sang its torment. What would she ever say to him?

Eternal rest grant unto him oh Lord as it was in the begin-
ning is now and ever shall be the fruit of thy womb Jesus who
trespasses against us and all the souls of the faithful departed to
ransom my soul with the blood of thy faithful.

Prayers were dashing together against the walls of Grace's
mind. She felt grateful that her ransom consisted of gumbo and
not blood. A small wind overtook her shoulders and gently
pushed her onward. She was at the grave.

Grace looked at the stone. The wind had blown grass clip-
pings over her father's name, but she could still make out her
mother's inscription: *My presence shall go with thee and I will*

give thee rest. Perhaps it was T-Papa's presence that would go
with them. Grace gave a sigh, bent down, and placed the jar of
gumbo on T-Papa's stone. *There. I have done what thou asked.
Now give me some rest!*

Suddenly, a car appeared out of nowhere, horn honking like
a wedding carriage, wheels screeching to a halt just down the
slope from where Grace was standing. She wiped her eyes, refusing to believe what she was seeing. Mr. Pep sprang from the
driver's seat of Camille's Ford Falcon, ran around to the other
side and opened the door for Camille. He waved to his Pretty
Miss Grace—*Do you think you could take your mother
home?*—and roared off again.

Grace was awed by this spectacle. There were so many
things wrong with the picture, she didn't know where to start.
Her mouth was moving but no words were coming out. How
long had she been here? And where was T-Papa? Whose voice
was calling her name? She blinked at the apparition advancing
up the slope.

To the grave Camille marched, a procession of one. In her
hands she cradled an unlit candle, a holy card, a sprig of daphne,
and a Styrofoam cup. A rosary dangled from her coat pocket.
She appeared to Grace as someone in a dream.

Grace closed her eyes and turned away. When she looked
back, Camille was getting closer. It could not be. Camille was at
home—wasn't she?—right where Grace had left her. When
Grace realized that this was indeed her mother and not a mirage
or Fear personified, her first instinct was to run. Not the way a
child runs when she's about to be caught doing something
wrong, but rather the way a soldier runs when he's about to be
ambushed by an advancing enemy.

Grace might have run but she was frozen to the soil, embed-
ded in the grass. All she could do was shield her eyes against the

heavy artillery heading straight for her. Camille hobbled up the
slope to where her husband lay. With nowhere to hide, Grace
would have to face her mother.

Camille was not doing well. She was facing her mortality for
the first time—Ash Wednesday was right around the corner—
and she was not doing well at all. *Remember man that you are
dust and unto dust you shall return.* Surrounded by dust, unable
to dust, unable to effectively command that dusting take place,
Camille was feeling like so much dust. Sackcloth and ashes. Is
that what she would need to wear in order for people to see her
brittleness? A reputation for unbounding strength can be a serious impediment in times of trial.

Something about this last loss—the loss of her womb—had
set Camille to mourning all the previous ones. T-Papa. Michelle.
Her own dear mother, whose Louisiana grave she hadn't visited
in nearly four years. Joseph, who had risen from the ashes of
war only to waste away in this foreign country called home. It
had not helped him that his mother had protested the war,
Camille could see that now. And then there was Grace. Grace
had been missing in action since she was about twelve. Camille
did not really know that kid standing at the top of the slope. She
would just have to go and make her acquaintance.

"Grace Desirée!"

Grace hated to be called by her middle name. *Desirée*—her
mother could stake her claim in a word. She could say *I know
you, I know your name, I named you, you are mine, you have no
say in the matter, you are still mine* in one word.

Grace froze.

Camille would have to handle it. It always fell to her to
handle the tough ones, the ones who couldn't believe unless
everything was spelled out for them. No single word would help;

they needed whole sentences. Broussards were thick by nature, and Grace was thicker than most.

Camille could see that this whole story could have been avoided if people had behaved differently. Most stories are that way. Being young and feeling odd, Grace didn't know how to leave without separating. Leaving is one thing, but separating is quite another. Camille reacted to attempts to separate the way a nation reacts when one of its states tries to bolt. People leave all the time, but every leaving implies a return. If not a return, a reunion. If not here, then in heaven. Separation holds no such promises. If leaving is the worst thing a body ever does, then separation is unthinkable. Before letting somebody separate, you'd better be ready to say *goodbye good riddance I don't care if I ever lay eyes on you again.* The Broussards would never be ready for that. It wasn't in their blood.

Besides, Grace was their favorite. Didn't she know that? She was like California to them. They made relentless fun of her. They sometimes pretended they wanted her to fall into the ocean—she sometimes jumped in just to shock them—but who can imagine a world without California? Who wouldn't miss her if she actually took the dive? The Broussards of Compton Avenue would be the first ones there, tugging on the rope, yelling from the shore, making waves, clinging by their teeth to what belonged to them. They would never let go if Grace didn't intend to come back, if she wasn't going to be there forever, allowing herself to be tormented by their love. She just didn't get this. Camille would have to spell it out.

When she finally reached Grace, the girl was on her knees frantically trying to wipe up something she had spilled all over T-Papa's stone. Smelled like gumbo. Camille, deciding to take advantage of Grace's humble position, got down on her knees.

"Let's pray," she said, placing her things on the ground in front of her and taking Grace's hand.

Lord, lay thy body next to mine that I might see the love of thine who knew me from my op'ning breath and leaves me not in sainted death.

"I've never heard that prayer."

"Made it up."

Grace's hand was hot. Camille was holding on for dear life. She was pleased to find Grace at her father's grave. They would have a chance to talk. She held tight her daughter's hand. Grace struggled to get free.

"Mama, what are you doing here?"

"I belong here. What are *you* doing here? I thought you and Rouby were showing Paul the town."

"I left them at the beach. It's too soon after your surgery for you to be running around. And where was Mr. Pep going in your car?"

"He got a call from some of his relatives saying they spotted Miss Alma in Inglewood. His car was in a wreck, remember? I told him he could borrow my car if he brought me by the cemetery."

"Isn't his license suspended?"

"That's just because he can't afford to pay his tickets."

"He drives too fast. I don't want you riding with him."

"Don't you think I'm old enough to make my own decisions? Anyway, I brought my Sacred Heart Auto League card for protection." Grace recognized the wrinkled holy card staring up at her from the grass.

"What happened to everybody else? Why didn't one of them drive you?"

"Oh, most of them raced out the door right after you all left. Raymond said he didn't have enough room in his car to take me anywhere. Anthony claimed he had a job to go to. And you know how I can't stand going anywhere with Louis an'em. Who wants to hear all their problems? I didn't bother to ask Marc and Vanessa. They don't want anybody messing up their car. I wonder what they're going to do with a baby! Joseph was still asleep on the couch. Yvette was in her room crying. And you weren't available. So, Mr. Pep to the rescue!"

"That's not funny, Mama. I'm worried about you. What are you going to do after I'm gone?"

"Where are you going?"

"I have to move out sometime!"

"You do, do you?"

This was the moment Camille had been dreading. She remembered her own mother waving goodbye to the train that would carry her youngest daughter from Lafayette to Los Angeles. Camille was determined not to make such a scene. She knew Grace was moving out. While she was making the gumbo, a man had called with a message about an apartment. "The check cleared," he said, and Grace could move in anytime.

Camille had not been altogether surprised, but she was worried about Grace and her ability to make good decisions. The world Grace was entering frightened her. It was not Dade County, Florida, but large numbers of Angelenos had voted to bar gay teachers from the schools. Though the Briggs Initiative had not passed this time, Camille was worried about the future. Harvey Milk and Mayor Moscone had paid with their lives for the intolerance of the country's most tolerant city. And whose children were they who ended up in Jonestown sipping a punch spiked with death? At home, Grace was protected.

Camille had been putting off making decisions about her life without children. She knew the time had come. She tried to picture waking to an empty house. No chattering Yvette. No sulking Grace. No Joseph distraught and devoid of purpose. Just her. No chickens. No ghosts. Just never-ending decisions about when to get up, when to go to bed, when and what to eat, whether or not to cook. Camille had never been alone in her life. It might be nice.

She picked up the Styrofoam cup. *Bless this humble offering and praise him for all he hath given us, O Gracious Father.* Gently she poured a little gumbo where T-Papa's mouth would have been. At his feet she placed the sprig of daphne from Mr. Pep's garden.

Grace watched dumbfounded. "What are you doing?" she wanted to scream. But she knew what her mother was doing, and she remained quiet.

Camille wrapped her rosary around Grace's palm. *As it was in the beginning, is now and ever shall be, world without end.*

"Let's walk." Camille squeezed Grace's hand.

"Where to?"

"I want to visit Michelle. The candle is for her."

"She's too far away. I don't want to get locked in here."

"Why not? It's the safest place around. Don't worry. Some gentlemen will come around and warn us before they close up."

Camille introduced Grace to several folks who were buried along the way to Michelle's grave. Here was a fellow she remembered going crawfishing with as a teenager. "He would never marry anyone if he couldn't have me, that's what he told me. He was something else!"

"Did he?"

"What?"

"Marry?

"Never. But he told that to all the girls. Now, this lady here traveled all around the world. Slept with men in every corner of

the earth. Was sterile, she was. And a good thing, too. Otherwise, she would have had to stay home and take care of all of
them babies!" Camille laughed heartily. Grace wondered what
had gotten into her mother.

"And here's a gal who spent most of her days in L.A. pining
for her best friend who stayed behind in Grimelle. How was she
going to live without her only friend? Well, she didn't live
long—anybody can see that."

"And over there, that's Yvette's first-grade teacher and the
reason she's teaching now. Sister Agnes never looked down on
the children. She truly loved them all. She only became a nun
after losing a child of her own."

Nuns with babies. Globe-trotting Creole nymphomaniacs.
Camille's long-ago boyfriends. Grace struggled to take it all in.

"Do you remember this name? He was the only boy from
church killed in Vietnam. A gentle soul really, never wanted to
fight. His poor father drank himself to death. They're buried
together, see? Oh, but the good die. Every day."

Camille prayed for them all.

Slowly, slowly, ever so slowly, what her mother was saying
began to register with Grace. She was not gossiping, the way
Yvette did, about those who could not gossip back. There was
no lust in her eyes, no ardor in her voice. She was just passing
along some simple information, which Grace could either take
or leave. Grace listened to all she said.

After fifteen minutes of walking, they reached Michelle's
grave. The stone was rimmed with cherubim. "Too weak to
live." That was how Camille explained it. Thirty-five years and
the guilt was still there. Because she had been depressed, Camille
hadn't eaten well during the pregnancy and Michelle was born
premature. "We don't *all* survive. Sometimes, life is just too

much for a body. I think that's what happens to a lot of people. They just despair of living. Michelle was my *real* Depression baby. It took her passing for me to come back to myself."

"Maybe you didn't want any more children…"

"I never looked on it that way. Been having children since I was seventeen. It was the most natural thing to do. I never thought about what *I* wanted until you came along… so far after Joseph, all by yourself. Desirée! My saving Grace, the child of my desire. The one who looked like me. I could see my beauty when I looked at you. You were the child of my old age. I waited for you. The others I just made, like making gumbo. In those days, there was never any thought as to whether you wanted a child or not. You wanted them all. Because you were going to have them whether you wanted them or not. So, best to want them. You love what you are given."

Grace considered this last statement and its possible implications for her life. What was Camille trying to tell her? Love what you are given. Did that only apply to children? Grace had been given a lot that she didn't especially want. At the risk of appearing ungrateful, she had often appealed to her Creator to "take this cup." She prayed now for the courage to surrender—to fate and family both.

"Oh, you can fight it, but that won't do you no good. Not if it's your nature. You always be a Broussard. Can't nothin' change that."

There were worse fates.

They said a prayer and started the walk back to the car. "That must be where your friend is buried." Camille gestured toward a fresh mound covered with flowers. "How's his family doing?"

Grace shook her head. "Not so good."

"It's a horrible thing to lose a child," said Camille. "Let's go say goodbye to your father."

It had been more than a month since Camille had seen her husband. Before she went into the hospital, he had visited her every night for three years. She didn't know why he hadn't visited her in the hospital. He must have hung around the house for a few days before becoming thoroughly dejected at not finding her there. Apparently, she had miscalculated in not telling him about the surgery. She didn't want to worry him. Now he had gone away for good.

Had they finally arrived at the point of no return? During their forty years of marriage, they had taken what was given and multiplied it sevenfold. Over and over, she had pulled him to her, his fleetness on top of her sturdiness. After his death, it was he who lingered. No more.

"Never really could bring myself to talk much about your father's death. Maybe it's my fault that you're all tied up inside. I didn't know how to talk to you. I was so crushed. Even Yvette, I couldn't talk to. Our closeness was coming here."

Grace didn't say a thing. It was her turn to pray. How many times had her father's hand kept her from falling? He was her defense against earthquakes and heartaches and ridicule. She missed him.

"You're so much like your daddy—determined to have your way at all cost. He suffered over things like you do. Worried and planned, just like you."

They had reached the grave. The Broussard women stood in silence. No prayers, just thought. Camille looked at Grace with affection. She shook her head. Then, spreading her arms like a hawk, she surveyed the land as if it were hers. "He planned for this too. First thing we did was get the house. Second thing we

did was purchase these plots. We talked about being buried in
Grimelle, but we knew you children would likely be here. If we
wanted you to visit us, we'd better be planted where we
dropped! The dead get lonely too, you know. We all got our
ways of holding on." They started back to Rouby's car.

"What changed your mind?" Grace could see her mother
struggling. "I mean, about holding on."

"Oh, it was in the hospital. I took a good long look at myself. Hollow. A hole taken right from the middle of me. When I
was alone in the hospital at night, after all the visitors were gone,
I'd cry over myself and the state I was in. I realized I'd been
trying to hold on to everything and everybody so nobody else
would leave me. Not fair to you and your sister. I kept saying to
God, 'You mean, I'm going to have to go the rest of the way by
myself?' God never said a thing in reply, which is His way of
saying, 'That's right, sister.' But I didn't want that answer, so I
answered myself, 'You're not by yourself. You have Yvette and
Grace.' I couldn't see being alone in that house without your
father. After all those years, I was still in love with him. We drew
on each other for strength. You'll know that kind of love. It's a
wonderful thing... but, Lord, it's hard when it goes!"

Grace regarded her mother with wonder. There was nothing
to say.

A man in a green truck drove up beside them. "We'll be
closing in fifteen minutes, ladies."

"Don't you dare lock us in here, Junior!"

"Miss Camille, is that you? Good to see you, sugar. How
was your surgery?"

"I'm still here. So I guess it was okay."

"All right, then. Don't rush. We'll hold the gate for you."

Camille laughed and waved. Together, she and Grace

waddled to the car. "I prayed to your father. He told me to let you go."

"What?"

"He told me you was going to be all right."

"How did you know I was leaving?"

"Oh, you started acting funny… like all the children do when they're ready to go. It took Anthony years."

Grace puzzled at this revelation but said nothing. They had reached the car. She opened the passenger door, rearranged the seat, and helped Camille climb in. Circling around to the driver's side, she paused to regard the back of her mother's head—the familiar roundness, the black curls going gray, the strong brown neck. She would miss that woman. Too much to think about. Grace opened the door and climbed behind the wheel.

"That Rouby sure keeps his car clean. I like that." Camille patted the dash and hung the rosary around the mirror. Grace started up the car. Camille pointed out all the landmarks they were passing, but Grace was no longer paying attention. Without comment she rounded the corners, pausing by the pond.

They both stared in silence.

Grace looked out at the park of stones. Against the fake pearl buttons, she felt for her heart. There was love there, but it was not a love she could bask in. It was only one thing among many. Love tempered with pride, sautéed in shame, bolstered by loyalty. Secrets that are buried don't die with their owners. What would they say about Grace after she died? This was Camille's daughter, the one who never married, who had a best friend for whom she pined, who couldn't have any children of her own, a gentle soul who never wanted to fight.

Camille gave her last prayer to the wind and bid goodbye to her husband. A new season was beginning without him. Soon

Lent would be here, clutching in its jaws the palm of rebirth. Camille Broussard was, essentially, a mother. She felt in no way diminished by this fact. With Grace growing up and leaving home, her work was all but done.

Children grow quickly. They do so while you're away. Even if you're there the whole time watching, they grow when you turn your back or lean out the window to catch a falling wish for them. Camille's youngest was moving out. Where to, she didn't know. It didn't really matter. Nobody ever left the Broussards. Grace would be back. They always come back.

Grace guided the car through the wrought-iron gates. In the rearview mirror, she watched the gatekeeper perform his happy ritual. No ghosts would pursue them, no voices would cry out as they waded into the stream of traffic. Maybe they could watch the sun set over the ocean before heading home to Watts. A space opened up, and Grace rushed into it, a prayer of thanksgiving hidden within her smile.

About the Author

Nancy Rawles writes plays as well as fiction. She grew up in Los Angeles and spent her early years as a professional writer in Chicago. She currently lives in Seattle and enjoys teaching creative writing as an artist in residence in schools in Washington state. *Love Like Gumbo* is her first novel.

Other selected fiction from Fjord Press

Plenty Good Room
by Teresa McClain-Watson
$14.00 paperback

Nelio
A Novel of Mozambique
by Henning Mankell
Translated by Tiina Nunnally
$14.00 paperback

The Five Thousand and One Nights
by Penelope Lively
$12.00 paperback

Runemaker
A Margit Andersson Mystery
by Tiina Nunnally
$12.00 paperback

Maija
by Tiina Nunnally
$12.00 paperback

Niels Lyhne
by Jens Peter Jacobsen
Translated by Tiina Nunnally
$14.00 paperback

Please write, fax, or email for a free catalog:
Fjord Press, PO Box 16349, Seattle, WA 98116
fax (206) 938-1991 / email fjord@halcyon.com
Visit our web site at www.fjordpress.com/fjord
for more information and reading samples